GODS OF MANHATTAN

The boot pressed down on his back. Johann tried to say a prayer, but he had no breath to say it. There was only the sound of the rain. And then the sound of a bullet.

Johann felt the weight of the boy's boot come off his back, then heard the splash of the heavy corpse hitting the puddles of the grimy alley floor.

For a moment, there was no sound at all, bar a kind of high-pitched squeak, an animal whimper that crawled out of the throat of the boy with the swastika shirt, as if he was some small burrowing thing caught in a wire trap.

Then there was laughter.

A terrible, echoing laugh, of a kind one might find in the pits of Hell, a laugh that bounced and rolled off the brick and steel and seemed to echo from every corner at once, booming, roaring, growing louder and louder. Johann felt ice in his chest, and began to stumble through the *Kaddish*, eyes shutting tight, as if warding off imaginary monsters the way he had as a child. When he opened his eyes again, the monster stood in front of him.

He was close to six foot, and the long coat of black leather gave him the appearance of being half shadow, a silhouette picked out against the gaslight of the street beyond. Johann blinked the raindrops from his eyes – or were they tears? – and tried to make out further detail, but there was none, only a sea of black, a black hole in space in the shape of a man. Black suit and shirt, black gloves with an odd texture to them, holding a pair of automatic pistols. And a black slouch hat that covered his face–

–oh God, his face!

An Abaddon Books™ Publication
www.abaddonbooks.com
abaddon@rebellion.co.uk

First published in 2010 by Abaddon Books™, Rebellion Intellectual
Property Limited, Riverside House, Osney Mead, Oxford, OX2 0ES, UK.

10 9 8 7 6 5 4 3 2 1

Editors: Jonathan Oliver & Jenni Hill
Cover: Mark Harrison
Design: Simon Parr & Luke Preece
Marketing and PR: Keith Richardson
Creative Director and CEO: Jason Kingsley
Chief Technical Officer: Chris Kingsley
Pax Britannia™ created by Jonathan Green

US & Canada ISBN: 978-1-906735-86-9
UK ISBN: 978-1-906735-39-5

Printed in the USA

PAX BRITANNIA

GODS OF MANHATTAN

AL EWING

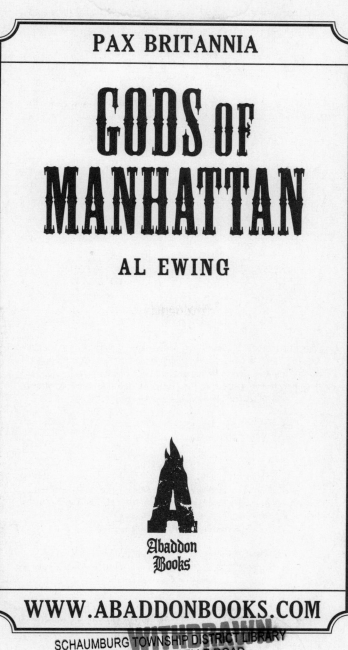

Abaddon Books

WWW.ABADDONBOOKS.COM

PROLOGUE

Night and the City

WHEN THE NIGHT came, you could hear Manhattan coming to life.

Stagecoaches clip-clopped down the wide streets, oil lamps burning on the sides. Rickshaws clattered through back alleys, seeking shortcuts, yelling at each other if they got too close. *Watch it, Mac! You blind?* Newsboys catcalled as they waved the evening editions. *Wuxtry, wuxtry! Blood-Spider sighted in the South Bronx! All in colour for a dime! Wuxtry, wuxtry! Don't ask, just buy it!*

Coloured lanterns picked out theatre signs, reflecting from the silvered letters. In Times Square, great paper advertisements for Sake-Cola and *Jonny's Daily Show* at the Chinese Theatre glowed softly from the arrangement of gas-lamps behind them. On every corner there was the scent of cooked sausage meat as the hot-dog vendors grilled their wares over barrel-fires, the smell hitting your nose as their calls and cries met your ears. *Mustard and sweet onion! Red sauce and yellow! Hot dogs, hot dogs! One dollar five! Wrap a nickel in a bill and eat your fill!*

You might start off surrounded by tourists and suits, bowlers and top hats on every head around you, and then turn the right corner and walk down the wrong alley and everything would change before you'd even noticed. You might find yourself face-to-face with a sneering young tough-guy in leather and studs and an injun haircut streaked with pink and green, with a safety-pin through the nose to complete the effect – an apparition you could only find here, in the City Of Tomorrow. Futureheads, they were called – an ironic gesture, considering their creed and battle-cry was "No future for me, no future for you."

According to the futureheads, some vital step towards progress had been lost along the way to the present day, and human civilisation had entered a period of stagnation, of cultural inbreeding. The familiar bred with the familiar and created more and more outlandish results. Futureheads were the self-proclaimed end result of this degradation, their clothing a forest of symbols repurposed and détourned, all original meanings subsumed into a new and terrible message – that history had stopped, the roaring train of time had crashed and humanity were now only playing around in the wreckage, finding what uses they could for the junk.

Still and all, a futurehead rarely wanted trouble. That swaggering tough was most likely on his way to a bar, happy with his own, in no mood to give you more than a filthy look and a wad of spit at your feet. No, if it was trouble you were after, you kept an eye on the bikers – the treaded rubber tyres of their Off-Road Bicycles rattling with steel spokies as they bunny-hopped and weaved through the crowds with practiced ease, swapping charged looks and predatory grins as they sped down streets and alleys. The better they were on those things, the more likely they were to be purse-snatchers. You could spot them because they rode no-handed, keeping their hands free to cut straps and grab bags, slinging their prizes into a basket on the front of the machine before grabbing the handlebars again to swerve away, leaving pursuit far behind.

Turn another corner and you might find a gothic Lolita-lookalike waving shyly at you from under a streetlight, kitten ears poking from her hair. Or a man wearing hard eyes and a trilby hat, shooting you a dirty look and opening his coat just enough to show you his gun, then strolling into a nightclub and putting four in the belly of some poor schmoe who hadn't made the payments. Or a fellow in shirtsleeves and zoot trousers, spinning like a top on his back and his head, on a cardboard sheet right there on the sidewalk. Music provided by three sharp-dressed men with steel drums and tom-toms, tapping out a beat so complex and layered that no formal dance would ever do, so catchy and contagious that not dancing wouldn't do either. White boy off to the side, throwing shapes with his hands and laughing like a drunk, even though he'd never touched a drop in his life.

That's a top one, fellahs, oh that's a nice one, he'd shout, and the answer would echo back from around the corner, *red sauce and yellow! One dollar five!*

Turn another corner and you might find yourself back in the world, back among those who made sense to you. Or you might find yourself face-to-chest with a powder blue t-shirt and a lightning bolt decal, and a soft deep voice that might have belonged to the Lord on the mount, wishing you a good night and good luck. Or you might find yourself where you'd never known you belonged until now. That place that couldn't exist in any other city in the whole damned world.

This was Manhattan, after all. There were stories here.

And when the night came, they came to life.

HERE'S A STORY.

Out on the water, there were two men. They were sitting in a small sailing vessel, drifting in the darkness towards Manhattan.

Willis was looking at the Statue. The arm holding the torch had been destroyed during the Second Civil War – the Statue was French, after all, so there was no surprise in her being a target – but most people liked the replacement arm and the new torch a lot better anyway. Something about having an actual fire roaring out of that torch – an eternal flame, the politicos had called it – made the Statue seem a little more defiant, somehow, and Willis liked that. He breathed in, watching the way the flames danced from the torch, reflected on the water below. He never did get tired of that view.

The other man glanced up briefly, then returned to his sword. He'd been inspecting it for the last hour, and it was starting to make Willis uneasy. The Mexican was a tall, muscular figure, strikingly handsome in an odd way, with scruffy black hair, long in back, and a thick moustache – but he slouched, round-shouldered, and his hair was greasy and hung in his face. He wore a pair of classy tuxedo pants and little else. The only things he seemed to own, once he'd paid for his passage, were his sword and a strip of red cloth poking out of his pocket.

He kept scratching the back of his skull. It made Willis uneasy.

"So. Up from Mexico, huh?" Willis grunted. Talking made the sailing go a little faster sometimes, and besides, he wanted to break the silence. Part of him wondered if he could throw the other man overboard, if it came to it.

The Mexican nodded.

"You know, most folks up from Mexico come via land, if you don't mind me saying. You serious about taking boats all the way around Cape Horn and up the other side?"

The Mexican shrugged. He spoke softly, with a strong accent, but with no hesitation, no fumbling for the right words. "They'd have been waiting for me in Russia. And somebody once told me there was some interesting art in New York. I wanted to see for myself."

Willis nodded, though in truth he hadn't the faintest idea what the fella was talking about or who 'they' might be. "I, uh, I don't know if they'd let you into a gallery wearing that."

The Mexican laughed, dryly. "Maybe not. I can find something to wear. Or Djego can..." he scratched the back of his head, wincing. "It's hard to tell sometimes who's who. You understand." He stared at his fingers for a moment, then gently felt around his eyes and at the bridge of his nose. "I'm Djego. Of course I am! I'm Djego the poet. Museums are exactly the sort of thing I like. Museums and avoiding trouble." He lowered his head. "Ask anyone. Djego hates fighting. Djego is a coward. Everyone knows." He spat the words.

He gazed out across the water, at the flickering torch.

"That was the problem. Djego ran away when they murdered everything he loved. Poor old Djego. He just wasn't equipped to handle that kind of thing. He needed someone else to take over. Someone better. Stronger. *More.*"

For a moment, there was steel in his voice, and in his eyes – and then he blinked and shook his head, scratching the back of it for a moment. "Djego... *I*... I am just looking after this." He held up the sword, looking at it in the light. "It's not mine."

Willis swallowed, looking nervously at the sword. When the half-naked man had hired his boat, back in Fort Hancock, he'd been happy with the payment offered. Six hundred, half in cash and half in valuables. Gold and diamond watches, tie pins. A couple of Nazi medals, which had been a little strange. Still, Willis had turned a blind eye. Now, he was wondering if he'd been right to be so mercenary about it. This man was crazier than a three-dollar bill in a windsock.

"So, what, uh, what kind of art are you interested in, Mr. Djego?" He smiled, wetting his lips and keeping his eyes on the sword.

"The soup cans. And I heard some things when I was talking to people on the way here. The kind of people who wear gold and diamond watches. And have Nazi medals in cigar boxes that they keep hidden and lovingly polished." He snarled, and started scratching the back of his head again. "Bastards." He shook his head, as though trying to focus his thoughts. "It seems... it seems as if I might have some business in this city. Well, Djego won't. Djego couldn't. But somebody will." Idly, he pulled the strip of red cloth out of his pocket. There were two holes in it.

His other hand continued to scratch, as if it couldn't stop. As if some itch in his skull was building and building.

"Business?" Willis took a shaky breath. "What, uh, what sort of business are you in?"

The Mexican blinked at him for a moment.

Then he tied the red cloth over his eyes in one quick movement.

Then he looked at Willis again.

Willis cried out and stumbled back, falling on the deck.

Behind the improvised mask, the Mexican's eyes were terrifying.

He stood – back straight, hair no longer in his eyes – and picked up his sword, gripping it as though it was a part of his arm. He gave a short, barking laugh, and even his voice was different; bold, mocking and macho. The Mexican had become a completely different person.

"I'm an exterminator, amigo."

He grinned – a madman's smile – and flipped Willis a quick salute. Then he jumped over the side.

Willis ran to the edge of the boat, looking into the water, but there was no sign the masked man had ever existed.

Willis sat down, trembling, trying to remember if he'd even heard a splash, and he wondered just what he'd let loose on New York City.

HERE'S ANOTHER STORY.

In Japantown, under the pink light of a shaded lamp, an otaku-kid took a steel flick-comb from his pocket and dragged it slowly through his Jesse Presley quiff, idly transferring a toothpick from one side of his mouth to the other. Hisoka looked at his reflection in the mirrored window of one of the idol stores, and it was acceptable. The weight of the nunchuks on his back felt good, felt right. It was a mark of status in his zoku to have hand-made nunchuks. He'd carved these himself from hardwood, and they were weighted perfectly, so that he could draw them from his back in one smooth motion, spinning and whirling them through the air in a dazzling display, never making the new-kid mistake of banging himself in the head or thigh with them. They were the only thing he'd ever been proud of in his life. With these – he knew with a cold and terrible certainly – he could kill a man.

Maybe he'd have to kill a man tonight.

There was trouble in the zoku between him and Orochi. It couldn't be helped. They were in love with the same girl, the neko-catgirl Akemi. Hisoka didn't have much time for catgirls – they were twee, silly, overdone – but that just made Akemi more remarkable to him. She carried the look in a way that was utterly unlike any of the others, that made the velvet ears and tail seem strangely exotic instead of an affectation so drastically out of fashion as to be simply absurd. The moment Hisoka had seen her, he'd known that this was the woman he would live and die for.

Probably die. But there were worse ways to die than for love.

Hisoka turned his head, hearing the soft whirr of metal and rubber. An ORB – the off-road bicycles the bosozoku ran with, with their thick-treaded rubber tyres. Just one, though. He knew what that meant. A visit from the Inspector.

He turned, looking contemptuously at the slowing bike, lip curled in an imitation of the King's sneer. "Inspector West."

The inspector bunny-hopped and skidded the ORB to a halt, the glass beads on the wheels rattling like the tail of a deadly snake as the sudden lack of centrifugal force left them clattering down the spokes. His eyes were hidden, as usual, behind black sunglasses, and his expression was as unreadable as ever. West was ex-bosozoku himself, the Americanised name hiding his Japanese heritage. The rumour ran that he'd been raised from birth by an outlaw vigilante who lived in a graveyard, and on reaching adolescence he'd formed his own outlaw bike gang to keep the peace in Japantown in the face of a corrupt police force, only joining the pigs himself once he'd burnt the corruption out at the root, and even then only to catch his mentor's killer. It was a good story, and it bought him a lot of respect in the Japantown gang culture, more than for the other cops. But it didn't make him a friend.

"Big night, Hisoka."

Hisoka shifted the toothpick to the other side of his mouth and shrugged, a studied display of indifference.

The Inspector spoke the language. He knew that too much talk was a weakness. He'd already said everything he needed to say – that he knew what was likely to happen, that he knew where, that he'd be watching. Whoever won in the coming clash between Hisoka and Orochi, the winner would walk away in cuffs and spend the rest of his life locked up in Rackham, and Akemi would find another boy, some handsome neko like herself, perhaps.

So be it. To be otaku was to live a manga, and the best mangas were the noirs. Hisoka shrugged again, enjoying the thrill of fatalism that shot through him, and turned his back, showing the

Inspector his nunchuks as he walked away.

On Inspector West's face, there was the faintest trace of disappointment. He could pull the kid in, check if he had a permit for those things, but it would only postpone what was coming. He stood off the saddle, driving his feet down hard on the pedals to bring the ORB up to speed, and raced off into the night, leaving Hisoka to his destiny.

Hisoka never made it to the meeting. They found him the next morning, with six bullet holes in his chest. On the body, someone had left a white business card. On one side, there was a spider design, in red. On the other, a haiku:

> *Where all inhuman*
> *Devils revel in their sins –*
> *The Blood-Spider spins!*

His nunchuks were never found.

HERE'S ANOTHER STORY.

Just off Broadway, the man in the tweed coat sniffed, sipping the pint of bitter he'd ordered, and grimaced. O'Malley hated that – the little grimace. Sons of bitches came all the way from Magna Britannia and the first thing they ordered when they came into O'Malley's was English bitter. And then they grimaced, because it was made in New Jersey and they hadn't got it just the way they served it in Assrapeshire or wherever the hell they came from.

Screw it. It was O'Malley's own fault for opening an English bar in the first place.

The man frowned. "It's not quite the way it is back home, is it?"

His wife pursed her lips, her mouth becoming reminiscent of a dog's wrinkled asshole. "Well, they don't know any better. They're all socialists here. No education to speak of. Dreadful little country."

So what the hell are you even doing here, O'Malley didn't say. Instead, he just kept on cleaning the glasses and counting his blessings that there weren't any other New Yorkers nearby to make the kind of scene he couldn't get away with making. Tourists were his lifeblood, especially the rich limeys from across the pond who flocked in their thousands to get a first hand look at the City Of Tomorrow. A few even stuck around. These two wouldn't.

One look told the story. They just didn't get it.

The man snorted, not bothering to lower his voice. "Well, obviously. Have you noticed they don't have any flags here?"

"We've got a flag. We don't use it much." O'Malley scowled despite himself. It'd been a sore point since 1954.

"Well, there you are. And they go on and on about all the culture here, and then you go to the gallery and it's all just nonsense, just a lot of silly colours and shapes. My five-year-old nephew could do better. And the music..." He turned to O'Malley, as if he was responsible for everything he'd seen and heard. "I've never heard anything like it in my life! The *noise!* There was one fellow playing some sort of – well, I'm not sure what–"

"Guitar." muttered O'Malley.

The man flushed; his wife tutted and sniffed, her mouth shrinking even tighter. "He wasn't even wearing a suit. When I go to a concert back home, we expect the performers to be dressed properly and to play proper instruments. And proper music. Not three-minute bursts of jingles and shouting."

O'Malley shrugged and picked up another glass. "Who was it?"

The man in the tweed shook his head angrily; his wife's mouth had almost disappeared. "Oh, I don't know. They were singing something about 'taking Berlin'. Probably your socialist friends. Well, that sort of propaganda doesn't wash with me. As far as I'm concerned, I'd rather have a thousand like Herr Hitler than one Bolshevik like Bartlet or Rickard. If you ask me, a strong leader like that is what this country needs."

O'Malley scowled. Typical Brits – half of them probably mailed checks to Untergang from their cosy little armchairs back home. "Yeah, well, he's not exactly a good friend of ours, so you might want to watch that kind of talk while you're here."

The man drew himself up to his full height – roughly a foot and a half shorter than O'Malley. "And you should watch your tone, Sir. I'm a guest in your country, and a customer, and the customer is always right."

O'Malley breathed in, then out. *Don't get mad at the customers.* All it took was one bad report spreading through Assrapeshire and he could end up losing a hundred customers. Keep the Brits happy, that was the rule. That was the price for running an English bar.

He could've taken his brother's advice and started a futurehead club, but no, he wanted to serve a 'better class of person'. What a schmuck.

"Sorry, Sir," he muttered, concentrating on cleaning the pint glasses.

There was a long silence. The Brits didn't say anything else for a while, and O'Malley was glad of that.

After about a minute of strained silence, the bell over the door rang and a skinny guy with long, dirty blonde hair and a ratty beard walked in, sniffing the air like a dog. He looked as though he hadn't bathed in weeks. The Brits shrank back, looking daggers. The long-haired man just smiled, good-natured.

"Hey, Larson." O'Malley smiled.

"Uh, hey, O'Malley." Larson grinned, nervous, fumbling in his pocket. "Listen, can I borrow your phone?"

O'Malley nodded. "Just remember to pay for the call. How's the fight against the Man? The cops still hassling you?" He took a perverse pleasure in needling Larson about his police phobia, especially with those damned supercilious Brits hanging on every word he said. Larson couldn't have come in at a better time.

The man with the dirty blonde hair laid twenty bucks down on the counter. Larson was notorious for being broke – chasing the dragon would do that to you. This was more money than O'Malley had ever seen him with. "Damn, Larson, what have you been getting into?"

Larson chuckled nervously. "Oh, uh, this and that." He wandered back behind the bar, heading into the back room, and O'Malley found himself surreptitiously listening in, trying to hear what was said over the loud tuts of the British heifer and her grim husband.

"Disgusting," the British guy kept saying, over and over. "Disgusting country. Disgusting people."

O'Malley ignored him.

"Uh, never mind how I found you," Larson whispered into the phone. "I've got something you want..."

Jesus, he'd better not be dealing drugs on my phone, O'Malley thought. Twenty bucks wasn't worth that.

"Who was that *awful man?*" The woman hissed, her eyes wide with indignation.

"College professor." O'Malley murmured, still trying to keep an ear on Larson. He didn't even seem to be speaking English any more. What was that, Spanish?

The British man took another sip of his bitter, shaking his head. "I suppose that's the sort of person who enjoys your American 'concerts'. It's disgusting. Disgusting. They didn't even play your national anthem at the end. Shocking behaviour."

O'Malley frowned, turning his attention back to the tourists. "Yeah, we don't use that much either. Mind if we drop the subject?"

The man sniffed, as if something smelled bad. "Not very patriotic, are you? Not proud of your flag, not proud of your anthem. If some chap was like that back home, we'd say he was rather un-British, what? I suppose that would make you un-American or something!"

The glass in O'Malley's hand cracked.

His knuckles were white, and so was his face. He was sixty-three years old, old enough to remember the last time he'd heard that word, the word nobody ever said anymore. Old enough to remember where it had led. Old enough not to be able to hear the name McCarthy without flinching. Old enough to remember The Second Civil War, the six days of hell when you didn't know who was your neighbour and who was Hidden Empire. Six days when people you'd lived next door to for years took a knife to you, calling you a monster, a *liberal,* like it was a curse word, a fake American. An *un-American.*

And the un-Americans didn't get to live.

Sure, it was all mind control, or that's what most had told themselves so as not to tear the country apart for good when it was all over. Still, after that week, there wasn't a USA anymore.

There couldn't be. So the big boys had made it official – sent the message that there'd never be another McCarthy, another Hidden Empire. This was the USSA, and that's how it was staying.

There was a sign behind the bar: *Doc Thunder drinks free.* Pretty much every bar in New York had a sign like it, and everybody knew what it meant.

Everybody except the tourists.

Rudi O'Malley – who'd seen his parents hung in front of his eyes on his sixteenth birthday, who'd seen a man's entrails torn from his belly and wrapped around a flagpole while people laughed and cheered, who'd killed twenty-eight people in the battle for the White House and dreamed of twenty-eight screaming faces every single night of his life – excused himself, dropped the broken glass into the sink, and went into the back room to bandage his hand.

Larson popped his head around the door. "Listen, O'Malley, thanks for the, uh... the... O'Malley?" He gingerly reached out a hand, as if to touch O'Malley's shoulder, then withdrew it awkwardly. "Are, uh... are you okay?"

O'Malley looked at himself in the mirror, at the fat, lazy tears running down his old, worn face. At his lousy, horrible bar and his lousy, horrible clientele and his whole lousy, horrible life.

"Yeah." He said. "Yeah, Larson, I'm fine. Go watch the bar for me, will you? I'll be out in a sec."

Rudi O'Malley was a New Yorker.

What else could he say?

HERE'S A FINAL story.

In the penthouse suite of the Atlas apartments, Heinrich Donner looked out over the city. The twinkling lights of the gas and oil lamps shone up at him like fireflies, and for a moment he remembered other fires. And chimneys that belched black smoke laced with human fat.

That had been a long time ago. He was old now, his white hair almost gone, his beard snow white, his blue eyes turned grey and clouded with the years. He leant on a stick, and rarely changed out of his dressing-gown. What was the point? He never left. Even his landlord had never seen him, or the man who brought his food – even the prostitutes who he took his frustrations at this half-a-life out on came and went blindfolded, so they couldn't see his face.

He remembered once a blindfold had slipped. He'd found the strength to bludgeon her to death, then made some calls to the people he could trust, those in Untergang who still felt he had some value to the organisation. They'd come and cleaned up the mess, and warned him that further mistakes could not be brushed under the carpet so easily. He had to chuckle at the irony. After all, wasn't he a mistake? And had he not been brushed under the carpet, installed in this palatial tomb, a battered relic kept against the day when he might have value again?

Once upon a time, Heinrich Donner was the heart and soul of Untergang. It had been his idea; a fifth column of Nazi operatives, working within American society to corrupt and disrupt from within, blurring the line between criminal activity and terrorism. After the disasters of the Russian campaign, it had been a reasonable success in terms of destabilising the country and spreading panic among the populace. And because the Führer could plausibly distance himself from Untergang – a terrorist organisation operating outside his mandate – Britannia had little to say on the matter beyond a tired shrug and a veiled warning to keep such tactics on American shores and out of the way of the Empire.

Of course, Heinrich Donner was not the 'leader' of the group. That honour fell to a man named Mannheim, codenamed 'Cobra', whose job was to send long ranting missives to newspapers claiming full responsibility for the Untergang's actions. It served a dual purpose. Since 'Cobra' was only a man sitting behind a typewriter or a wax-cylinder recorder several miles away from any action, he could never realistically be caught – and if Mannheim was apprehended, another 'Cobra' would take his place. The public would see that those charged to defend them could not even catch one man, and panic and disquiet would spread.

And, of course, Donner's hands would remain clean and pure.

Heinrich Donner was a prominent industrialist, a noted businessman, a beloved philanthropist. All of New York had celebrated him when he'd stepped in to help rebuild the city after the horrific events of the Second Civil War. (And damn that fool McCarthy for his stupid, failed attempt. If he'd only swallowed his damned pride and worked with the Führer – but the past was the past, and there could be no going back.)

As far as America was concerned, Heinrich Donner was a saint among men. They cheered his modest speeches, filled with gentle humility, wept at his tearful account of fleeing Germany as a young husband and father to escape Hitler's tyranny, of losing his wife and child to the madman's grasp. The only one who knew the full truth was Doc Thunder, and he could prove nothing in a court of law, of course. Besides, he knew that to expose Donner's secrets would mean exposing his own. He was effectively stalemated.

It had all been going so well.

Why had he become so obsessed with Thunder? Why had he never simply given up, washed his hands of the whole situation, focused on more achievable goals? All those endless attempts to kill him, to steal his blood, to have America's great symbol brought down, brought low... it had brought attention to him, over time. The wrong kind of attention. Eventually, he was caught in an explosion and believed dead, and the Führer had quietly suggested that he should remain that way. For a few years, he had continued to run Untergang's operations, but his heart was no longer in the work, and gradually it passed to other hands, younger hands... until finally he had nothing but this apartment, a monthly allowance for food, drink and whores, and handlers who were only seeing to his needs until the kill order came through and they could dispose of him once and for all.

And the order would never come, he knew. The Führer had long since forgotten him. Untergang's latest leader had his own master plans and never gave Donner the slightest thought. He was a relic, a battered old antique, a souvenir of a bygone age. His place in the scheme of things had been taken by younger men with bigger and better ideas. The world had moved on.

He still hated Doc Thunder. That was the worst thing. That burning, black hatred would never go away, and now it was matched by a bitter, bottomless frustration. To know that you would never look into your enemy's eyes again, never watch them squirm, know the sweet taste of their fear... to know he could never *hurt* Thunder again... it was unendurable.

His lips moved, and he began to whisper.

Please, mein Gott. Please. Give me one chance. Let me hurt him once more. Let me be the catalyst that brings misery and torture down on his head, him and all his kind, all the strutting fools in their masks and their ridiculous outfits, all the ones who made me suffer, who reduced me to this shell. Let me take my final revenge on them all...

Be careful what you pray for.

The sword slid through his back, between his ribs, piercing his heart. The man standing behind him twisted the blade, and Donner shuddered, his eyes bulging, then rolling back.

El Sombra withdrew the sword from the man's corpse and wiped it on the curtains. He'd come straight here after he'd gotten the information, and by the look of things – he prodded the corpse onto its back with a bare toe, studying the features – his information had been correct. He'd half-expected the old man to go for a gun when he'd broken in, but he hadn't even heard. Probably deaf, or nearly deaf. Idly, he took a step backwards, listening to the ugly, wet sound of the bowel letting go, and then turned on his heel and wandered off to check for papers, or lists of names, or maps. Executing one of the Bastards was always fun in and of itself, but he didn't want this to become a dead end. If the Ex-King Of The Bastards had fallen from grace, maybe he'd gathered some insurance on the way down. Or at least something that could be used to find more of them.

He found what he was looking for in the bedroom.

Ignored, the body on the carpet began to cool, and stiffen. Two days and eleven hours later, it would be found by patrolmen after Donner's downstairs neighbour complained about the spreading stain on his ceiling, and the stench from above. The newspapermen would hear of it, and it would become front page news – the dead man who died a second time.

And then all Hell would descend on Manhattan.

And a lot of stories would come to an end.

CHAPTER ONE

The Case of the Stolen Lightning

NIGHT WAS FALLING, and the city was coming to life once again.

As Rabbi Johann Labinowicz shuffled into the deli, he closed his eyes for a moment and took in the sound of the bell. A small, perfect little object that tinkled softly and gently, with a clear, resonant sound whenever the door opened, Johann had found himself wandering three blocks or more out of his way simply to hear it, and as a result this particular deli had, over a span of years, become his regular haunt.

Johann was a man who took pleasure in small things. The ring of a shop's bell, the taste of a perfectly made salt beef hoagy with pickle and mustard. Having your habits and tastes known by your deli. Little things of that nature.

"One salt beef, pickle and mustard." Mrs McGregor said it like a hello, as her husband had. Bill McGregor had passed away five years ago, but Alma had taken over the running of McGregor's Fine Deli and it was as though nothing had happened. She'd mourned, a deep and terrible wound in her had healed over time, but she'd done her mourning in between chopping egg and scattering cress, frying onion for the beef dogs and fine-slicing gherkin the way her husband had taught her. Only her regulars had noticed any change at all, and no change at all in the food. Mrs McGregor was a close and private woman, who played her emotions like cards against her chest. Johann had known her twelve years, and still considered being greeted in such a way to be an honour worth more than rubies.

He'd already counted out the three dollars, fumbling in his pocket as he walked the last few steps from the door with its wonderful bell, and now he laid them out on the counter with a smile, before picking up the sandwich that had already materialised, prepared in advance of his arrival. "You know, Alma, maybe the day comes I don't walk in that door, eh? And then, you'll be out a fresh sandwich."

Alma snorted, shaking her head. "Oh, that will never happen, Rabbi. You're an addict, you are."

Johann shrugged. "What, I have no will of my own? A slave to the salt beef? Suppose I'm trampled by a runaway horse, eh?"

Alma shook her head and went back to slicing pickles. "Then I'd come to the hospital and throw the damned sandwich in your face for being such a god-damned fool as to not look both ways and you'd apologise to me for being so foolish and the sandwich wouldn't have been wasted at all, now, would it?"

Johann chuckled to himself. "Such language!" He sniffed the sandwich, enjoying the tang of the pickle and the waft of the fresh bread.

The bell rang again.

The boy who walked in was barely more than sixteen, but he was six foot and muscular with it. He slouched as he walked, and his hair was carefully shaved into three stripes – blood red, bone white and a livid blue that seemed garish and clown like against his black skin. He was wearing a powder-blue t-shirt with the familiar lightning bolt decal torn off and pinned back upside-down, with the same safety-pins that pierced both his ears. His jeans were ripped, and around each wrist was a studded leather band.

On his left bicep, he wore a tattoo of a scowling McCarthy and the word: AMERICAN.

A futurehead.

Johann stiffened, inspecting him carefully. Futureheads could be trouble, and this one was dressed to provoke. Still, usually with futureheads that was all it was – provoking a reaction. Shocking the old men. They were harmless. Oh, they'd turn the air blue if you crossed them, call you everything under the sun, but that was all they'd do.

Johann allowed himself to drift into a daydream of the moments ahead. The young man would at the very worst say something he imagined to be shocking to the ears of an old Rabbi – little dreaming that an old Rabbi could already tell him stories that would make him faint – and the old Rabbi in question would play his part and tut and speak of *kids today* or *it's just noise they listen to now* and the dance would be complete. The two of them would go their separate ways, each having played a different game and each, in their own eyes, the winner.

And in maybe five years, no more, Johann would see the boy grown to a man, dressed in ordinary clothes, and the boy would raise his hat respectfully and both would have forgotten this meeting had ever taken place, lost as it was in wild youth.

It was a story Johann had played out countless times with countless disaffected young people, and it was a story he almost enjoyed. It was the story he would have preferred.

"Gimme a sammich." the young man growled, and spat on the floor. Johann winced. Alma wouldn't take that well. Part of him felt he should leave, but he owed it to Alma to provide support in the face of what was sure to be an unpleasant customer interaction.

Alma took the bait, as Johann knew she would. "May I have a sandwich *please,* you young hooligan! And no you may not after you spat on my clean floor! Were you raised in a barn?"

The futurehead scowled. "I want a sammich."

"Well, you're not getting one. Now clear off out of my shop before I throw you out! And don't think I can't!" Alma heaved and shook with indignation, her face beet red. In that moment, Johann believed that she really could have thrown the young man bodily out of her door, as big and surly as he was.

The young man blinked, the scowl still on his face. Then - without a word - he simply reached, took the sandwich from Johann's grasp, and bit into it.

"S'a good sammich." he grinned, in between chews.

Johann simply stared.

"You get out now! You get out of my shop!" screeched Alma, purple with fury. The futurehead smirked through a mouthful of the Rabbi's bread and beef, and moved to the door. He'd won the battle. He'd walked in and taken what he wanted, and now he would leave.

"Wait." said Johann, softly.

The young man turned, looked at him, and bit into the sandwich again.

"You can have my sandwich."

The young man narrowed his eyes.

"No, you can have it. You can come in here and cause trouble and spit on a clean floor, if that's what you enjoy. You can steal from an old man, take what you haven't earned. You can do what you like." Johann felt the blood rushing to his cheeks and heard the anger in his own voice. "You can! You can dress like you're in the Hidden Empire, like good people never fought and bled and died to make you safe from them! You can do all of that, because you're taller than we are. It's just a matter of height. You're taller than we are, and stronger than we are, and you look more threatening than we do! And in your world that is the only thing that matters! That, I understand! That is the path you have chosen for yourself – good luck to you! *Mazel tov!*"

He paused, gathering his fury, his fists clenched. Then he reached out and grabbed a hold of the upside-down lightning bolt, the safety pins popping away as he pulled and the ragged patch of blue cloth came away in his hands. "But you will not disgrace *this* while you do it!"

The boy blinked, shock written over his face. Johann's fist shook. "Now get out. Get out of here."

The futurehead threw Johann's sandwich onto the floor, spat, and left, the door slamming violently behind him.

The bell rang furiously for a second, then came to a stop.

"Oy..." Johann breathed. He felt drained. He hadn't meant to lose his temper that way.

"Give me that." Alma smiled, taking the square of cloth from his hands, then pinning it up behind the counter. "It'll make a good conversation piece. You want me to call the cops?"

Johann shook his head. "No... no, I just lost my temper with him." He let out a sigh, feeling his heart hammering in his chest. "I'm too old for such nonsense. For a three-dollar sandwich! And what have I achieved? For you, a conversation piece and a dirty floor. For me, almost a heart attack, maybe worse if that schmuck had taken a swing at me... ah, let me help you clean this up."

Alma smiled. "I won't hear of such a thing, Rabbi. You sit yourself down and catch your breath and I'll make you up a fresh one."

"No, no..." Johann sighed. "I couldn't eat it now. I'll head back to my apartment and take some soup when my stomach is settled."

"Then take your three dollars back, at least."

"Three extra dollars would throw my whole budget off. I'd become extravagant. You keep it, or give it away to a hungry orphan." He shuffled towards the door, swinging it open and listening to the sound. "Wait, wait – promise me one thing, Alma, if you think you owe me something for acting like an old fool."

Alma raised an eyebrow.

"Don't ever change that bell."

FOUR BLOCKS LATER, Johann found himself chuckling over the incident. The look on the young man's face! He'd think twice in the future, perhaps, about bullying old men. And perhaps he wouldn't. Still, it was nice to dream.

Johann's eyes flicked up to the solitary gas lamp that lit the dark alley, his little shortcut home. Someone had cut little stars and moons from coloured paper and stuck them on the glass, so that they threw great coloured shapes onto the ground below. The effect was quite charming. A square of cardboard propped against the wall told the rest of the story. Breakers had, sometime the night before, made the alley an impromptu dancehall, at least until the residents had run them off.

Breakers and bikers, futureheads and Warhol-girls. And that lightning bolt on blue cloth watching over them all. Manhattan was a strange place, and yet occasionally it threw up little wonders, pink stars cast in light on the concrete floor of an alleyway. A small thing, but representative of all the strangeness and charm of this unique place, this City Of Tomorrow...

Johann took pleasure in small things.

At that moment, he became aware of footsteps behind him. A cold chill seized his chest, and he swallowed hard, that terrible certainty of who those footsteps might belong to racing through his mind. *No, surely not,* he told himself. *I'm an old man.*

There was a low, mean chuckle from behind. He steeled himself. He would look around, and he'd see a group of young men, and he'd recognise none of them. And they'd walk right by him, never thinking to bother an old Rabbi. It was a story he'd played out a dozen times in this alley. A good story.

So Johann turned his head, and found himself looking at three stripes of hair coloured red, white and blue, and a t-shirt with a square torn out of the front and a couple of safety pins hanging from that ragged edge, and a pair of eyes with hate and humiliation in them.

It was the boy from earlier. And not alone. Two others, the same age, walked either side of him, one black, one white, both of them in the same mish-mash of ragged clothes held together by safety pins and charged symbols. The other young black man's face was a mass of steel piercings and studs that made the handsome features alien and ugly.

The white boy wore a swastika.

It was beginning to rain.

Johann sped up, walking faster, as the spattering raindrops hit his cheeks like tears, trickling down. Behind him, the footsteps sped up to match. The rain intensified, suddenly coming down in sheets, the filthy alley lit bright white for a split-second before a crash of thunder formally announced the storm. *Why didn't I bring my umbrella?* Johann thought, madly, and then he found himself running, feet splashing in the growing puddles.

He ran, and they ran after him. It was a race now. At the end of the long, dark alley, he could see trotting horses, smell hotdogs, see bright lights, a finish line. If he could just get to the lights, he might be safe–

And then he tripped.

He landed face-down on the wet, dirty floor of the alley, knocking the wind from his lungs. He lay there a moment in the wet and the dirt, coughing weakly, and then a heavy boot pressed down on his back, pinning him.

He heard the quiet *click* of a switchblade springing from its casing. Then another. Then a third.

"Gimme my bolt back, old man." The voice was flat, emotionless, as it had been in the Deli. Another voice beside snickered softly, barely audible over the sound of the rain coming down.

"Yeah," said the new voice. "Old man. Give him it before we cut you."

Johann tried to croak out a response – something, anything – and then the boot on his back stamped down harder. Why were they doing this? He was an old man – but then, that was the reason, of course. He was an old man who had humiliated a younger one. With a sudden cold clarity, he understood that they would kill him. They would murder him in this filthy alley and then the three of them would go back to the deli, and see what they were looking for, what Alma had tacked to the wall, and they would want it back, and Alma would stand up for herself and they would kill her too. If they had to, they would kill her quickly, but if they could get away with it, they would kill her slowly. Because they could, and that was all the justification they needed.

But they would kill him slowly first.

The boot pressed down on his back. He tried to say a prayer, but he had no breath to say it. At the end of the alley, he could see the lights, and the horses, and the people passing by, rain dripping off their umbrellas.

Not one of them looked at him.

"Gimme my bolt." the futurehead growled, in his dead, emotionless monotone.

Johann could not speak. His lips moved, but no sound came.

There was only the sound of the rain.

And then the sound of a bullet.

A bloody rose bloomed at the back of the young man's head, opposite the hole that had suddenly appeared just below the white strip of hair. His eyes bulged, lost focus, and then he toppled backwards, dead.

Johann flinched, feeling the weight of the boy's boot come off his back, then heard the splash of the heavy corpse hitting the puddles of the grimy alley floor.

For a moment, there was no sound at all, bar a kind of high-pitched squeak, an animal whimper that crawled out of the throat of the boy with the swastika shirt, as if he was some small burrowing thing caught in a wire trap.

Then there was laughter.

A terrible, echoing laugh, of a kind one might find in the pits of Hell, a laugh that bounced and rolled off the brick and steel and seemed to echo from every corner at once, booming, roaring, growing louder and louder. Johann felt ice in his chest, and once more his wrinkled lips began to stumble through the Kaddish, eyes shutting tight, as if warding off imaginary monsters in the way he had as a child.

When he opened them again, the monster stood in front of him.

He was close to six foot in height, and the long coat of black leather he wore gave him the appearance of being half shadow, a silhouette picked out against the gaslight of the street beyond. Johann blinked the raindrops from his eyes – or were they tears? – and tried to make out further detail, but there was none, only a sea of black, a black hole in space in the shape of a man. Black suit and shirt, black gloves with an odd texture to them, holding a pair of automatic pistols. And a black slouch hat that covered his face–

–*oh God, his face!*

Johann gasped, and behind him the boy in the swastika made another strangled cry, as though the wire around the struggling animal had tightened.

His face! That terrible mask!

As the monster tilted his head to stare at his persecutors, Johann could see the whole of it. A head of black leather, with a mask of shining metal, and that metal mask coloured a burnished bloody red, featureless but for the eight lenses that shone in the half-light like the eyes of some terrible spider, hiding all evidence of humanity. The effect was terrifying, an emotionless blank visage that spoke of remorseless, unstoppable vengeance for unimaginable crimes. Behind him, Johann heard the boy in the swastika shirt scream.

"What are you? You ain't human!"

The man in the blood-red mask hissed, like escaping steam, and then the hiss turned into a laugh, that devil's laugh, mocking, sneering, rolling across the wet stone.

Then he raised his twin pistols.

The boy with the piercings – the one who'd remained silent up until now – let out a yell and hurled himself towards the figure in black, switchblade gleaming. In response, there was the roar of automatic fire as shot after shot slammed into his bare chest and burst from his back in fountains of blood and bone. His face twisted in an agonised rictus as he took two more steps forward, propelled by the momentum of his charge, and then dropped to the alley floor, a foot from the Rabbi's trembling, prone form.

Johann felt the warmth as the young man's blood pooled against him.

The boy in the swastika shirt took a stumbling step backward, his face deathly pale and slick with sweat. His own blade slid from his grasp to clatter on the ground at his feet, and his hands slowly jerked upwards, as if on puppet strings. "Please." he croaked, tears streaming down his face. "Please. Please."

The man in the mask stopped laughing.

He stepped over Johann's shaking body, walking towards the boy, gazing down on him with those eight expressionless glass eyes. Again, there was a hiss, like steam escaping from some dreadful engine of death.

Then he spoke.

"You... surrender."

The boy blinked, slowly shaking his head. The crotch of the ripped denim jeans he wore darkened as a stream of piss trickled down his leg to mix with the rainwater and the blood.

Gently, the man in the mask pressed the barrel of one of his twin automatics into the centre of the Nazi emblem on the boy's chest.

"For show?"

The boy let out another whimper, eyes wide and wet. He tried to find any sign of mercy in that cold, red metal mask, any humanity shining back at him from those eight monstrous lenses.

He saw nothing at all.

The masked man hissed again, softly.

"You should start mixing with a better class of people."

Then he turned his back. The boy stood for a moment, face white, hands still raised, swaying gently in the air like balloons on strings. Then the spell was broken, and he ran back the way he came, sobbing like a child.

The man in the mask bent down and began to help Johann to his feet. The Rabbi flinched at his touch, surprised by the gentleness of it. He swallowed, and spoke softly: "Thank you. I think they would have killed me."

He stood, the adrenaline making him quiver, unsteady on his feet. His clothes were sticky with blood. He looked down at the two dead young men – boys, children – and then up at the blank mask. "Please. I am grateful, you saved my life, but..." He swallowed. "Was there no other way?"

There was a chuckle from behind the mask, dry as kindling.

"Not for them."

Johann swallowed, and nodded, feeling like a coward. He wanted to go home and wash the blood from himself, to be far away from this terrible creature that had saved his life. He wanted to be sick, to sleep for a hundred years, to feel something besides the cold weight of horror coiling in his gut.

"Well. Thank you again." he said, quietly, and turned away. He wondered whether he should call the police.

The man in the mask laid a hand on his shoulder.

"A moment."

Johann's blood froze.

The man's grip on his shoulder was soft, almost gentle. *"Did you think you could escape me, Rabbi Labinowicz?"*

"What? What are you talking about?" Johann swallowed, feeling a cold trickle of sweat at the base of his neck. Helplessly, he tried to jerk away from the hand, but the grip on his shoulder was suddenly like a steel vice.

The other hand still held a squat, smoking automatic pistol.

"Did you think I came here by accident? That I don't know every detail about you?" The laughter came again, and the eight blank lenses reflected the terrified, sweating face of the Rabbi back at him. *"You take a special interest in the children of the neighbourhood, don't you, Johann?"*

Johann licked dry lips. "What of it? The schooling here – they need to learn! I teach them!" His voice sounded hollow in his ears, like a murderer pleading for clemency. *Oh God, how had it come to this?* "Mathematics, and sciences..."

The masked man hissed slowly, dangerously, like a snake about to strike. The blank, emotionless lenses seemed to bore into Johann's soul, uncovering his every secret.

"I know exactly what you teach them." The voice was cold, mocking, deadly. *"You take pleasure in small things, don't you, Rabbi Labinowicz?"*

Johann cried out as if he'd been struck, trying to struggle free again. "Please," he begged, his voice hoarse, "whatever I've... whatever you *think* I've done, please. You don't have to do this. I'll do what you want, I'll, I'll go to the police–"

The man in the mask laughed again, a low, throaty cackle, redolent of cobwebs and deep graves. He raised his pistol to Johann's face. *"I have a surer way of dealing with your kind. Open your mouth, Rabbi. I have another small thing for you, but this time I doubt you will take much pleasure in it at all."*

"Please–" begged Johann, but he got no further. The bullet entered his mouth and blew the back of his head out across the brickwork. He slumped to the floor and the man in the mask put another into his head for good measure.

In the street beyond, the men and women still walked to and fro. They paid no heed to the sound of gunfire, nor did they notice the trickle of blood running from the alley across the sidewalk and into the gutter. They knew better.

In the alley, Johann's corpse, and the others, began to stiffen, the pouring rain pooling in the bullet-wounds and the sockets of their eyes. Sitting atop each of them was a small white business card with a red spider motif on the back, and a short haiku on the front:

> *Where all inhuman*
> *Devils revel in their sins –*
> *The Blood-Spider spins!*

Of the Blood-Spider himself, there was no sign.

CHAPTER TWO

Doc Thunder and The Queen of the Leopard Men

As a rule, Maya Zor-Tura woke late.

Each morning, she floated slowly to awareness like a bubble of air rising up from some bottomless ocean trench, the half-remembered fancies of her dream breaking apart and dissipating into the morning sun as it poured through the skylight and splashed onto the silk sheets. Her eyes fluttered open, blinking away the last crumbs of sleep, and she stretched like a cat, arching her back and opening her mouth into a wide, luxurious yawn. And straight after that, on most mornings, she went back to a light doze, finally deigning to grace the household with her presence at eleven, or noon, or perhaps a little after lunch.

At the appointed hour, she'd appear in a gown of translucent yellow silk, or a sharply-cut suit, or her 'adventuring clothes' – black leather corset, boots and coat, with a royal purple skirt in a ragged style on the cutting edge of current fashion – or, quite often, nothing at all. On Maya, nudity seemed as elegant and refined as the evening clothes of British royalty.

She was tall, with flowing dark hair, skin the colour of rich, dark coffee and cat-like green eyes that seemed to constantly radiate a kind of amused superiority, and none of these traits had faded in several thousand years of existence.

For Maya Zor-Tura, time was something that happened to other people.

This morning, she paused in mid-stretch and for just the smallest moment she tried to recall exactly what the dream had been about. Dreams were important, despite Doc's occasional and somewhat half-hearted insistence that they were only a natural function of the brain. He'd learned a more unscientific and unpalatable truth in their time together – that dreams, and especially Maya Zor-Tura's, contained messages. Soundings from the past, and the future, and places beyond human understanding, often all at once. Warnings that should not be ignored.

And this dream seemed especially potent and vivid.

A dream of murder.

Murder, and a man in a mask the colour of blood.

She shook her head, brow furrowed. Did the mask cover his whole face, or just his eyes? She frowned, marring her beauty with her frustration for a single instant. Trying to catch a dream and remember it was like trying to hold smoke in your hands. This one was gone.

She dismissed the remnants of it from her mind for the moment and stretched idly, enjoying the emptiness of the bed. There was something rather decadent about having it all to herself, lounging in that vast, warm space, with the scents of the linen and the bodies that had lain there mixing as she breathed in. It made her almost feel like a goddess again. Maya wondered occasionally about going back to that life, to the forbidden kingdom of Zor-Ek-Narr and the half-human, half-leopard men who'd been her concubines and worshippers. It had been luxurious in a way that the townhouse in New York could never be, even on a morning like this. But it had been so very dull, at the end.

That's why she'd gone with the Doc, when he'd come bursting into her serene existence. The excitement, and the thought of a new world to explore.

She purred, remembering the first thing he'd ever said to her. He'd been chained to the wall of the Temple Of Serpents, and she had just drawn the tip of a red-hot iron across his bare chest – the scar had long vanished, as scars did with him, but occasionally she traced her finger along where it had been. She remembered that she'd paused, admiring the way he endured without flinching, and then he'd looked at her with those icy blue eyes.

"I never knew evil could be so beautiful." he'd said.

That was the English translation, of course. It wasn't quite so impressive unless you knew that in the secret tongue of the Leopard Men of Zor-Ek-Narr a particular synonym for 'evil' and the most common word for 'beautiful' sounded almost exactly alike, depending on how you rolled your tongue around the 'r'.

So in that one single moment, he'd shown how little pain or fear meant to him; he'd paid her a compliment, albeit a backhanded one; and, most importantly, he'd made a pun in a language he'd first heard spoken perhaps forty hours previously.

After that, Maya had to admit, she'd been intrigued. She'd allowed him to escape, had him recaptured and ordered him to fight in her personal arena against a cadre of Jaguar Warriors armed with poisoned spears, and all the time the flirting had continued. Once he'd saved her from the giant roc her treacherous high priest had attempted to feed her to, they'd both known exactly where things were leading.

It wasn't forever. He'd age, over the centuries, and she wouldn't. Eventually, he'd die, or she'd simply grow tired of him and walk away, and she knew herself well enough to realise that it was going to be the latter. Lately, she'd found herself thinking more and more about home, feeling an ache that was partly homesickness and partly a feeling of being stifled, of playing a role instead of living a life.

But for now, she was here and it was now and it was more exciting to spend her limitless time this way, in this wonderful city, in this wonderful life of science and adventure and danger, than any other way she could think of. Perhaps in a hundred days or a hundred years she'd think differently, and return to the forgotten temples and palaces of Zor-Ek-Narr to reclaim her queendom and become once again embroiled in the endless intrigues of her people. Or perhaps she wouldn't.

Right now, she decided, it was time to get up and have Marcel prepare her a strong coffee and a croissant. Opening the spacious walk-in closet, she combed through her wardrobe, settling on a simple light blue kimono, and then padded down the stairs to greet the rest of the household.

PASSING THE GYM on the second floor, she heard the soft creak of the chain supporting the heavy bag as it swung. If Monk was doing his morning workout, that made it a little after ten – earlier than she was used to. It was the dream that had woken her so early, the killer in the red mask. In the dream, was he standing over a body?

Yes. Someone she cared for, dead or about to be.

Worth noting.

She swung open the door to the gym and looked upwards. As usual, Monk was hanging by his toes from the ceiling rings, aiming fists big as hams into the big leather punch bag, his grotesque, simian face twisted in familiar effort.

Monk Olsen could best be described as a curiosity.

At the age of six months, he had been found on the doorstep of the Clark Olsen Orphanage in New Jersey, where presumably his parents had been unable to bear the thought of caring for such a monstrous child. Even at that tender age, his face bore the simian cast that would mark him for the rest of his life, while his arms were elongated, with a light coating of fur and already some muscular development, and his toes were large and long, bending and clutching instinctively at the end of his too-big feet. A doctor, called to minister to the baby, suggested that he be put down on the spot; Clark Olsen politely showed him the door.

Clark named him Eustace, after an uncle, but the child never did take to that, choosing instead to repurpose the cruel nickname the other boys taunted him with – Monk.

"If folks shout a word at you in the street, that's an insult. If they shout your name, it's like they're cheerin'. That's the way I figure it, anyhow."

He was five years old when he came up with that little bit of homespun wisdom, but Monk was far ahead of the curve as far as intelligence went. He had a keen eye and an analytical mind to go with his ape-like strength and gait, and on leaving the orphanage found himself a job as a photojournalist with a great metropolitan newspaper, where he showed a penchant for investigating the unusual. The paper touted him as the Gorilla Reporter, a nickname he accepted with a graceful shrug of his sloped shoulders.

Monk found himself used by the paper as a sort of in-house freak, a news story in his own right, and he allowed the editors to exploit him in that manner purely because it gave him access to the strangest, most bizarre stories in the city – impossible crimes, unbelievable inventions, crazed geniuses and the occasional dash of sexual oddity to add spice to the broth. With such a mandate it was only a matter of time before his path crossed with Doc Thunder's, and the outwardly unlikely friendship between the City Of Tomorrow's greatest hero and its ugliest citizen continued to fill untold column inches until Monk finally got bored of the daily grind and went freelance, mailing in the occasional story as Doc's assistant and sidekick.

Together, Maya and Monk were Doc's most trusted associates; 'the beauty and the beast', according to the papers. Rumour had it that the three of them formed a polyamorous triangle. Like all the best gossip, it was both difficult to believe and completely true.

"Hey, Princess!" grinned Monk, waving to Maya from his high perch, before swinging off the rings and somersaulting down to the floor, landing on the pads of his feet. "What happened, did the bed burn down? When have you ever been up so early?"

Maya laughed, kissing him and enjoying the feel of those strong simian arms thrown about her slim waist. "I think around 1647, by the Roman calendar. What can I say? It's a beautiful day and for some reason I didn't feel like wasting it." She kept the dream to herself, for the moment. She had hardly any clear details beyond that blood-red mask and the smell of death, and it didn't seem worth troubling Monk with it – not until she had some clear sign of what it meant. "Have you seen the Doc?"

"Doc?" Monk nodded, scratching his chin. "Down in the lab, last I saw. Looking over some forensic work. You remember Easton West over in Japantown?" Without pausing, Monk did a standing jump, leaping up in a backflip and stretching his thick legs so the long toes could grasp the ring, all with as much forethought as another man would spend in stepping onto a kerb. "He sent some paperwork and a little physical evidence over this morning from some vigilante killing – that spider guy, the one Doc doesn't like much..." Monk let the sentence trail off as he aimed a combination of punches at the heavy bag. Visitors to the brownstone often wondered why Monk Olsen might need a gym at all. He could break a man's skull like another man could crack open a fortune cookie, and there'd been times when he'd done exactly that. When asked about this, he would gently change the subject, not letting these curious souls know that the reason for his continuous training wasn't to practice throwing punches, but rather pulling them.

"I might be a monster," he'd say, "but I'm not a murderer. Not by choice."

The rain of blows landed on the bag with soft, agreeable thuds, sending it swinging back and forth on the sturdy chain but not bursting it asunder as he once had. These blows might break a man's neck, or flatten his nose, or crack his jaw down the middle. But they wouldn't kill. That was the important thing.

"I'll see you later," Maya called, and then left him to his work.

"Oh, and check *The Bugle.* I've not read it yet, but there's a howler of a headline on the front page." yelled Monk, and then unleashed another volley of restrained punches against the leather.

WHEN MARCEL BENOIT looked in the mirror, the Devil looked back.

The Devil used to smile, or laugh, or wink, but these days he assumed a contrite expression, looking over the top of his glasses as if to say – *mea culpa. It seemed like a fun idea at the time, but let's face it, it's starting to get a little tired.*

The Devil, according to Marcel, was a man of certain iron habits. He liked games of chance and chess, he liked a good trade and a better haggle and he liked to tell an incomplete truth, which is easier than a lie and a good deal more fun. He was easily reached, if you knew your way around a chalk circle, and always willing to let a fool bargain something precious away for a trinket he thought he wanted. Marcel was one such fool.

His tragedy had been a simple one. He would never be anything in the kitchen, not even a dishwasher. He could not use a knife without slicing open a finger or thumb, his palette could not distinguish a jalapeno pepper from a clump of mud, and his nose, constantly thick with cold, dripped regularly into any pan or open container he happened to lean over. He was *mal carne,* bad meat. And yet he wanted nothing more, in this life or any other, than to be one of the great chefs.

Of course, he could not sell his soul. What is a great chef without his soul?

Instead, he sold his reflection.

Nobody else could see it. Just him. But slowly, his deteriorating appearance, his lack of grooming and his hissed arguments with mirrors made him *persona non grata* in the restaurants of Paris. He was indeed a great chef, one of the greatest in the world. But when your best chef starts to have a blazing row with his own meat cleaver, he has to go, no matter how good the terrine is.

Marcel drifted, passing through the great culinary meccas of the world as he went, landing work as a line cook, or a pastry-chef, or a saucier, or any one of a hundred jobs far beneath his true talent. The cycle was always the same – he would come into a new kitchen and dazzle his fellow workers and the customers with his incredible culinary skills, and the bosses would look on him with favour. They would sample his fresh-baked bread or his reductions and state that they were never letting him go, that they would be fools to dismiss this wonderful man as so many others had. And then, one day, the Devil would say just the right thing from a mirror or a shiny piece of cookware or the back of a spoon, and Marcel would snap and rage against him at the top of his lungs, and it would all come out.

Who wants to employ an obvious madman in a place with knives? Marcel had to go.

Over time, his hair turned white, and the word spread, and even the smallest doors were closed to him. He ended up sprawled under a sheet of flat cardboard in a filthy alley, drinking bathtub gin and bursting into tears whenever the rain left enough of a puddle to see the Devil's face.

That was where Doc Thunder found him.

The circumstances were complicated.

Lars Lomax, the most dangerous man in the world, had attempted to use him as a guinea pig, understanding that he would not be missed. In the aftermath of the whole affair, as the emergency crews attempted to clear away the wreckage of Lomax's gigantic steam-powered Robo-Thunder, Doc had turned to him, laid one large hand on his shoulder, and asked what he could do to help.

"Let me cook for you," said Marcel. And Doc Thunder did. It was the best meal he had ever tasted.

Marcel had told Doc his story, and – rather than laughing or shaking his head in disgust or simply making a quiet call to the local sanatorium – Doc had done what he could. He'd had a new kitchen built, without reflective surfaces, and stocked it with cookware that would, likewise, not reflect, much of which he designed himself. And Marcel cooked, at first for the Doc, and then as time went by for Monk and Maya as well, and slowly he began to mend.

Occasionally, he would still catch sight of the Devil in a shop window or a puddle, and the Devil would only shrug. What was there to say? He had other games, and Marcel just wasn't that much fun anymore.

Maya had met the Devil herself, of course. You didn't get as old as she had without running into him sooner or later. She'd found him rather boring, and made her excuses. They'd not met since.

As she entered the kitchen, she breathed in the smell, as she did every morning; the powerful, sweet scent of the bacon fat, the subtle spice of cinnamon, the warm comforting aroma of the fresh bread, and under it all, as always, the dark, rich tint of her favourite coffee, waiting in a cup for her. "How do you always predict just when I'll want my coffee, Marcel?"

The Frenchman blushed and looked at his shoes. "I paid quite a price for the ability, Mademoiselle. But your smile is worth it all." He reached for the tray which he'd left on the side of the counter – a sumptuous Italian espresso, a perfectly cooked croissant and the morning paper. Even the paper was folded just so.

Maya cast her eye quickly over the paper, and frowned slightly. There was the headline Monk had spoken of: DEAD MAN FOUND MURDERED IN PENTHOUSE.

She could see Monk's point. It was a clumsy headline. If the man had been murdered, to say he was dead was a tautology. Still, something made her look more closely.

Heinrich Donner, the wealthy industrialist and German expatriate, had been found in a penthouse apartment across town, stabbed through the heart. The police believed a sword had been used. The title was referring to the fact that Donner had been missing for decades and was believed dead.

Maya frowned. A sword... had the masked man in her dream carried a sword? Or a gun?

She smiled sweetly at Marcel, finished her coffee and croissant, and then took the paper downstairs to the lab. Doc would want to know.

THE MAN IN the lab coat stood six foot seven, and his body seemed to be carved from bronze, a massive sculpture of hard muscle and sinew.

If he put his mind to it, the man could use that muscle to bend steel three inches thick, or jump an eighth of a mile. The bronze skin looked as tough as leather, and if put to the test it could shrug off bullets and leave only small bruises to mark their passing. An exploding shell might penetrate his skin, if applied directly, but it would not do much more than that.

The man needed to sleep no more than one hour out of every forty-eight, and during emergencies he had been known to stay awake a full week or more. He was more than seventy years old, but he barely looked half that age. If you shaved off the thick beard he wore, he could be mistaken for a man in his late twenties. His blue eyes could see further than an eagle, while his ears could hear frequencies normally reserved for the bat. He had bested three of the world's grandmasters at chess – he preferred speed chess to other varieties, as he often found himself predicting the exact move his opponent would make if they were left too long to think, which ruined the element of surprise.

He also painted, on occasion.

In fact, there was very little the man could not do. Except fully understand what it was to be a normal human being.

Occasionally, that troubled him.

His name was Doc Thunder, and he was widely recognised to be America's Greatest Hero. Occasionally, that troubled him more.

He'd talked to John about it, once, late at night, after that ugly business with Professor Zeppelin and his terror gas attack on Washington DC. He'd sat in the darkness of the Oval Office, nursing a scotch that he knew couldn't do a damned thing to him, letting the words tumble out of him one by one.

"Bullets bounce off my skin. I can stop a traction engine with my hands. I can be killed, but I honestly don't know if I'm going to die, John." There'd been something close to dread in his voice, as if the gas had affected him after all. "There are people who fought just as hard as I did against the Hidden Empire, and they died doing it. They knew they'd die and they fought anyway, because it was right. There are firemen and police officers and soldiers who risk their lives every day, without any of my advantages. Because it's the right thing to do. And I wonder if I'd do the same, if I wasn't... this." He'd sighed, shaking his head. "And I wonder what'll happen if I ever make the wrong decision. What the consequences would be."

John had just laughed and poured him another whisky. "You're a symbol, Doc. It's not an easy job."

Doc had smiled, then made his excuses and got up to leave. John had given him a strong handshake on the way out, and a last piece of advice: "Keep wearing that shirt, Doc. People like the shirt."

It was the last time they'd spoken. Two months later, in November, John had gone to Dallas and N.I.G.H.T.M.A.R.E.

had shot him in the head to announce themselves on the world stage. Forty years later, Doc had only just managed to put them down for good, breaking their organisation until no stone was left on another stone. Even Silken Dragon, still beautiful, still deadly, still quite mad, had died in those final moments in Milan, despite all Doc Thunder's efforts to save her and bring her, at last, to trial – although they never did find the body, as so often happened with so many of these people, and a part of Doc knew that nothing ever stayed buried.

Still, John could sleep a little sounder now.

Doc was still wearing the shirt. It peeked out from the open lab coat – a light blue t-shirt with a yellow lightning bolt pointing down and to the left. The symbol of the Resistance against McCarthy, back in '54. It still meant something, even now. A lot of people flew it from office buildings instead of the old flag, although the stars and stripes still got wheeled out on state occasions.

John had been right. Doc's job wasn't exploring lost continents or fighting insane scientists. It was just standing up and doing the right thing, and being seen to do it. Because there were a lot of folks who didn't, and the more of those there were, the more the average Joe might start thinking he didn't have a chance, that the only way to play the game and win was to play it with no rules at all, golden or otherwise. Screw the little guy, stamp him down. Hate the different ones. Why not? They're Them and you're Us and spitting on them might make you more Us, might win you some power. Tell any lie that'll serve your purpose, print them and distribute them to the people while swearing you only speak truth. Believe what you're told without question, or shrug, because what can you do? What can anybody do? The bastards run the world, we just have to live in it. What can you do?

Keep thinking that way and soon you're looking in the paper at an article that says they're building a camp on the edge of town for all the people who are bad for the country, or bad for the company, there's no real difference anyway, and just keep looking the other way a little longer, friends, just keep nodding along, just keep shrugging, whatever, you're not in danger, you're one of Us and nobody's ever going to come for you, pal. Promise.

It couldn't happen here, is what we're saying.

Would we lie to you?

Doc knew where that road ended. He'd seen it with his own eyes.

So he wore his beliefs on his chest, and he always tried to do the right thing, and when he needed to stand up, he stood up. And because he was who he was, everybody saw it. And maybe someone took a look at him and realised that they could question what they heard, or they could step in when they saw something bad happening, or they could just try and treat people just a little better. Maybe just one person that day looked at him and thought: *I should start trying.*

That was Doc Thunder's job.

Right now, part of that job was to help the police solve a murder.

"The shooting in Japantown?"

Maya's voice. Entering the lab unusually early. Doc nodded, flashing her a brief, tight smile.

"A gang member, executed in the street. There was a Blood-Spider card left on the body. Inspector West wanted me to check if the forensics matched his pattern." He sighed. "And they do."

Maya nodded, frowning. "Shooting children." She shuddered. "Are they any closer to catching him?"

Doc shook his head. "Unfortunately, a lot of the police don't want him caught. A lot of the citizenry feels the same. They see him as being on their side – cutting through the red tape, even. You know he shot a rabbi last night?"

Maya gasped. "That's monstrous."

"They found pictures of naked children in his home. A lot of the police are saying the Blood-Spider should get a medal." He rubbed his temples. "That's the problem, Maya. The people whose job it is to arrest him don't want to arrest him. The only reason Easton wants him off the streets is because... well, you know his foster father was a vigilante?"

Maya nodded. "The Blue Ghost. You worked with him occasionally. I remember you telling me."

"He never took a life. He was shot up more times than I can remember because he refused to. The man had an almost inhuman capacity for taking punishment, but eventually he had to retire."

Doc looked into the microscope, double-checking the scratches on the shell cases. "He was murdered three years ago, just before Lars Lomax died. Someone strangled him and dropped him off a pier. By the time the body was found, it had been underwater for weeks. They only identified it as Danny Coltrane with dental records. Any clues had been wiped out." Doc shook his head. "Not pretty. The Blood-Spider popped up soon after that, and, well, I think Easton feels as if he lost his father only to have him replaced by someone who defiled his father's memory." He shook his head again, sadly. "I can't really disagree with him. I don't see killing as ever being necessary."

Maya raised an eyebrow. "Even for a child molester?"

"The man deserved a day in court." He sighed, rubbing the bridge of his nose as if to stave off a headache. "You didn't get up this early to debate moral philosophy, though, did you?"

"No." Maya sighed, then looked Doc in the eye. "I had a dream. I can't remember all of it, but... I dreamt about a man in a red mask, standing over someone I loved. Ready to kill. Perhaps having killed already." She paused. "You know I wouldn't tell you if I didn't think..."

"It's coming true. Say no more." Doc frowned. "A red mask."

Maya handed over the paper. "And I think this might be involved somehow."

"Let me see that." Doc took hold of the paper, scanning the article.

Almost immediately, he went white.

"Donner. Heinrich Donner. My God." His voice shook. A bead of cold sweat trickled from his forehead down his cheek. Then he looked up at her, and his eyes burned with a cold, limitless fury.

"Get Monk in here. *Now.*"

He scowled.

"I've got a job for him."

CHAPTER THREE

The Case of The Man Who Died Twice

EVEN IN THE United Socialist States of America, the old-fashioned Gentlemen's Club was still an indicator of social status among the idle rich.

There was the Union Club, the oldest but no longer the grandest; the Cornell Club; the Down Town Association, although it increasingly attracted beatniks, pop artists and generally quite the wrong sort of people; and The Leash, which allowed female as well as male applicants, although the stringent rules of membership put off many.

The Jameson Club was perhaps the most exclusive of them all. A new member, upon applying to the club, would be asked for references from no less than five senior members. Having produced these, he would be allowed one visit to one of the lesser smoking rooms, where he would be jovially, but thoroughly, interrogated by the Club President or one of the deputies to determine whether he was of the calibre required for membership. Should a prospective member meet the high standards required, there would then be a probationary period of one year, during which time the new recruit could be dismissed from the club without warning and for the smallest social infraction.

These iron laws kept the Jameson Club satisfyingly free of the riff-raff and nouveau riche who infested other, lesser, gentlemen's establishments like a plague of cockroaches. It also meant that the average member was at least forty years old, if not fifty.

Parker Crane was not the average member.

Where most members of the Jameson Club had soft, doughy faces, with great jowls and wrinkled brows, worn from the countless demands made of New York's elite, Parker Crane's face was thin and angular, with a large nose that seemed from some angles almost like the beak of a predatory bird. He was a young man, no older than thirty, and it was generally agreed in the society pages that his sharp features and severe grey eyes, as well as his air of coldness and distance, lent him a powerful charisma. Many starlets and society beauties had fallen foul of the 'Crane effect', though he was careful not to allow his dalliances to sully the image of the Club. One must, after all, have priorities.

Crane had inherited most of his wealth from an uncle who had died – murdered by a burglar, according to the rumours – and was now a gentleman of leisure, dabbling in photography. It was one of those professions that allowed the independently wealthy to squander their time in its margins, and Crane was a noted presence in fashion-forward circles; the futurehead trend was slowly but surely giving way to pop and op-art creations informed by a return to the Warhol era. Warhol himself, in his old age, was consumed by the idea of inaugurating a new style, a basic, simple look combining jean trousers in denim with a clean t-shirt and athletic plimsolls, perhaps with a workman's shirt over the top. This, he said, was the costume people would wear in the world he saw in his head.

"Imagine, uh, a world where everything was simple, where you could just clap your hands and, uh, light would appear. That's the basis of all this. What if you could make light without effort? We have so much machinery, so much industry, and I feel like, uh, in New York we're on the point of breaking through into a different aesthetic. Machinery without machinery."

He would talk for hours about the possibilities of his mental world. Restaurants where people ate flavoured foams and used liquid gases to create astonishing desserts. A means of recording all human information and calling it up at a moment's notice, so every man could have a whole library at his fingertips. A global telephone system, so there could be calls from New York to London, from London to Paris, as easily as calling across town.

"If, uh, we had all this, if we could do all this... what would it look like? That's where all my work is headed. To try and break into this other world, this dream world, to try and replicate it and bring it here so, uh, so I can live in it."

The newspapers called it *dreampunk*.

Crane was a presence on the edges of Warhol's Factory, often featured in fashion magazines on either side of the camera, although his work was competent at best. Mostly, those in the know were intrigued less by his talent as a photographer and more by his wealth and status, and the dichotomy he represented – on the one hand, the cold, severe traditionalist, the youngest member of the Jameson Club, and on the other, the young photographer with a model on each arm and an eye for the future of fashion. The usual line taken by gossip columnists was that Parker Crane had 'a secret identity'.

They could not have been more right.

"Master Parker?"

Jonah was a tall, deferential man with an impeccably trimmed toothbrush moustache. As majordomo of the Jameson Club, he commanded an army of servants and maids whose function was to be silent and invisible until they could be of service, and then to simply appear, as if by magic, without being asked or even looked for. To speak to Crane in person, instead of sending a servant for the task, was a mark of supreme respect, and Crane took it as such. He put down the fashion spread he was reading and gave Jonah his full attention.

"Ms. Lang left a message just now enquiring as to whether you would be free to join her for coffee at the Rockefeller at noon, Sir." He pronounced *Rockefeller* with the slightest inflection of disapproval.

Crane nodded. Marlene Lang was a model he'd been seeing on and off for some time, in between other conquests. She was easily bored and favoured open relationships, so the arrangement suited her enough that she kept in touch. Currently, they were enjoying some time apart, but Crane was certain this meeting was about business rather than pleasure. The mention of the Rockefeller was a signal. It was a tourist spot, quite beyond the pale. The only reason Marlene would go there would be to discuss her 'hobby', as she put it.

Crane was one of the few who knew that Marlene Lang was a member of the Spider's Web.

THE BLOOD-SPIDER'S network of operatives numbered around twenty people, stretching over the whole of New York and reaching into every corner of society. Few knew about the Spider's Web, and those who did spoke of it in hushed, reverential tones, mindful of the importance of secrecy in their great work. Marlene was more open about it than many, but the Blood-Spider was willing to tolerate her idiosyncrasies for the sake of her driving skills.

Her father had been a mechanic, one of the first to combine the raw power of the traction engines and the intricate steam-hydraulics that drove the robots of Europe into a new kind of motor vehicle. The automobile was a young science, but great strides were being made – enough to get the Blood-Spider interested in owning an auto and employing someone to drive it. Having learned to drive the new vehicles almost as soon as they'd been invented, Marlene was a natural choice.

"I'm his personal chauffeur," Marlene had cooed to Crane once, her blonde hair spilling onto his shoulder as they shared a post-coital Gauloises. "It's ever so thrilling. You should see how he makes me dress."

Crane had raised an eyebrow, drawing on the cigarette for a moment before passing it along. "Why on Earth would the Blood-Spider need an auto? They're so unwieldy. They still haven't found a way to fit a decent boiler and furnace into the damned things. You can't get more than five miles in one, and god help you if you're idling at a stop-signal, you'll end up stuck there forever. Autos are a passing fad. Strictly for hobbyists."

"Not this one. The Silver Ghost, I call it. Goes like a bullet – top speed of almost forty miles per hour, once it's warmed up."

Crane had snorted – "Little liar!" – grabbed hold of her wrist and yanked her to the side, spilling her over his lap, her cigarette nearly burning a hole in the silk sheets as he brought the palm of his hand down against her quivering derrière. Afterwards, she'd wiggled coquettishly on his lap, smiling a secret little smile of her own. A smile with a hint of the devil in it.

She was wearing the same smile now as she waited, sipping her espresso, surrounded by the tourists excitedly discussing their visit to the viewing deck. Nobody would be listening to them. She could speak freely.

She pushed a large cappuccino at him as he sat down, which he ignored. "You know my coffee by now, surely?"

"They don't sell it here. I wouldn't even call mine an espresso, frankly." She smirked, enjoying his stiffness in this setting. She was dressed impeccably; a black and white op-art top that hurt the eyes if you looked too long, with a jet black pencil skirt and stilettos to match. Such an outfit should have stuck out like a sore thumb here, among these awful people, but somehow she managed to blend in.

"I have a message for our mutual friend," she breathed, letting the words hang deliciously on her tongue. Crane frowned. She was entirely too much in love with her role, but he was prepared to tolerate it.

"By which you mean the Blood-Spider. Why not tell him directly?"

She pouted. "You know I can't, darling. He contacts me, not the other way around. The only way I know to contact him is through you. The human mail drop." She smirked, taking another sip of the not-quite-espresso. "Do you think he's trying to keep our relationship alive?"

"Such as it is. Still sleeping with that artist?"

She smiled. "He bored me. Détourned symbols are so very yesterday. How do you take something seriously when every scruffy teenager can do it? Let him play with his futurehead friends." She finished her coffee, looking through lowered lashes at the lumpen proletariats milling around their table. "No, the most fabulous thing to do now is believe in something utterly and completely, without restraint."

"Like Warhol? He's going senile." Crane's lip curled, approaching a sneer. He had little time for dreampunk.

"Like the war on crime, darling." Her green eyes flashed dangerously as her smirk widened.

Crane nodded. He was bored of this game. "Give me the message. I'll see that it gets to him."

"If he reads the paper, he has it already. That industrialist everyone thought was dead – Heinrich Donner. He's turned up again."

"Donner's alive?" Crane's eyes narrowed. Why hadn't he heard about this?

"Not quite. Stabbed through the heart, poor man. With a sword. It's very unusual. The sort of thing *you-know-who* might be interested in."

Crane frowned, thinking for a long moment, then stood. "Go home. Wait by the phone. He'll want to get moving at sunset, no later." Absently, he pulled out fifty dollars and left it on the table.

Marlene raised an eyebrow. "You'll give the waitress a heart attack. Or is that for me?"

"I'm sure you'll think of a way to earn it." He nodded a cursory goodbye, then turned away.

"It's a date." Marlene smiled, then snapped her fingers at the waitress for a second cup.

JONAH GREETED CRANE on his return with a barely-perceptible raised eyebrow. Crane checked his pocket-watch, noting that enough time had passed to allow him some plausible deniability with Marlene, then gave Jonah the slightest of nods.

Jonah took a small copper key from his pocket and moved to unlock the door to the lower library.

In the Jameson Club, there were two libraries. The upper library was one of the club's great treasures – a repository of famous first editions culled from private collections, including a folio of Marlowe's *Faustus Redeemed* and the original manuscript for *Edwin Drood,* complete with the famous epilogue. Had the Jameson Club been a museum, visitors would have flocked to see such exhibits. As it was, most of the members saw these priceless artefacts of literary history only as decorative touches, adding a touch of class to the room where they went to do the daily crossword. The books simply sat and looked pretty, in the manner of a trophy wife or a set of elephant's tusks.

The lower library, meanwhile, was all but forgotten. While there were several first editions stored there, they were the kind of thing you'd find on the bookshelves of any dedicated collector with money to spend, and thus their value as items of decadence was next to worthless. Since the building of the upper library, the room had fallen into disuse, and now it was used as a junk room by the serving staff, a place of dust, cobwebs and bric-a-brac, forgotten by all. Crane was the only member who ever bothered to go inside, and if the other members noticed, they dismissed it as a minor eccentricity. If Crane wanted to poke around amongst piles of dusty old ephemera, they thought, then it was his business.

Surely there was no harm in it.

In one corner of the lower library, underneath a bust of Catullus, there was a locked trunk, to which Parker Crane had the only key.

Inside the trunk, there were three black slouch hats, two black trenchcoats, three pairs of black shirts and slacks, five pairs of strangely-patterned black rubber gloves, three pairs of black shoes with the same intricate pattern on their soles and one pair of black automatic pistols, which were kept in perfect condition.

There was also a mask.

It was made of leather and designed to fit over the whole head, with a blood-red metal plate in the front that covered the face, with eight lenses set into it, like the eyes of a spider.

The last thing in the trunk was an ornate box containing a set of immaculately-printed business cards. On one side, the cards showed a spider design, in red. On the other:

Where all inhuman
Devils revel in their sins –
The Blood-Spider spins!

AS HE POPPED the buttons on his white dress shirt and slid it off, Crane felt a strange sense of peace and contentment envelop his mind. It was a wonderful feeling to strip away the cares of the world, the outward show that was Parker Crane, gentleman of leisure, and to become his true self. How had that editorial put it? The spider at the centre of a web of blood and vengeance.

How true, thought Parker Crane. *How very true.*

He lifted one of the black shirts, inhaling the fresh scent of the laundry. Jonah had done a capital job, as ever – bloodstains were hard to get out of any fabric, and black clothing had a tendency to turn grey if improperly handled. "You're quite the most invaluable member of my web, Jonah," Crane murmured, as he slid an arm into a black sleeve.

"One does one's best, Master Parker." nodded Jonah, deferential as ever, then turned respectfully around as Crane continued changing.

The mask was the last thing to go on. That was the moment when it really happened. When he felt the weight of that dreadful playboy pose – that vicissitude, that narcissism, that languid sloth that felt as heavy as lead on his back – all fall away, replaced by the cold, bright, beautiful clarity of his cause. His mission. To purge the world of the criminals. To wipe out the inhuman.

It was Parker Crane who raised the mask to his face, but it was the Blood-Spider who tightened the straps.

Occasionally, he wondered if there was anyone else who felt as he did, who could lift a mask to his face and become an entirely different person, stronger, faster, harder, colder, *better*. If such a person existed, he should like to meet them one day. To compare notes.

If they were in agreement with the cause, of course.

Otherwise, they would have to die.

"*Telephone.*" hissed the Blood-Spider. Jonah bowed, then turned to open a small cupboard near the door. Inside was a black telephone, connected to an unlisted line separate from the club's own. The gloved hands snatched it up, fingers dialing the numbers, stabbing savagely at the apparatus as if possessed. Then he lifted the receiver to that strange, almost-featureless mask and waited, as the spider waits, patiently and remorselessly, for the fly.

DAVID SIKORSKY JUMPED as the phone on the wall rang. "Christ!"

Marlene smiled, shifting her weight on the couch. "I was expecting that. Be a dear and fetch it for me, will you?"

David frowned. He was a man in his mid thirties, lean and twitchy, with a mop of black hair resting on top of his head like a bird's nest and an unkempt goatee sprouting from his chin. He had a penchant for dark-coloured turtlenecks, cheap black coffee and 'breaker' music, which blared tinnily from a clockwork gramophone in the corner of his studio; the thumping, insistent beat of the drums colliding with the insistent jangle of the telephone. He stared at it for a moment, then looked at his model, brow furrowed with impotent irritation. He'd asked her not to take calls while she was modeling. He'd told her a dozen times, he couldn't have his concentration broken during a shoot, but did she listen?

For a moment, his eyes dueled with hers – two sapphires, gleaming with superior amusement – and then his will broke and he turned to the ringing phone with a heavy, theatrical sigh. Passive aggression had always been David's forte. Rather than answer it himself, he simply lifted the receiver off the hook and, adopting an exaggerated air of indifference, carried it across the studio, the long extension cord stretching as he held it to Marlene's ear.

She was not in a position to take hold of it herself, of course. The black leather singleglove cinching her arms prevented her doing much more than rolling the balls of her shoulders, while the leather straps keeping her ankles bound to her thighs kept her in a kneeling position on the red velour couch, the heels of the tightly-laced ballet boots pressed tightly against her bottom. The black ribbons that kept her hair piled up on top of her head, and the one wound decoratively around her throat, formed the rest of her *couture* for the afternoon.

Marlene enjoyed working with David. If only he wasn't quite so spineless, she might have added him to her catalogue of lovers. She smiled sweetly at him, then spoke into the receiver. "Marlene Lang."

The voice on the other end was a muffled growl, a hiss like steam escaping from some terrible industrial press.

"You were told to return home and wait."

"But if I'd gone home, darling, you'd have called here and you wouldn't have reached me. So I was just being efficient, really." She smiled sweetly, for the benefit of no-one. David was staring moodily into one corner, as if to give her some measure of privacy, though his arm still held the receiver stiffly in place. There was silence on the other end of the line.

"What's the matter?" She purred the words lazily, like a cat. "Am I being terribly immoral? I suppose I am, really. I shall have to watch that."

The voice on the other end was cold. *"Bring the car around to the usual place no later than nine tonight. We have a murder to investigate."* The line went dead.

Marlene wondered for a moment if she'd made him jealous. But then, to feel jealousy, one would have to feel, and Marlene was not entirely convinced the Blood-Spider had any feelings beyond that cold, hard anger that informed all his movements. Perhaps that was what made him so fascinating to her – or the deliciousness of the cause, their shared war on crime. She had never imagined that a life of pursuing the common good, without recognition or reward, could be quite so wonderfully decadent.

"There, done. You may put the receiver back, David." She smirked, watching him bristle as he marched stiffly back to replace the apparatus in its cradle, then adopted a contrite look, pouting as he turned his wounded eyes back on her. "Have I been very naughty?"

David shook his head, stuttering a response and blushing. "It's not that, it's... I kind of wish you wouldn't... I mean, I've told you before..." Frustrated, he moved to the equipment he'd laid out on the table, out of the camera's view. "You're not going to be taking any more calls, right? I just need to concentrate for this."

"No more calls, darling. I promise." Marlene smiled, arched her back, and opened her mouth for the ball gag.

THERE WERE STILL little phantom shivers of rubber on the tip of her tongue and a pleasant ache in her shoulders as her hands gripped and spun the steering wheel of the Silver Ghost, tearing it around a corner in a cloud of billowing steam.

She was dressed somewhat more conservatively now, although not by much. The belted leather jacket that formed the top portion of her uniform certainly covered up her torso admirably – although the tight fit drew the eye somewhat – and the peaked cap added an air of authority. The leather miniskirt was slightly more of a problem. It only came down to mid-thigh when she was standing, never mind sitting down, and the high heels on the black pumps she was made to wear did little to distract any passengers from the curves of her legs.

Not that the Silver Ghost carried any passengers apart from the Blood-Spider himself, of course. Perhaps he did have human feelings after all.

Or perhaps he saw her as merely a luxurious component of a luxurious vehicle – for 'luxurious' was really the only way the Silver Ghost could possibly be described. A sleek silver bullet, filigreed with the thin, clustered piping that kept the high-pressure steam turning the wheels and driving the whole apparatus forward, the air-intake surrounding the nosecone looking like the maw of some strange and terrifying undersea animal, the blazing twin gas lamps on either side forming its eyes. It looked delicate in its majestic complexity, but Marlene had been in the driving seat when the agents of E.R.A.M.T.H.G.I.N. – that strange reverse-organisation, a gang of madmen existing to mock, détourn and destroy all symbols, the futurehead ethos gone wild and rabid in the streets – had roared out of an alleyway in their own patchwork auto, looking like nothing so much as a squat metal slug, and raked the Silver Ghost with machine-gun fire.

"*Us am vigilantes! Am us not men?*" they'd howled, a terrifyingly accurate parody of the Blood-Spider's hiss, distorted as if played through a sped-up gramophone, the bright red clay headgear they wore to signify their 'de-evolutionary status' refashioned into crude, cruel mockeries of the Spider's signature mask. "*Us use violence to effect social change! Am us not men? Us bring terror to underclass, make streets safer for overclass! Am us not men? Am us not men?*"

The Blood-Spider had turned, bullets missing him by inches, and dispatched each of them with a single shot, shattering the clay helmets and painting the fragments a different shade of red. A final shot had smashed through the slug's bonnet, bringing forth an explosion of hissing steam and sharp metal fragments and sending the auto careening into a nearby gas lamp, a charnel-display of rotting meat left as an example to any others who might consider impeding the Blood-Spider in the performance of his terrible duty.

The Silver Ghost, meanwhile, had suffered barely a scratch. It was built to last.

Marlene parked the auto near the mouth of a secluded, seemingly deserted back alley, filled with shadows and scurrying rats. As she opened the door, one shadow detached itself from the others, uncoiling like a snake, pitch darkness suddenly assuming form and substance. Marlene smiled.

"Darling."

Eight blank lenses gazed back at her as the Blood-Spider took his seat.

"*The Atlas building. West thirty-eighth.*" He opened the glove compartment of the sleek silver machine and withdrew a large grappling hook, connected to a loop of strong steel wire. "*I have a personal call to make.*"

"Yes, Sir." purred Marlene, gunning the engine and sending the Silver Ghost on into the New York night.

THE HARD PART had been getting to the roof without being seen.

After that, it was a simple matter of placing his hands on the smooth stone of the wall and then vaulting over the roof edge, letting the intricate network of suction-cups on his gloves and the soles of his shoes affix themselves so he could climb down the wall to the window. This was his great secret – how he appeared and disappeared without warning, how he could strike from everywhere at once. The powerful suction of the rubber allowed him to cling expertly to any surface and reach the highest and most inhospitable nooks and crannies, there to watch and wait, as the spider waits in cracks and crevices for his prey.

The Blood-Spider clung, like a spider clinging to a wall, over a drop that would not only shatter and pulverise his bones but liquefy his very flesh if he fell – and he thought no more about it than a normal man would if standing upon the edge of a high kerbstone.

Danger was meaningless. The risk of death had been weighed, judged and found to be acceptable. All that remained now was the task at hand.

The cause.

Slowly, patiently, the Blood-Spider used a glass-cutting tool from his belt to carve a circle in the window large enough to gain him entry, pushing gently with his palm until the circle of glass popped into the room, landing almost silently on the deep plush carpet. He disliked compromising the crime scene in such a manner, but the police department had taken their turn with it. His job now was to find those things they had missed, in the places they had not bothered to look.

As he crossed the threshold of the window, he looked to his left, at the dried blood still mixed with the fibres of the carpet. A man had died there. He had been stabbed in the back by a coward, and it was the duty of the Blood-Spider to find out who that coward was. As the soles of his boots sank into the lush carpeting, he devoted all his attention to that stain of blood, to that spot where Donner had been killed. That was the first piece of the puzzle. He would find the others, and piece by piece he would build up the truth of the matter. Strand by strand, the Spider would spin his web.

He sank to one knee, brushing his fingertips over the dried, crusted stain, the map of a forgotten continent. Slowly, he examined its contours, his whole attention focused on determining its secret meaning, the clues buried in its unique shape.

And so he never noticed the hands reaching for the back of his neck.

Not until they were at his throat.

CHAPTER FOUR

Doc Thunder and The Ape Detective

MONK HAD BIG hands.

Large, hard things, they were. Great clubs of meat and bone and sinew, flexing dangerously, constantly twitching and moving. A carpet of rough hairs growing from the back of each, dirt and grime under the thick fingernails that he could never quite get out. Rough calluses on the fingertips, like sandpaper.

Killer's hands.

He'd taught them gentleness, painstakingly and over too many years. But every so often he would pick up a boiled egg and the shell would crack, or he'd handle a paperclip and it would bend between his fingers. Monk would wince, imperceptibly, and it would haunt him for days, making him hesitant about shaking a hand or putting his arm around a shoulder.

For at least a week after such an incident, he would sleep on the couch downstairs. Doc and Maya had grown to accept it. Gradually, his confidence would return, and so would he. But it always took time.

He had to be careful. So careful, all the time. And he was careful. He was careful when he twisted the cotter pin in the lock of the penthouse suite to let himself in, and careful when he examined the room Donner died in, lifting, inspecting, replacing exactly, each object treated like a Faberge egg, every clue a museum piece of untold worth.

"Go take a look at the crime scene," Doc Thunder had said. "Pick up what you can, then get straight back to me. No risks, understand?"

Monk had shrugged. "Sure, Doc. You think Donner got mixed up with something?"

Doc had laughed humourlessly. "Mixed up isn't the word. He was the man behind Untergang. I could never prove it, but he was. The secret figurehead – businessman and philanthropist by day, inhuman monster by night. And he hated me more than any human being I've ever known."

Monk had raised an eyebrow. "Lars Lomax?"

Doc had almost smiled. "Lars hated me, all right. He would have burned the entire world to see me dead. But... Heinrich Donner would have burned the world to see me stub my toe on the ruins. He was the one who murdered–" Doc had suddenly gone quiet, as if he'd almost said too much. Monk waited.

"We finally had it out in 1959. We were fighting in Paraguay. He had this secret bunker set up... the whole damn place was full of nitro-glycerin and he pulled a gun on me." Doc shook his head sadly. "I had him. I really did. I had hard evidence, I was going to bring him to trial, but he just..."

He'd tailed off, looking into the middle distance. "He knew bullets didn't work on me. He knew that. One of them bounced off my chest, hit the nitro... and boom. Goodbye, Heinrich. Nearly goodbye me." He'd paused. "I think the evil little son of a bitch just wanted to kill us both." Monk remembered being surprised at the venom in Doc's voice. He'd never spoken that way before about anyone, even Lomax. Donner's hatred hadn't all been one-way. "I really thought he was dead. I've taken down Untergang leaders since then – the Purple Wraith, Queen Tiger... they must have been figureheads, like Cobra was. It was Donner.

All the time. All the time..." He'd shaken his head, covering his eyes, and Monk had flinched. He'd never seen Doc look that way – that look of despair. "I need to know what he's been doing since 'fifty-nine. I need to know who killed him, and why, and if he's really dead this time. I don't think I can go to the police yet. I just... I don't know, Monk. I don't quite know what to do."

He'd looked at Monk with those steel-blue eyes, and they'd looked lost, like a kid's.

I don't know what to do.

The most frightening words Monk had ever heard Doc say.

"So... you want me to take a look? Bring back some intel?"

Doc had nodded, and suddenly the old certainty was back. "That's what we need." He'd smiled. "Remember, no risks. Take the flare gun. And listen, the slightest hint of anything and you get out of there. This is Untergang we're talking about – old school Untergang. They don't play games. Oh, and one last thing. Maya's had a dream; a man in a red mask, standing over one of us. She thinks it could be connected, so... keep an eye out."

Monk had just smiled. "Sure thing, Boss. No risks. You can rely on me."

And here he was, putting the picture together. A jigsaw puzzle. A portrait of a man's life, a life now ended. Under his breath, he began to murmur to himself. At the orphanage, some funny guy had given him a copy of *The Jungle Book*. Real funny, a laugh and a half for the popular crowd. The joke was on them. He'd devoured it, cover to cover, maybe just to show them, but that one book had started a fire for reading, for knowledge, that'd never gone out. Monk wished he could remember the funny guy's name. He'd wanted to thank him a lot in the years since. Send him a pound cake for Christmas or something.

Anyway, after *The Jungle Book* he was hungry for more Kipling, so he'd moved on to the *Just So Stories*, and there was a verse in that one that came back to him sometimes, on a case like this one.

"I keep six honest serving-men, they taught me all I knew. Their names are what and why and when and how and where and who."

Six questions. Get the answers to all six and you had the puzzle solved.

He was in the where. The police knew the when and the what. They even figured they knew the how.

According to the police, Donner had probably known his killer enough to let him in the door, and to turn his back. There'd been no sign of forced entry.

Monk wasn't so sure. He'd just forced his way in and left no sign of it. Easy enough with hands like his.

They were strong, and they were sensitive. Even under that thick layer of callus, they knew weight, and give, and push. They knew how to open a door with a cotter pin and make it look as though you'd used a key, even to the smartest cop in the world – which the ones who'd checked this place over weren't, not by a long stretch. And more. He knew, instinctively – and it was the smallest twinge in the middle of his gut and on the edges of his subconscious but by God, he *knew* – he hadn't been the first to force that lock.

So the police had it wrong. Donner didn't know his killer. Didn't even know his killer was there until the sword was in his back.

Monk considered it, weighted it in his mind for truth, then continued along the mental path. Donner hadn't gone to the window after letting his killer in. He was already standing, looking out on the city, when the killer had let himself in silently, padded across the carpet, and stabbed Donner in the back. No mercy. Not even an explanation. Just the kill.

That was the how.

He ran his fingers over his sloped brow, as if coaxing the thoughts into life, a physical tic from his childhood. He had the why, too. If Doc was right – and Doc was *always* right – Donner was the leader of Untergang, and that was why enough for a hell of a lot of people. So, five out of six. One to go.

Put the why together with the how, the silent entry, the quiet, instant kill... secret service? Or the Special Tactical Espionage And Manouvres unit? But no, they wouldn't let it reach the papers. And Doc would have been told. Him and President Bartlet had been the best of pals ever since that brain transplant stunt Lars Lomax tried.

Someone else? No love lost between Untergang and N.I.G.H.T.M.A.R.E. – but they weren't about to go to war, either. Besides, N.I.G.H.T.M.A.R.E. was finished. After what Doc had done to them in Milan, they didn't have the manpower to go after a stray dog, never mind a top-flight bad guy. And E.R.A.M.T.H.G.I.N. was just a joke taking itself a little too seriously. It didn't have the chops for this.

Someone new, then.

Monk needed more information. He frowned, took another quick look around the room, then padded across to the bedroom, reaching behind him as he went, unconsciously mussing the pile with his fingers, making sure he left no tracks. An old habit.

In the bedroom, he let those fingers – rough and gentle, club-like and dexterous – tease lightly over the fabric of the bed, while the eyes under the ridged, furrowed brow of his ape-like face scanned every passing detail.

The lamp beside the bed; gold, with a German eagle motif. Monk wouldn't have been surprised to see a swastika there too, but that would've given the game away.

A little rectangle on the bedside, where the dust wasn't so thick. Something had lain there for a while, by the side of his bed. It wasn't there now.

A dent in the wall, like a crescent moon.

The sheets. Expensive. Silk? Or a blend? Either way, they were a little sweaty, a little scummy. Not quite as clean as might be expected.

He looked around, taking another look at the dust on the bedside table. Then he closed his eyes, thinking back to what he'd seen of the living room. Norman Rockwell print on the wall. An ashtray, filled with old cigarettes, a pyramid of them. Not emptied in too long. Food particles caught in the carpet – he'd stopped eating at the table.

Filthy sheets. Filthy ashtrays. He'd stopped doing a lot of things.

On a whim, Monk picked up the heavy lamp and held the circular base to the dent. It matched. A struggle?

No. He'd just thrown the damn thing at the wall.

Depression. Hits a guy that way sometimes. Things stop mattering, people stop caring. The detectives probably wouldn't have noticed. They hadn't been there.

Why hadn't he hired a maid? Because he needed to stay hidden. Stay reclusive. Nobody could know.

Why?

Monk's mind was racing now, cogs whirring in his head, switches flipping. *Think, ape-man.* Why can't the leader of Untergang hire a maid?

Because he wasn't the leader of Untergang any more. He wasn't anything. That stunt in Paraguay Doc had talked about – that was his last run. He might have been the big boss across the big pond, but that didn't mean he didn't have superiors back in the Fatherland. If Uncle Adolf figured he'd been compromised – out he'd go. Exiled.

Monk shook his head, frowning. No, not exile. Storage. He'd been locked away like last year's gramophone, just in case he ever came good again, in case any of the secrets in his head were ever useful to anybody. Instead, he'd been forgotten and left to rot.

So Monk was back to the why. Why now? He scratched the back of his scalp with great club-like fingers. If he only knew why, he'd know who – but then, if he knew who, he knew why. Sometimes it shook out like that.

He needed to know what it was that had been taken from the bedside table. Some kind of book?

He shook his head, then took a last look around the bedroom, hoping against hope that he'd see the damned book or framed photo or whatever it was under the bed or something. No joy.

Best thing to do now would be to head back to Doc, give him what he'd found out, let him figure the next move. One last look around the main room and –

Monk froze.

There was somebody in the main room.

A tall guy, all in black leather, with a big coat and hat. He'd cut his way in from outside, through the window, leaving a big circle of glass on the pile carpet. How the hell had he done that? They were more than forty floors up.

The tall guy bent over the bloodstain on the carpet, brushing gloved fingers over the matted fibres. Monk stilled his breathing, the gentle eyes under that ugly slope of brow narrowing. He moved forward, silent, the soles of his big bare feet falling light as snowflakes on the thick carpet. Silent as the grave.

He was wearing some kind of helmet under that hat. Or a mask.

A red mask.

Almost without thinking, Monk reached forward, those big hands moving towards the back of the tall guy's neck. This was going to have to be done carefully. He was going to have to choke this guy out without killing him.

And he had killer's hands.

He moved fast. Those big, brutal killer's hands wrapped around the tall guy's neck and squeezed – hard, hard enough to cut off air and blood, but at the same time Monk knew he had to be gentle. So, so gentle.

Too gentle, in the end.

The tall guy in the red mask twisted out of the grip and brought the butt of one pistol hard across Monk's face. It would have broken another man's jaw, and it sent him sprawling to the right, cracking his head against the wall and leaving a dent. Red Mask was up on his feet in an instant –

– *Jesus, his face!* –

– and Monk forced himself not to look at those eight featureless lenses, lashing out with those big feet, those ape's clubs on the end of his legs, driving them up and into the taller man's gut. The impact sent the man in the coat flying back in a short arc, landing with a crash that demolished an occasional table.

Monk spat blood, and a molar, then flipped back onto his feet, loping towards the downed man like a charging gorilla. He didn't have room to be gentle any more. He needed to finish this fast, and if that meant mashing that metal mask into the tall guy's face so he never quite looked human again, well, that was just too bad. He'd done his best, but now it was kill or be –

– the revolver in the masked man's gloved hand swung up and spat a bullet into Monk's kneecap, then another into his lung.

Monk went down like a freight train crashing, rolling over from the force of his own momentum, coming to rest next to the destroyed table. He reached, fingers trembling, a last attempt to grab hold of the masked man's coat as he scrambled upwards, but he only caught air.

Then he caught another bullet.

This time he didn't even hear the shot, just felt his head knocked sideways, saw his vision double, then triple. He felt nauseous, the pain in his ruined knee and deflated lung joined by a screaming cold iron spike right through the meat of his brain. He figured he must be dead.

He wasn't. The bullet had glanced off his thick skull, cracking it, and into the wall. The masked man fired another two – one in the gut, another in the chest about three inches from the first.

The last thing Monk saw was the masked man lifting the gun up and aiming it right between his eyes. Those eight lenses didn't have a shred of mercy in them. They didn't hold anything human at all.

Then it all went black.

IN THE BLACKNESS, he thought he saw a star explode, far away. A little supernova that took the shape of a thunderbolt for long moments while it faded. He felt something metallic in his hand, and realised he was awake and pointing that metallic something-or-other through a window at the night sky. There was a big circular hole in the window, which was a little strange. Had that been there before? Was it his window? He figured he should head up to bed, but then he remembered this wasn't the brownstone. It was some fancy apartment.

Whose apartment? Heinrich somebody.

Monk suddenly had a very clear sense that he'd missed something very, very important. Something obvious, something that could have changed the whole game, changed everything – if only he'd thought of it sooner.

He passed out before he could think what it was.

*   *   *

HE DIDN'T REMEMBER using the flare gun, but he must have, because he came round to find Doc shining a torch in his eyes. "Con cushion. Sirius." Something like that. Monk couldn't think straight.

He was alive, anyway. That red mask guy must have left him for dead, gone out the way he came in. He should tell the Doc.

He tried to speak, and went away again into blackness. He felt as if he were out for hours.

He came back around, and Doc was still shining the light in his eyes. No time had passed at all. Monk wondered if he was going to die.

Talk, ape-man. Ook ook.

"Duh. Drrr."

Doc put a hand on his shoulder. "Don't try to talk, Monk. I have to stop the bleeding and then I need to get you across town to the hospital. It's going to be bumpy."

Maya broke in. How long had she been there?

"You can't be serious."

Doc's voice was cold and terse. Deadly serious. Monk realised there was a good chance he was dead, and he tried to say something, tried to say what he'd found, but all he managed was to cough blood.

"Look at him!" Maya's voice held an edge of anger that Monk had only heard a few times in his life. She was furious, which meant she was scared. Which meant... *talk, ape-man. Talk while you can.*

"Look at him! He might die if you move him. If you try to – I can't even say it..." she drew in a breath, her emerald eyes flashing green fire. "If you try what you're planning, he'll die for certain."

"He'll die if I don't. By the time the paramedics get here and get him to the hospital, he'll have bled out. I've already done the math, Maya, there's no way to play this that won't probably kill him. But at least he's got a chance, if get him there myself. *If.*"

Maya gripped his massive wrist, and her grip was like steel. Where there'd been fire in her eyes, there was nothing but a sea of ice.

"If you kill him, I kill you."

Doc pulled his hand away, not speaking, not looking at her, just dressing Monk's wounds with whatever he had – torn silk shirts from the wardrobe, alcohol from decanters on the sideboard. He didn't speak.

It was Monk who broke the silence. "Duh. *Doc.*"

"I said don't try to–"

"Important." he coughed again, and spat more blood. He didn't know how much he had left. "Donner. Not... not Untergang." He flicked his eyes around the room. "All this... exile. Ret... retirement..." He breathed in, weakly, trying to get some air into the lung he had left. Why was this so difficult? He just wanted to go to sleep.

"Monk!" Doc was yelling in his face. He forced himself to spit out some more words and prayed they made some sense.

"Guy who... did this. Red mask. Red mask." *Eight lenses. Black coat.* He tried to say it, but his brain and his tongue seemed disconnected. The blackness seemed to be closing in on him again. He had to try. *Ape-man. Talk. Say it. Eight lenses.*

Talk, ape-man!

"Eyes... crazy eyes..."

That was as far as he got before his head fell away, down into a black ocean with no bottom to it.

And maybe this time he wouldn't wake up.

"RED MASK. DAMN it." Doc was cursing himself. He should have known. Maya's dreams didn't lie. Why hadn't he thought about it? A man in a red mask, standing over the man he killed, a man Maya cared for. Monk, of course Monk, it couldn't be anybody *but* Monk because Doc was all but invulnerable to anything except his own damned stupidity. And he'd sent him into the lion's den anyway. How had he been so damned careless with his best friend's life?

He shook his head, spitting out another curse under his breath. It was Donner. Always and forever, it was Donner. Even beyond the grave – especially beyond the grave – Donner had the power to blindside him, to get under his skin, to get him making mistakes. And now Monk had paid the price for one of those mistakes, and he might not make it through.

No wonder Maya was mad. She stood behind him, those green eyes burning into his back, as he gently cradled Monk in his arms, holding the immense dead weight of the man as if he was carrying a baby. He took a deep breath, stilling his mind and steadying his nerves.

And then he threw himself out of the window.

The important part was to get the landing right – every landing. If he fell from this height and he didn't take the whole impact on his leg muscles, he'd break Monk's neck and most of his other bones. Even so, it'd be a hell of a jar.

"Hold on, Monk." he breathed, almost whispering it. "Hold on, buddy."

The sidewalk rushed up to greet them both like an eager lover. Doc braced, and when his feet hit the pavement – hard enough to crack it – he bent his legs, softening the impact, then straightened them quickly enough to hurl himself over the rooftops. If he'd aimed right, he'd come down on Madison. After that, a leap to Third Avenue, and then one more would get him there. Hopefully that wouldn't be one too many.

Below him, citizens craned their necks, pointing, witnesses to the miracle of a man who could leap more than a thousand feet in one bound, carrying a human gorilla. None of those who saw – not the carriage-drivers whose horses bolted as Doc Thunder landed in front of them, shattering the tarmac and then taking off into the sky again like an eagle; not the secretaries working late in high-up, high-class advertising offices, who turned their heads at just the right moment to see a god sailing past their window with an injured ape-man in his arms; not the kids staying up late on the fire escapes and feeling them rattle with every shockwave – not a one of them would ever forget the sight. Some of them would carry a fear of Doc Thunder around with them the rest of their days, the arachnid response of those confronted with the alien, with a man who so plainly could not be a man. Others would close their eyes in hard moments and bring the memory back, to give them strength in a difficult time.

For Doc Thunder himself, it was three short leaps and nothing more, with the clockwork of his superlative mind crackling as he performed the calculations that would allow him to do it without killing his best friend. He felt no triumph as he landed for the last time in front of Saint Albert's, only a great wave of relief.

Monk was still alive.

"Get this man stabilised!" he yelled, kicking open the door hard enough to send it off one hinge, nurses and orderlies running to fetch stretchers and gurneys. "And get me Hamilton! Miles Hamilton! He still works here?"

A tall man with longish grey hair, haggard cheeks and eyes that had seen far too many sleepless nights stepped forward from the relative calm of one of the wards. He showed little emotion, even while his staff fought to fit their huge patient across two gurneys strapped together, his blood slicking the floor as they wheeled him down the corridor towards the operating theatre. Instead, his cold blue eyes looked up at Thunder's, accusingly. The name on his badge read Dr. Miles Hamilton.

Once upon a time, Hamilton had been Doc's closest ally, his personal physician – the one man Doc had trusted with the secrets of his strange, inhuman physiognomy. He'd been a warm, uncommonly gentle man, a man who would rather die than cause bad feeling to anybody. Then there had been that final, ugly business with Lars Lomax, the most dangerous man in the world, almost three years ago. Lomax had kidnapped Hamilton and tortured him for hours in an effort to get hold of any secret that might destroy his enemy once and for all. Perhaps it was the torture breaking his mind in a way that couldn't be fixed, or perhaps Hamilton blamed Doc for allowing it to happen in the first place, but after it was all over – after Lomax had plunged to his fiery death in the Amazon rainforest – Hamilton had never been the same. The old gentleness was gone, replaced by a cold, hard demeanor, almost cruel. He snubbed old friends in the street, and even his closest colleagues at the hospital felt uneasy around him.

Doc had tried to bring him back to himself, but Hamilton had only grown colder, a new and barely-disguised hatred for Doc Thunder bubbling under the surface of his frosty attitude. Worst of all, he now bugged Doc constantly for a sample of his blood, insisting that the recuperative qualities inherent within it could revolutionise medical science, and even if it were weaponised, well, that would only allow America to spread its military might across the entire world, which could only be a good thing. Imagine an army of soldiers with Doc's powers...

This was the kind of talk that had caused the end of their friendship. Doc had stopped calling, stopped feeling anything for his old friend but sadness at the change in him. Now, Hamilton stood, looking superciliously at Monk, like a man looking at a sideshow freak, and Doc felt again the pain and anger at how far Miles had fallen from his old self.

His voice was curt but without emotion, as if he simply didn't care. "Doc, what on Earth is the meaning of this intrusion?"

Thunder shook his head. He wasn't about to get into an argument now. "There's no time, Hamilton. Trust me, I'm not exactly relishing this encounter either, but you were the closest person I could trust. I can trust you?" Even as he asked the question, he reached down to his bicep, grabbing the skin and pinching, digging in with his thumbnail. "Get a catheter."

Hamilton looked up at him, his face still not registering the situation. "You can't mean to −"

"A catheter!" Thunder shouted the words, angrily. "You're getting what you wanted, Doctor. My blood! A full pint of it! And unless you want it on the floor, you'll get me a damn catheter!"

He was yelling now, partly from his anger at himself and at the situation he'd created, and partly from the sheer effort it took to tear a hole in his own skin. A thin rivulet of blood began to trickle down towards his elbow.

Hamilton fetched the catheter.

By the time Maya arrived, it was all over. Monk was in the theater, with a pint of Doc's blood hanging over him, being fed to him a trickle at a time along with several pints of his own blood group. Doc's blood would have a healing effect, in time, and from the sound of it Monk was critical but stable and passing further out of danger with every moment.

For a few minutes at a time – just enough to keep him from dying – Monk would have the recuperative powers of Doc Thunder himself. They were the same blood type – O Negative – or there'd have been nothing he could have done. And even among the O-Negatives, there were those who overdosed, who died instantly as their hearts inflated and burst against their ribcages, whose brains hemorrhaged, whose spines were snapped by the growth of muscle in their backs... he had to pray Monk wouldn't end up one of those. "Small doses," he'd said to Hamilton, and the old man had nodded coldly and said something about how he didn't intend to waste any. Doc had felt like punching him. Instead, he'd shaken his hand, resisting the urge to crush it.

They'd been friends once. It seemed like forever ago.

"You were right," smiled Maya as she walked back from her conversation with one of the orderlies. "Monk's alive, thanks to that little stunt. I don't know why I doubted you. Being right is what you do for a living." She leant in to kiss him, and he shook his head, placing a finger at her lips.

"If I'd been right, I'd never have sent Monk in there alone. I was a damn fool, and he paid for it." He shook his head, wincing. "It's Donner. He's haunting me. Making me sloppy."

Maya frowned, curious. "I've never seen you like this. You're... almost afraid of him. Even now. What is he to you?"

Doc Thunder scowled. "It doesn't matter. He's dead. It's his killer we should worry about – and whoever did that to Monk, if he's not the same person." He stood, suddenly, and stalked towards the exit, making her run to keep up. "I'm missing something. Smart as I am, I'm not smart enough..."

Maya blinked, trying to guess his meaning, then her eyes flew wide open. "No. Doc, no. It's too risky. Every time you use that thing, you run the risk of it killing you. You know that."

"Monk could still die because I was stupid, Maya." Doc Thunder scowled, cracking his knuckles as the rain began to spatter on the sidewalk. "My mind's made up. First, we get some sleep. Then, it's time for desperate measures."

He took a deep breath, then turned to her.

"It's time for the Omega Machine."

CHAPTER FIVE

The Case of The Man
Who Never Smiled

After he'd finished cleaning the blood from the front of his mask, Parker Crane went to a cocktail party.

It was a low-key affair at the Astoria; a mere one hundred dollars for a ticket, and thus hardly worth bothering with for most members of the Jameson. A couple even looked askance at Crane's rousing himself for such a mediocre get-together. However, most understood that a large number of strumpets from the fashion 'scene' that Crane was involved in would be there, and young men would always be young men – it was only to be expected that Crane would want to sow a few wild oats. Besides, he was so awfully good at keeping his many and varied affairs from tarnishing the name of the club.

Crane decided not to call Marlene; she would either be there herself, or more likely embroiled in her own sordid affairs, in which case he knew where he could find her if she was needed. Instead, he made arrangements to go with two of the models he worked with regularly. A pair of twins, attractive enough to dabble in the modeling world, pneumatic enough to preserve his image and wealthy enough to be deemed worthy of his company, although they were, regrettably, new money. Blonde, naturally. Their father was something in dirigible construction. Crane had quite forgotten their names over the course of the carriage ride from their city apartment, where he'd picked them up – something that rhymed? Mandy and Sandy? Chloe and Zoe? He hadn't bothered to find out, or even talk to them beyond what was absolutely necessary. They spent the journey giggling and whispering to each other, while he looked out at the rain falling down on the city.

His city.

He was regretting not putting a bullet through the ape man's head. He'd assumed the throwback had died, but he'd seen the flare lighting up the Manhattan sky as Marlene had driven him back to his regular drop-off point, and he knew what it meant. The Gorilla Reporter had called in his lovers to bail him out.

The Blood-Spider disapproved of Doc Thunder – his permissive attitudes were the least of it – and he had no doubt that Thunder's simian sidekick had planned to kill him, perhaps in order to cover up an involvement in Donner's murder. Could he add Thunder to the list of suspects? And if so, how could he be dealt with? What bullet could bring down the bulletproof man?

Something to consider for the future. If Thunder turned out to have been the one to take Donner's life, neither he nor any member of his freakish entourage would live to regret it. Perhaps it would be best, he considered, if Olsen did not die from the bullet wounds, although it would be an unlikely outcome. If he survived, he could be interrogated.

The Blood-Spider would have his answers, once way or another.

On pulling up to the Astoria, Crane and his two dates were greeted by the expected barrage of flashbulbs. As usual, there was a gaggle of photographers armed with box cameras, and a secondary crowd of sketchers scribbling away with coloured pencils on small notepads. He set his face in a careful, studied mask of contempt, one girl on each arm, their matched backless dresses complimenting perfectly the cut of his tuxedo – a Gunn original, hand-stitched by the master himself. Crane felt the mask becoming real as his hands drifted down to the naked smalls of their backs, and the myriad documenters of his social life clustered about him to record the moment for posterity. To them, all he was was this persona, this disguise he'd created for himself. For them, his entire self boiled down to a string of listless, bored copulations, to parties and openings, launches and premieres, rumours and scandals and endless, beautiful women. And not one of them knew the truth – that was what filled him with that cold, coiling hatred, lying like a snake in his gut. Not a single one of these vultures knew the reality of the man they were so desperate to tell the world about in their filthy little publications.

The corner of his mouth twitched, almost involuntarily, in a smile. And if they did know... if the great unwashed who pored over these yellow rags, these scandal-sheets, if they knew his intimate secrets – what? Would they praise him? Understand the cause that burned in him like a fire? He liked to think they might.

Some would want him dead, of course. The criminals. The inhuman. But he and they were at war, a war that never ended. Nestled against warm, yielding flesh, his trigger fingers itched, unsatisfied, denied their kill.

Inside, the girls ran quickly to powder their noses, leaving him blessedly alone. As he plucked a glass of champagne from the tray of a passing waiter, he felt his ears burning, and he turned his attention to the source – a rather loud argument near a potted plant, which the waiters were studiously avoiding as if attempting to starve it into silence, but which had drawn a small throng despite their efforts.

"What you don't understand, Mister Big-Shit Doctor *A-hole,* is the Blood-Spider's keepin' our streets safe, capeesh? Every one of these pieces of crap he puts down means lives saved! People *in the line* walkin' away from the jackpot and breathin' for another day! You ever told an officer's widow her husband's lying in the ground because some spic had more rights than he did? Huh? You ever did that, asshole, 'cause I have!"

The voice was loud, belligerent and rough, sandpapery from decades of nicotine abuse. Crane recognised it immediately. Detective Harry Stacey, forty-three years old, five feet and two inches tall. Hair a muddy grey with still the occasional streak of red. A handlebar moustache to match. A tan suit that had seen better days. He stank of whiskey, cheap cigars and light corruption. Crane had no doubt that he'd scrounged up the hundred dollars admission though gambling or stealing cash from the evidence locker, and presumably he was only here in the first place to grease a few palms or find a new mistress to put in the apartment he kept for that purpose across town.

In many respects, the man was a human sewer, but he had qualities that Crane couldn't help but admire. For example, he had an iron determination to protect the decent people in society from the undesirables, those who would prey on them – those inhuman devils who would revel in their sins, as it were – and he never allowed his weaknesses to compromise that. Not to mention that his deep connections with the more squalid elements of the police department allowed him to be useful to the Blood-Spider as a member of the Spider's Web.

Of course, if he hadn't proved himself so useful, he would have probably been killed by now. That made his blind loyalty a source of endless amusement to Crane, although naturally the Blood-Spider would never allow it to show. Idly, Crane looked over at his opponent in the one-sided debate.

`A tall, thin man, dressed in a grey suit and leaning on a gold-handled cane, with longish white hair and beard, hollow cheeks and grey, sunken eyes with large bags underneath them. The face was emotionless, almost supernaturally calm in the face of Stacey's tirade, and the only movement the man made was to occasionally take a long sip from the champagne glass in his left hand.

What had Stacey called the man? A doctor?

"It just seems somewhat unconstitutional, doesn't it? Shooting a young man in the street in cold blood. What about the basic freedoms?" The voice was cold, disinterested, and this attitude only enraged Stacey more. The scotch in his glass spilled over his clutching hand as he aimed a stubby finger at his debating partner.

"Freedoms? Screw your god-damn freedoms, Mister Med School! What about *my* freedoms? Where's my right to take a walk through the South Bronx at night without some freakin' jig sticking a knife up my ass? Where're the freedoms of all the decent folk, like – like schoolteachers, not the stinking commie ones, the ones who teach sports, where's their freedom not to have to look over their shoulders all the time in case there's a Jap with a giant freakin' pair of, I don't know, those sticks with the chains, what are they called, standing there waiting to knock their balls right off 'em and wear 'em like a friggin' hat? If it was up to you, Hamilton, you'd just give all the chinks and the spics who're terrorising the streets of this city a, a little slap on the wrist and a don't-do-it-again–"

"Can we do this without the racial invective?" murmured the doctor – Hamilton, that was his name. His expression had not changed, and he looked bored by the whole discussion. There was something about him that rubbed Crane the wrong way. His stoicism in the face of Stacey's drunken tirade seemed unnatural, somehow.

Not to mention his disapproval of the cause, which was suspicious in itself. This Hamilton would bear watching.

"Racial – up your *ass,* pal! I'm no racist!" Stacey flushed red, knuckles white on his glass as he tossed the rest of the scotch down his throat. "You god-damned *progressives,* you're pretty damned quick to call a guy a bigot just for speaking his mind, aincha? Maybe *you're* the racist, pal! Ever think of that? Maybe you're racist against people like me who friggin' work for a living – *in the line* – keepin' the streets safe like my buddy the Blood-Spider! Friggin'... friggin' *cop racist!*"

"I think we're done here." Hamilton turned on his heel, taking the bulk of the crowd with him. Stacey stared balefully after him for a moment, hurled his dead cigar angrily onto the polished floor and then charged off in the other direction, banging immediately into a waiter carrying a tray of canapés and sending miniature smoked salmon rolls scattering in all directions. Crane watched Stacey curse the man out and then head down a corridor in the direction of the gents' toilets.

Crane checked that no eyes were on him and then surreptitiously followed, making sure to keep several paces behind the detective, moving silently. Once they were out of sight of the main throng, Stacey stopped, digging in his inside pocket for a fresh cigar.

Crane smiled, taking a handkerchief from his own pocket and using it to disguise his voice as he crept up behind the older man.

It was all in the timing. Crane, silent, waited until Stacey had raised the stogie to his lips and was attempting to light it with a book of matches he'd taken from one of the city's many strip clubs. Then he spoke.

"Detective."

The Blood-Spider's voice. That unearthly hiss, low, sibilant and menacing. Harry Stacey nearly leapt out of his skin. "Christ–" The match went flying, thankfully going out before it burned a hole in the carpet. The cigar slipped from suddenly trembling fingers, bouncing off an unpolished shoe.

"Turn around and you will be killed, Detective. Do we understand each other?"

Stacey had been half turning, but now stood straight as a ramrod, beads of sweat appearing on goose bumped flesh, staring straight ahead. "Aw, crap. I mean yessir. Whatever you say. I won't turn around, you can count on your buddy Harry Stacey, Mr. Blood-Spider, sir, 'cause I'm right there with you *in the friggin' line,* pal –"

"Be quiet."

Stacey was quiet.

"Two days ago, a man was found dead, Detective. Murdered in his home. He was killed with a sword."

Stacey frowned. "Killed in his home... wait, was this that recluse guy everybody thought was dead? Danner, Donner, what was his name –"

Crane thrust the tip of a finger into the man's back, and he jerked as if he'd been stung by a wasp.

"Be quiet, I said."

Stacey nodded, dumbly, trying to swallow.

"I need information, Detective. Anyone who's been killed or injured with a sword in Manhattan. If you bring this information to my... mail drop..."

"Aw, not that douchebag Crane! Jesus, every time I set foot in that friggin' rich-boy hellhole I get a case of the hives –" The finger jerked in his back again. "I love that guy."

"Crane. If you bring him the intelligence I require, I will allow you to continue serving the cause. If not... your sins are deep and steep, Detective, and they lie black upon your heart. I know about the gambling, the bribes, the kickbacks, the whores. Some would say the Spider's Web has no place for you."

"So what, you'd kick me out?" Stacey scowled. "Just 'cause I cream a little off the top here and there? A guy's gotta make a living, buddy – uh, sir."

Crane jabbed the finger into his back once more, leaning closer. *"Yes. I would kick you out."*

His hiss dropped slightly. *"Of a window."*

Stacey stiffened, the sweat glistening on the back of his neck. Unconsciously, he raised his arms. "Please, I – I got a family! I got a grandmother with, with lumbago, she needs me – I got two! Another with the consumption! She needs me too! I'm needed in this world!"

Crane chuckled dryly.

"I'd hate to deprive your 'grandmothers' of your continued affection, Detective. The information. Tomorrow, without fail, as soon as your shift ends. Do we have an understanding?"

Stacey nodded, and Crane took a perverse delight in noting the dark stain spreading across the front of his tan suit trousers.

"Don't turn around."

Harry Stacey didn't turn around.

He remained, with his arms raised and the front of his trousers coated with his own urine, for six minutes and fourteen seconds, until finally the two pneumatic blondes who Parker Crane would spend the evening entertaining in various ways exited the ladies toilets and asked him if he'd had a stroke.

ON HIS WAY out, with the girls in place on his arms and another coming along for good measure – a statuesque redhead, the daughter of a Wall Street financier, who believed in seizing each moment as it came or some such philosophy, Parker Crane turned back and met the gaze of Doctor Hamilton. There was no emotion in that gaze. It reminded Crane of nothing so much as a dead fish on a slab, but all the same, he found something in it unpleasant. Threatening, almost.

"Can I help you?" he said, trying to keep the irritation out of his voice.

"Parker Crane, the fashion photographer." Hamilton thrust out a hand, which Crane didn't take. "A pleasure to meet you. I'm..." He seemed to be searching for the correct words. "...an admirer of your work. I think you've made quite a valuable contribution to the culture of this city."

Something in the phrasing bothered Crane. "What do you mean?"

"What I say. I've watched your career with interest. In fact, I think we may have a mutual acquaintance..." His eyes narrowed, speculatively, though his expression did not betray the slightest hint of what he was thinking.

Crane stood for a moment, before one of the blondes – Mandy? Sandy? – tugged his arm, giggling. "*Par*-ker, we want to see your place. You said you'd show us your etchings..." They dissolved into tipsy giggles and led him away towards a waiting hansom. As he walked out through the great double doors of the Astoria, Crane turned to look back at the strange man who'd accosted him.

But Doctor Hamilton was gone.

LATER, IN HIS palatial room, Parker Crane lay back on silk sheets soaked with champagne and the sweat of beautiful women, ears filled with drunken laughter and soft, wet noises, and mused that none of this seemed real to him. Occasionally, all of the luxury, these endless dalliances and pleasures of his other self, his fake self – all of it disgusted him. Yes, there was a release there, a form of pleasure, but it was nothing compared to that feeling in him when he pulled the trigger and removed evil from the world. True pleasure came from the barrel of a gun.

The thought amused him as he allowed sleep to steal over him.

In the hospital, Monk Olsen breathed through a tube. He would not die tonight, but his healing would be long and slow.

In the basement of the hospital, Doctor Miles Hamilton gently carried a vial of blood – the bulk of Doc Thunder's generous donation to his friend – down to the cold room where such perishables were kept, placing it in a chilled metal box in which it could remain fresh – a box to which only he had the key.

In the brownstone, Maya slept, and dreamt of a man in a red mask, and murder, and all the secrets of the past returning to haunt the future. Occasionally, she dreamt of home, and smiled.

Doc Thunder did not sleep at all.

CHAPTER SIX

Doc Thunder and The Omega Machine

"I HATE THIS thing."

Maya scowled as she adjusted the copper headband so that the contacts – small discs of sponge soaked in brine – rested against Doc Thunder's temples. His hands were strapped down to the arms, and another strap ran across his chest, with still more securing his legs. "To prevent convulsions," he'd said, "from the effect of the galvanic stimulation on the body."

The chair was linked up with copper wire to an odd device consisting of an array of magnets, which, when set to spinning in a certain configuration, would create an induction effect and charge the wires with pulses of pure galvanic force – 'omega energy', as the Doc had dubbed it. The shifting colours of the sunset streamed through the window, cascading over the massive, squat machine, reflecting from the shiny copper and burnished steel, making the apparatus look strange and otherworldly, like something out of a scientifiction chapbook.

Monk had once asked him if the 'omega effect' could be used to power a machine, like a steam engine – power a car or a robot, maybe. "Too dangerous," the Doc had said. "Omega energy can kill a normal man, and that's the first thing they'd use it for. Executions. If I can make it safe, I'll give it to the world. Until then, the Omega Machine will be the only one of its kind on this planet."

On Doc's signal, Maya would throw a switch mounted on the omega generator, closing the 'omega pathway' and sending pure omega energy from deep within the guts of the machine down the wire and through the chair. At which point, it would pass through the brine-soaked contacts and straight into the Doc's brain.

On a lesser man, the effect would be fatal, but on Doc's enhanced body, the 'omega effect' charged his synapses, opening up new doors of perception and allowing his conscious mind access to the subliminal, unconscious parts of his brain. Essentially, it boosted the power of his mind by a factor of ten or more and allowed him to make intuitive leaps that previously would have been unthinkable even to him. There was only one drawback.

If he was left too long in the Omega Machine, it would kill even him.

And nobody knew how long 'too long' might be. It could be as short as a few seconds or as long as ten minutes. But once his mighty heart ceased to beat, it would be beyond Maya's power to compress his chest. If his breathing stopped, Maya would not be able to reinflate his lungs any more than she could have reinflated a crushed metal can. CPR just didn't work on Doc Thunder – that was an unpleasant truth he'd lived with all his life.

"I hate it." Maya scowled, though it didn't mar her beauty. Then she laughed, without humour. "It's funny – when you risk Monk's life, I threaten you with death. So what do I threaten you with when you risk your own?"

She looked at him for a long moment, then, a sudden, strange, considering look crossed her lovely features.

Doc's voice was soft, gentle. "Don't go."

Maya smiled, caught. "I was just thinking about the Forbidden Kingdom. My home." She smiled, sitting down on his lap, reaching around to gently stroke the back of his neck with a fingernail. "Intrigues and betrayals. An endless succession of high priests and viziers – either sinned against or sinning. The number of times I had to intervene to break up some conspiracy or other... goodness knows what they've done without me." She leant to kiss him, probing for a long, delicious moment with her catlike tongue, and when she finally let his lips go, her eyes were considering, as if the kiss was an evaluation.

Doc tried to smile. "I'm sure they haven't done anything too..." He tailed off, the words sounding hollow and ridiculous in his own ears. She continued looking at him, head tilted to the side, and he stayed silent, not wanting to betray the sudden panic he was feeling. He'd nearly lost Monk – his best friend, his bedmate – and to lose Maya, too, to let her slip away from him, to be alone again, as he'd been before...

Eventually, he spoke. "Would you... would you really go back to that? I know the danger didn't mean anything to you, but you were so... bored..."

Don't let her be bored, he thought. *Please. Don't let her be bored of me.*

She smiled, reaching down past his belly, stroking, teasing, like a cat toying with a wounded bird. His muscles flexed against the straps, and she laughed. "No. I'm not bored. But... there are dangers here I didn't have to worry about at home. Worse than death. Worse than boredom, even."

She leaned in, her lips brushing his. "Are you going to break my heart, Doc Thunder?" Her lips blocked his reply, that tongue darting and delving in his mouth, her scent in his nostrils as the firm shape of her breasts and the weight of them pressed into him. She broke the kiss suddenly, looking at him with an air of cool consideration as she picked up the rubber bit-gag that would keep him from biting off his own tongue.

"Must I break yours first?"

He opened his mouth to speak, to tell her she was wrong, to ask her to stay with him, but she forced the gag in his mouth and secured it before he could. For the best, maybe. Maya Zor-Tura was not a woman who enjoyed the company of beggars. "Are you ready?" she said, crisply, padding over to the large switch mounted on the casing of the humming machine, the handle coated in rubber to prevent omega discharge.

Doc looked at her for a moment, then nodded.

She threw the switch and –

head full of lightning
sdrawkcab gninnips yromem
something in the past

– the flashes in his mind started to spark and crackle –

clue to discover
long-forgotten adventure
buried connection

– the first galvanised insights coming fast, in a rush –

thinking so quickly
that it becomes something new
not thinking at all

– a kaleidoscope of colour in his head, strange scents and audio hallucinations –

thousand days ago
something changed something went wrong
why think remember

– zoning in on a specific memory, something his subconscious had been screaming at him in the night for three years or more –

lomax was involved
lars lomax anti-scientist
implacable foe

– why Lomax? He hadn't thought of Lomax since he'd died –

hamilton as well
hamilton changed after that
why think remember

– Hamilton had been there, in the airship, over the Amazon,
what was the meaning behind that –

go into the past
memory unlocks the clue
think and remember

– think and remember –

Maya watched as Doc jerked and thrashed in the straps, teeth
biting into the bit-gag, eyes bulging as the omega energy tore
through his brain. When he was ready, when he had the answer
he needed, he'd tap out, hammer the arm of the chair with his
palm, signal her to turn off the omega field. If he could.

She wondered if this was the time she'd watch him die.

Think and remember.

The insights, the flashes and sparks in his mind, had calmed
as they always did, leaving him in a trance state, feeling the
pain and strangeness of the electric current flowing through his
synapses, and in that twilight world of semi-consciousness Doc
Thunder remembered Lars Lomax, the most dangerous man in
the world.

The twisted bald super-genius who had sworn to kill him a
thousand times, the evil scientist whose self-declared purpose
was to burn the whole world and raise his own civilisation in
its ruins, the ultimate foe, the one man who on his own had
caused more trouble than Untergang and N.I.G.H.T.M.A.R.E.
and E.R.A.M.T.H.G.I.N. and every other organisation he'd ever
fought put together, bar the Hidden Empire. Lars Lomax – the
enemy of Earth. The name that froze the blood in the veins of
law enforcement agencies the world over.

In some ways, Lomax had been a worse enemy over the years than even Heinrich Donner, the man Doc Thunder despised most in all the world. Strange, then, that they were so alike in their iron commitment to changing the world for the better. Lomax genuinely wanted to raise mankind to the stars, to make everyone in the world into a Doc Thunder, and if they'd only managed to work in unison, maybe that could have happened. Maybe they could have saved the world together.

But Lomax hated him.

Lars Lomax had hated him for his physical superiority, his perceived arrogance, his reluctance to destroy the status quo rather than change it slowly from within. Doc Thunder could never find it in him to hate Lomax back. He'd tried to save him, tried to bring him around, to persuade him that it didn't have to be that way, that there was a way that they could both get what they wanted without destroying each other. But that hatred had only grown, the terrible flaw in an otherwise brilliant personality. A single crack that turned this mirror-image of America's greatest hero into the world's greatest threat, that made Earth's would-be saviour believe that the only way to save the global village was to destroy it.

More sparks, more flashes. He had to remember something. Their final confrontation. The zeppelin, flying over the rich jungles of the Amazon, the struggle for the pistol...

No. That wasn't the important part. It was the part before, the part Maya had told him about. Something Lomax had said. How had it gone?

What had Maya said?

Think. Remember.

"I always enjoy our talks..."

"I always enjoy our talks, your Royal Highness. Tell me, what will you do when all this is over and your lover is dead? Go back to your forgotten kingdom? I can't imagine what the funeral service will be like."

One thousand days previously – in the sparks and crackles of Doc Thunder's memory – Lars Lomax smiled, and his shaggy red eyebrows lifted in amusement. "I imagine it involves feeding the deceased to a giant cobra, or possibly having a death-duel with a panther. That's about your speed, isn't it? Am I close?" He idly reached out to move his bishop a single square.

"Close." Maya smiled, readjusting herself on her seat. The ropes binding her arms and legs in place, securing her to the warm leather seat in front of the chessboard, were tight, but not so tight as to cut off her circulation. Lomax was considerate of his guests, as long as it suited him to be. "Actually the funeral service involves raising an army of my finest warriors to hunt you to the end of the world and flay the flesh from your living bones for daring to plot against my chosen consort. Never mind the temerity you've shown by daring to bind a Goddess... anyway, Queen's knight to queen five. Knight takes pawn. Mate in three moves."

Lomax frowned as he made her move for her. "Well, I'm not going to leave you free, am I? I'm not stupid. You'd kill me in five seconds. Three moves, you say?" He concentrated for a moment, and then took his own knight and captured a pawn himself. Getting rid of that white rook was a priority – in addition to all the other priorities, of course. Like killing Doc Thunder once and for all. "Well, I'm concentrating on several things at once, you have to understand."

Maya sneered. "King's knight to king four, knight takes knight, mate in two moves. And believe me, I understand. After all... you're no Doc Thunder, are you?"

Lomax cursed. Now he'd lost his knight, his queen was locked in one corner of the board and his king was looking dangerously under threat. How had he missed that? He'd walked right into it. Too many variables, that was the problem. Hurriedly, he captured the original knight with a pawn. Perhaps he could outflank her somehow.

For these few seconds of consideration, the game on the board was as important as the larger one taking place in the massive dirigible floating over the Amazon, towards his destiny. He'd rebuilt his Flying Fortress for the purpose, investing in hydrogen rather than cavorite to lift the structure – less expensive, and more suited to his purposes.

Of course, it meant that he was flying in a gigantic firebomb that could go off at any moment, but what was life without a little risk?

Whenever he had Ms. Zor-Tura as his guest – vastly preferable to leaving such a dangerous opponent free to provide aid and comfort to the accursed Thunder – he made a point of getting out the chessboard. Last time, he'd beaten her conclusively in one game and forced her to a stalemate in the second. No small feat, given that she'd been playing the game almost since its inception, and he was putting the final touches to his earthquake machine at the time.

Having made his move, he snapped out of his brief trance and turned his attention back to Maya.

"No Doc Thunder... well, I take that as a compliment. Anyway, pretty soon there'll *be* no Doc Thunder, just a moldy old corpse hanging off the front of my dirigible. Do you like it, by the way? After you broke the old one, I traded up. I particularly like the new furniture." He stood, walking across the metal flooring of the dirigible cabin towards the chair – his favourite chair, the one Doctor Hamilton was sitting in. "What do you think, Doctor Hamilton? How's my taste in antiques?"

Hamilton seemed restrained, drugged almost – not his usual self. He'd been Doc Thunder's personal physician for over ten years, and in that time Maya had gotten to know him well. A man with a dry wit, a gentle grip and a fierce light in his eyes, always ready with a smile, who cried at the injustices of the world openly and without shame. A truly gentle man.

The light in his eyes seemed gone now. The chair he was strapped in looked as if it would be most at home in one of the dungeons of the Spanish Inquisition. Hamilton's arms were strapped down to the arms of the chair, and there was a further studded metal strap wound around his temples and forehead, with a screw positioned at the back of the monstrous device that would tighten it as needed. Lomax had been slowly tightening the mechanism until it dug into Hamilton's flesh, and the agony must have been unendurable – the band was already visibly sunk into his forehead. Despite this, he remained still and calm, speaking through hitching breaths. "You can stop... stop asking questions. I'm never going to tell you what you want to know." The words held an edge of determination that struck Maya as almost out of character, and she felt shame at the thought. She'd misjudged him.

"But I really don't want to know very much, Doctor. Can't we compromise? Long negotiations can be such a headache." He reached to tighten the screw again, and Hamilton winced and inhaled sharply, gritting his teeth. "I really think you should reconsider. If nothing else, when your head cracks open like an eggshell it's going to make a terrible mess of my lovely Flying Fortress."

"I said no." Maya couldn't tell if that look of supernatural calm on Hamilton's face was despair, agony or something else. The words were low, almost rasping. "I'm not going to help you kill him. Good God, listen to yourself! You've tried shooting him, bombing him, stabbing him – now you want to find some ancient poison or radioactive metal that can kill him for you? You're a sick maaaagh!" His voice became a scream as Lomax tightened the band once more.

"Excuse me while I turn this a small trifle... you're right, Doctor, I am a sick man. I'm a very sick man. Sick of *him*. That pompous intellectual midget. That over-inflated stuffed shirt. I want him out of my hair for a while, Hamilton. Him and his trained ape."

"I beg your pardon?" hissed Maya, arching an eyebrow.

Lomax rounded on her, his irritation boiling into a sudden rage. "Oh, I forgot, the ape-man's your boyfriend too. Well, of course he is! The monarchy always did get their playthings, didn't they, Princess? King Thunder the first's big happy family can do what they like! *He* can do what he likes! Bend the ears of Presidents! God forbid the rest of us get the chance to make our voices heard! God forbid any *real* human beings ever go outside the stifling rules of this wretched, poisoned society, ever get to live their lives free from the taint of the status quo! Free from the *rules!* The ones *he* enforces!"

Hamilton didn't blink. "You're mad, Lomax. You're completely mad."

"Oh, I'm furious." Lomax was suddenly calm as he turned back to face the Doctor. "We have a superhuman being retarding our development. If humans had fought the Second Civil War alone, we'd have a paradise by now. My paradise. Instead, all we did was swap one flag for another. Well, I think it's about time we put the flags away with the rest of our childhood toys." He leaned in, close to the Doctor's ear.

"Listen, Doctor. You're Thunder's personal physician. You must know his weaknesses. You see, I was thinking... Poison. We're on our way to my Amazon lab, I've got a number of interesting toxins stored there. We'll experiment, see what might work. I just want a little input from you, that's all." He slowly twisted the screw, very gently now, applying only the slightest pressure. Hamilton screamed. "A little co-operation. That's all I want, and then the pain can stop. What do you say?"

"'First, do no harm.'" Hamilton gasped, his expression still unchanging as he gritted his teeth. "I took an oath. You can torture me all you want."

"Good. I'll do that, then."

"Even if I could help you –"

Lomax scowled, standing suddenly. It was all taking too long. He had to speed this up. "Fine. Fine, fine, fine, your own life isn't important to you. I get it. You're a big hero, well done, very good. How about *hers?*" He drew a revolver from his belt and pointed it directly between Maya's eyes. "Because one way or another I plan to hurt him, Doctor. I plan to hurt the big blue banana very badly indeed. And between you and me? I don't really care about methods."

Maya strained against the ropes, testing them again. Then she spoke, coolly. "Queen to queen seven, queen takes bishop. Check. And don't you dare threaten *me.*"

Without taking his gun off her, Lomax made the move. He chuckled, and called back to Hamilton. "Her Majesty speaks! And she's right, you know, Doctor, I am indeed in check. Seems a shame to end the game at this point, doesn't it? I'd look like a sore loser. It'd be sour grapes." He laughed again, eyes flashing fire, matching Maya's as his finger stroked the trigger. "Sure you won't reconsider my generous offer? I'd so hate to seem *unsporting.*"

"Go ahead and shoot. I may be more resilient than you think."
Maya smiled, daring him with her eyes.

"You are fascinatingly long-lived, I'll grant you that. A true
scientific puzzle. But immune to death by gunshot? I'd be a poor
scientist if I didn't test that little theory." He chuckled, spying
something on the chessboard. "Oh, and…" He took one of his knights
and quickly knocked the white queen over on the board before
picking it off. "Knight takes queen. That's game over, I think, Maya."

Maya looked back at him, and at that moment the entire cabin
lurched sideways, the pieces toppling off the board, the board
toppling off the table, the torture-chair sliding across the smooth
metal floor.

Maya smiled. "Game over. Yes, I rather think it is. King's knight to
king six." Her eyes sparkled. "Checkmate."

A hand tore through the metal siding of the cabin, peeling it away
like a can-opener, as the superhuman forced his way in. Lars Lomax
only smiled, and straightened.

"I thought he'd never get here."

He raised the gun and fired twice at Doc Thunder, aiming for the
eyes. They were the weak spots, where a well-placed bullet could –

wait something not right
i thought he'd never get here
why did he say that

The insight hit like a thunderbolt. They were starting again.
He needed to tap out soon, give Maya the signal, but he couldn't
yet. Not until he'd worked it out.

"I thought he'd never get here."

But Lomax hadn't found the answer he was after – hadn't
found his poison, the death-in-a-bottle that would end the life of
the man he hated most. But he'd sounded impatient–

what else had he said
out of my hair for a while
strange way to put it

Another flash. Stronger. He was on the edge of something, he knew. What had happened next?

There'd been a fight. An unequal fight, as always. He'd kept firing his pistol, even as he'd climbed into the cabin, even though he knew it wouldn't affect him. No, that wasn't quite true. He'd gone for the eyes. Always for the eyes.

The weak spot. A bullet in the eye would go straight into his brain and kill him, or at least brain-damage him. During the Second Civil War, he'd kept goggles with bullet-proof glass in them to wear during gunfights, but in the long run they'd limited his vision too badly to be worth it, especially after Silken Dragon's people had discovered inexorium –

inexorium
the metal cuts through my skin
no poison required

Doc gritted his teeth, tasting the rubber of the gag. He was almost seeing something, but not quite. The flashes were coming more quickly now. The insights. He travelled back in his memory, remembering the unequal fight, Lomax darting and ducking, aiming more bullets for his eyes, diving to the floor to escape a punch, rolling and snapping off one last shot – the one that killed him. The bullet had bounced off Doc's forehead, ripping up through the roof of the cabin and into one of the hydrogen chambers. It must have struck a spark on the metal, or at least he'd assumed later that's what must have happened, because suddenly the cabin was filled with flame and smoke. He'd heard the terrible roar and the rush of heat as the hydrogen went up –

but why hydrogen
antiquated and unsafe
why not cavorite

– and then he'd just reacted, grabbing Maya and Doctor Hamilton, ordering Lomax onto his back. He remembered that part very clearly, that oddly triumphant look. "You don't get to save me, Thunder." A coughing laugh. And then he'd run into the flames. Later, in the wreckage of the airship, they'd found his blackened skeleton. In death, it had seem to laugh at Doc Thunder, grinning with an empty skull-smile at his inability to save his greatest foe. It was the smile of the last enemy, of death itself.

Doc had blamed himself, but the simple truth was that hadn't had time to go after Lomax. He'd just hurled himself out of the crashing airship and into the waters of the Amazon, doing his best to shield Maya and Miles from the full effects of the fall. He'd dragged everyone to shore – Hamilton had nearly drowned – and then he'd freed him from the chair, the metal band across his brow leaving a deep indentation, although he didn't seem to be in that much pain. Hamilton had thanked him, without smiling –

was that when he stopped
after that he never smiled
and now we don't talk

– that was when he'd changed, that day that Lomax died. They'd been good friends before, and after that they'd drifted apart, and eventually Doc Thunder had stopped feeling the need for a personal physician. Now they were strangers.

He could smell skin cooking.

He wanted to tap out, but there was something he was still missing. He could feel it, right on the edge of his thoughts. That unsmiling thank-you on the riverbank –

holding out his hand
it caught me off guard somehow
his left hand shook mi –

And then it was over.

Doc slumped in the chair, panting, as Maya took her hand off the switch. When she took out the gag, he stretched his jaw, and then spoke, throat raw. "Too soon."

Maya shook her head. "You were in there for almost a full minute. Your skin was cooking. I thought you'd passed out."

He shook his head, gingerly feeling the burned patches at his temples after she undid the straps holding him down. "No such luck. I think I might have something. Or a lot of somethings that are going to add up to something." He shook his head, trying to clear the feeling of nausea – always the aftermath of an omega session. "We need to go back to the hospital."

Maya froze. "Is Monk in trouble?"

Doc frowned, thinking. "Maybe. More than we thought. But... I think I might be the one in trouble, Maya. I think I might have made my second mistake of the evening."

He stood, breathing in, trying to steady himself. Then he spoke again.

"Because when I met him... Doctor Hamilton was right-handed."

CHAPTER SEVEN

The Case of The Killer Caballero

THE NEW JUNIOR Under-janitor at the Jameson Club swept the floor slowly, methodically. Occasionally, he scratched the back of his head.

He was a temporary fix – quite the wrong sort of person for a permanent position, even as Junior Under-janitor – but the Club had needed someone in a hurry, as the previous Junior Under-janitor had sent an urgent telegram to say that he would not be coming in today, or any day. It was always difficult to measure a man's tone through the medium of something as impersonal as a telegram, but those who read it were of the opinion that the man had written it while frightened out of his wits. Some sort of psychological condition, perhaps. A poor show if he'd hidden it during his interview.

Fortunately, the new Junior Under-janitor had walked in the door only a few minutes later, quite literally begging for work. While he was quite the wrong sort of person – *quite* wrong – he did have a knack for making himself entirely unobtrusive, and thus was hired on for the day, with the possibility of being allowed back the next day if – one – the Club seniors could find nobody else on short notice and – two – he could keep his unfortunate racial handicap from bringing opprobrium on the Jameson Club.

He was, after all, *quite* the wrong sort of person.

Parker Crane certainly did not notice the new Junior Under-janitor as he breezed in, nodding a curt hello to Jonah, who hovered at the foot of the stairs.

"Sir, if I may, you have a visitor." The slight, nigh-undetectable pause before the word *visitor,* and the set of Jonah's eyebrows, communicated all of his feelings on the matter.

"Detective Stacey. Thank you, Jonah."

"I took the liberty of placing him in the Lower Library, Sir, as I felt your conversation would be best conducted in a private setting."

"Thank you, Jonah."

"Also, your guest has a somewhat curious smell and I fear allowing him into the more commonly-used environs of the Jameson Club would irreparably damage your standing as–"

"*Thank* you, Jonah. That will be all."

"Yes, Sir." Jonah gently ushered Crane through the door and into the room. Harry Stacey was waiting there with a near-empty glass of scotch – not the malt, thank goodness – and impatiently drumming his fingers on the dusty arm of the old leather chair he'd stationed himself in.

"About goddamn time! I been waiting here for close to an hour, you god-damned pansy!" He threw the rest of the scotch down his throat, then pointed an accusing finger at Crane. "Listen, pal, you better get on the *ball,* capeesh? 'Cause I'm in pretty tight with *you-know-who,* mac, and if *you-know-who* finds out you messed me about when I got important info for him, *you-know-who* might just figure on stickin' one of his guns right up your well-pounded rich boy *ass* and pulling the trigger until he friggin' breaks it off! Get me?"

"The Blood-Spider. You can say his name. This room is quite soundproofed." Crane was amused, despite himself, by the little man's bluster, but there was business to conduct. "You have the information he asked for?"

"Yeah, sword killings." He lifted up a manila file and opened it up on his lap. "You know, I didn't think there'd be this many. All recent, too – last few days."

"The last few..." Crane's eyes widened. He hadn't expected this at all. "Tell me." The urgency in his voice made Stacey look up, a trace of puzzlement on his idiot's face, and Crane scowled. It wouldn't do to even let this cretin guess his secret. He'd already risked too much with that little stunt at the party. "The... Blood-Spider will want to know the information urgently." His voice dropped, faking an air of concern. "I've... already angered him. I might have accidentally boasted of my connection to the Blood-Spider to, ah, guarantee success with a woman." Harry Stacey looked worried about that, which pleased Crane immensely. "He told me he might be considering getting another mail drop with a smaller mouth. I have to prove my worth to him, or..." He left the sentence dangerously unfinished. He was satisfied that he'd drawn Stacey away from any possible suspicion, and perhaps the ruse might keep him from flapping his own receding gums quite so often.

No such luck. Stacey's worried look transformed into a vicious grin, and he leant back in the chair, pointing a finger at Parker. "Too bad for *you,* buddy. I figure he'll probably cut your balls off you and bury 'em in concrete. Parker Crane, the richest eunuch in New York city. You oughtta get in his good books, like me. Me and the Spider, we're like *that.*" He pressed thumb and forefingers together. "Thick like thieves. Two old buddies from around the way. He told me once that I was the cream of his whole friggin' Web, y'know? I mean, compared to some of the things I've seen, y'know, *in the line,* this is just a hobby for me, kinda like stamp collectin'."

Crane sighed, shaking his head. He was probably going to have to do something about Stacey one of these days. "The sword killings." He forced a smile. "If you wouldn't mind."

"Don't want to make the Boss mad, right? I feel you, buddy." Stacey smirked, passing him the photos one by one; the crime scenes left behind.

"We got two futureheads here, found dead with sword wounds. One to the throat, one to the abdomen. That's down in East Village.

Both white, swastika tattoos, previous for, uh, 'racially motivated assault'. Roughhousin', I call it, but you know these progressive types. Another over in the Bronx, same. Three more over on Staten Island, one right in midtown, *five* in Central Park. Whoever this nutcase is, he sure gets around, I'll tell you that much."

"All the same man?"

Stacey nodded. "Sure. Wounds all match up. Plus, the vics all have a lot of things in common. All with previous for rolling jigs or queers, all heavily on the Kraut side of politics if you catch my drift. A couple of these dumbasses were actually killed during assaults in progress, while they were rolling other guys. We got witnesses who saw this guy work, said he saved their lives. 'Course, these are mostly jigs or spics, and you know they lie –"

"Stacey." Crane's voice was acid. "Let's have the facts without the editorial, please."

"Listen, rich boy, I don't see the *Blood-Spider* having a problem with the way I talk, so why don't you just –" Crane's look froze him in mid-sentence. "– ah, fine. Fine, whatever."

He rummaged quickly through the files. "Here's a witness statement for you. The five in Central Park. Apparently these guys pulled knives on a... on a *latino* couple, pardon your delicate friggin' ears, out for a late-night stroll. Went for the lady's purse, the fella stepped it, he got cut up some. Things were getting ugly, you know? Anyway, we got a clear description of what happened next. Just when our witnesses think they're gonna bite it, they start hearing this laugh."

Crane raised an eyebrow. "Laugh?"

"Sure, this big crazy laugh, like Santa Claus, big and booming. Like it's everywhere at once. I mean, I didn't hear it, but according to the witnesses it really got the perps freaking out, you know? Yelling 'who's there', 'come on out', all that jazz, trying to make this guy show himself..."

"So... they were scared?"

"Yeah, that's something I don't get either. I mean, it's just laughing, right? Some asshole laughs at me out of some bushes, I'd walk in there, grab his ass and introduce him to a little chin music, capeesh? Guy's probably a friggin' homo, ain't a jury in the world gonna convict me if I hand the guy his face. You gotta get a little rough with their kind, mark 'em up some, or next thing you know, the whole institution of marriage –"

Crane growled. "*Stacey.*"

Stacey shrugged. "Yeah, yeah, you've got your balls on the chopping block, I got you. So, yeah, I guess it must have been a hell of a laugh this guy had..."

Crane nodded, trying to hide the sinking feeling in the pit of his stomach. One of his tactics as the Blood-Spider – one Stacey had never been on the receiving end of – was a merciless, mocking laugh that froze the hearts of his enemies like ice in their chests. Was this a coincidence? Could it be?

"...anyway, suddenly this guy leaps out of the bushes. The witnesses didn't see exactly where he came from. It was like, one minute he wasn't there and the next minute, *bam*, there he was, large as life and twice as ugly."

Crane's brows furrowed. "Describe him."

"Go the description right here, let's see. Well, to start with, he's a wetback."

"A... what?"

"Mexican." Stacey shook his head, looking irritated that he had to explain the term. "Exhibitionist, too. No shirt, no shoes; just a pair of black suit pants. Oh yeah, and get this. He was wearing a mask. A red mask, wrapped around his eyes."

"A red mask..." The sinking feeling intensified. A red mask, like the Blood-Spider wore. Was he being imitated?

"Right. Anyway, this crazy bastard leaps out of nowhere carrying a sword and starts carving them up like Christmas turkeys. Lemme just repeat that for those sensitive ears of yours. One guy, not even wearing a shirt, against *five*. And these were big guys. They worked out, they'd done some time in juvenile. These were people who knew a little something about how to break a guy's head open, you know? Even if he did have a sword and a scary laugh."

"So whoever this... interloper is, he's very highly skilled."

Stacey frowned, looking around briefly as if checking nobody was in earshot. "Listen –" He leaned forward, as though imparting a great secret. "– I can handle myself in a fight, capeesh? I done a lot of stuff in the line. But five guys with blades – I couldn't have taken them. Seriously, they'd have cut off my dick and drop-kicked it into the East River. You ask any cop, they'd tell you the same. Even the Blood-Spider couldn't have taken all five of these guys with just a sword. Not all at once."

Crane raised his eyebrow again. "But the interloper..."

"Two decapitations, two fatal stabbings – one through the eye – and the last guy bled out from getting his junk cut off."

Crane blinked. "No wonder castration was weighing on your mind."

Stacey shrugged. "Like I said, it could be a lie, but *something* killed those assholes in the park. And until we got anything better to go on, I'm going with the sword-man theory." He frowned. "There's more, though. You know I got deep contacts in the FBI? Hell, I could have been a Fed myself, but I told those suit-and-tie assholes right to their faces: 'Harry Stacey is a man of the streets', I said –"

Crane rolled his eyes. He'd heard this story a dozen times, the day Harry Stacey turned down the FBI, and the truth was a little more prosaic. Harry was in a twice-weekly poker game with a filing clerk at the Bureau. When Harry needed minor information on FBI operations, he either forgave a debt or two or – on those occasions when he was not owed – leaned on one of the local whores to give the clerk a free ride. Like so much of the detritus that made up Harry's life, it was rotten to the core, and Crane found himself wishing he could simply reach forward and break the disgusting little man's neck. But it was necessary sometimes, when fighting the darkness that riddled Manhattan like a cancer, to perform acts that were themselves unsavoury – morally dubious, even. The Blood-Spider knew that very well.

Harry seemed to be coming to the end of his monologue; Crane forced himself to listen.

"– tried to pin a medal on me, but I told them I wasn't interested in none of that crapola. I don't need some piece of tin, that's what I told them. My place is on the streets, capeesh? A medal don't mean a damn thing in the line, you know? The only thing that counts is your shield and your gun and your *guts,* that's what I told ' em." He breathed in, as if showing off his gut for approval. "Anyway, like I said, I got contacts, and apparently this loon's been popping up in connection with some stuff the FBI's looking into. Kraut stuff."

"Kraut?" Crane's eyes narrowed.

"As in Untergang."

Crane blinked, slightly stunned. "Wait, this red mask fellow – he's working for *Untergang?* That doesn't make sense."

Stacey laughed, shaking his head. "Working for 'em? Hell no! Working *on* 'em, maybe. Look, the FBI keep some of those guys under surveillance. They figure if they keep watchin' the little fish, sooner or later they're gonna lead 'em to the sharks, y'know? Anyway, they're keeping tabs on this one cell, waiting for the chance to move in – and our guy just bursts in there and takes them apart. These are friggin' terrorists! With guns! Ten of them at least!" His eyes grew wide, staring into Crane's as if trying to infect him with Stacey's own incredulity at it. "He kills all but one of them – asks some questions – then kills that last guy too!" He drew a finger across his throat. "*Shlikk!* Just like that! The goddamn wetback is some kind of *machine,* capeesh?"

Crane leant back in his chair, lost in thought. "Who *is* he...?"

Stacey shrugged. "He hates the Krauts, that's for sure. Other than that – who the hell knows? Ain't like this town's ever been short of vigilantes. Hell, remember the Blue Ghost? I used to hang out with him when I was just a patrolman. Hell of a nice guy, even if he did get beat up a lot. Him and me were like *that,* even if I did used to smack that Jap kid he hung out with around a lot. I mean, yeah, he broke my arm, but it was all in fun, y'know?" He looked into the distance, furrowing his brow. "Vanished a little before you came on the scene, as a matter of fact..."

"I don't need to hear another tall story from you, Detective." The edge was back in Crane's voice, no matter how much he tried to keep it out. "I need to know who this masked man thinks he is and how and why he found Heinrich Donner." The why was obvious, Crane knew, if unpalatable. The thought brought him back to the ape-man's appearance at Donner's penthouse suite the previous night. "And we need to know how Doc Thunder's connected to all this." And there was a connection, he knew. Doc Thunder and Heinrich Donner had never been friends. Perhaps he was working with this Mexican, this red mask. Perhaps he was Thunder's secret enforcer, committing crimes to make sure Thunder's hero's hands could remain clean and unstained. If that was the case, it was one more reason for him to have earned Crane's contempt.

The Blood-Spider preferred to do his dirty work himself.

Stacey scowled, snarling at him like a dog straining at the end of a leash. "Listen, buddy," he snapped, "I don't know how you got so mouthy – considering you're just a jumped-up messaging service for the boss and all – but if I was you I'd quit flapping your gums, capeesh? You act like you're in charge of this caper because you were born with a goddamned silver spoon halfway up your stretched asshole, but lemme tell ya, pally, I'm in a lot deeper with the Blood-Spider than you are. And so help me, I might just decide to tell him how you been treating me."

"Oh, shut up and get lost, Stacey." Crane waved the Detective away, as Jonah, knowing as ever just when he would be needed, opened the door to escort him out. Stacey snatched up the file, let loose a few more choice epithets about Crane's education and background, and then left, leaving nothing but the stink of sweat, cigar smoke and whiskey to mark his passing.

Crane made a mental note not to lose his temper like that again. He'd spoken as the Blood-Spider, and while an imbecile like Harry Stacey might not think twice about it, he could be sure others would take notice. Parker Crane had always been a mask – a disguise to hide his true self – but lately the mask had begun to fray, and traces of the truth were occasionally visible. That would not do. Not after all the work he'd done.

He had too many plans to allow his temper to spoil them.

"If I might interrupt your reverie, Sir...? You received a telegram in the last five minutes, and while I felt it prudent not to interrupt your conversation with the Detective..."

"Yes, of course." Crane reached out a hand, taking hold of the folded piece of paper, and passed his eyes quickly over it.

HELLO PARKER STOP NEED TO TALK STOP HAVE
SOMETHING OF INTEREST TO YOU STOP BOTH OF
YOU STOP ALSO FIFTY FIFTY CHANCE OF OTHER
INTEREST STOP PLEASE COME TO THE ROOFTOP
OF SAINT ALBERTS ASAP STOP NO B S STOP

DOCTOR MILES HAMILTON

"Miles Hamilton..."

"Chief Administrator at Saint Albert's, Sir. At one point he and
Doc Thunder were very close friends."

Crane frowned. "'Fifty fifty chance of other interest.' What
does that mean?"

Jonah coughed gently. "If I may be so bold, Sir, I would be
more interested in the part that says he has something of interest
to 'both of you'. Add that to the, ah, 'no B S'... and unless the
good Doctor has developed a taste for the vernacular..."

"He knows." Crane's eyes grew hard. "He knows that I'm the
Blood-Spider. He's learned my secret, maybe *all* my secrets, and
he's telling me to leave the mask and the guns at home."

Jonah nodded. "And will you, Sir?"

Crane almost smiled. "Jonah, Jonah, Jonah. The mask and the
guns *are* my home." He stood, looking over at the trunk that sat
in the corner, squat and menacing, like some demon coiled up
and ready to explode. "Bring the telephone. I'm afraid I'm going
to need to interrupt Ms. Lang's evening again."

He turned to look at Jonah, and there was something quite
terrifying in his gaze. Something that spoke of brutal, merciless
violence yet to come.

"We're going to pay a little social call."

As JONAH LEFT the room, he paid no attention to the Junior
Under-janitor, still sweeping the floor and scratching the back
of his skull. If he had known the Junior Under-janitor had been
listening at the door, he would have been instantly dismissed –
and perhaps 'silenced' by the Blood-Spider.

But the Junior Under-janitor was beneath his notice. He was, after all, quite the wrong sort of person. A Mexican, and very likely an illegal immigrant.

If Jonah had known that the Junior Under-janitor was not only an illegal immigrant but was also suffering from multiple personality disorder – and indeed was prone to regular bouts of extreme violence –it's hard to say whether he would have been surprised. But he'd never bothered to ask such things. Could he push a broom, that was all that mattered. The next day, they would begin the process of finding a proper applicant for the post.

He barely even remembered the man's name.

It was Djego.

CHAPTER EIGHT

Doc Thunder and The Face of Fear

MORE THAN TWENTY years before, the clocks were striking midnight.
The Seventies were coming to a close, and the whole of America
looked set to follow.

The Blue Ghost watched through one swollen eye as Anton
Venger, Agent Of N.I.G.H.T.M.A.R.E., held the glass bottle aloft.
Inside, the blue ichor which would spell death to half a continent
– and perhaps the end of civilisation as mankind knew it – sloshed
lazily to and fro, seemingly glowing with its own internal light.

Venger chuckled, his handsome, tanned features lit by the fire
of Liberty's torch as he savoured the coming moment, when he
would uncap the deadly bottle and hurl the concentrated solution
off his perch on top of the Statue – where his men had taken
the Ghost at Venger's request – and into the harbour. There, the
final reaction would take place, the seawater combining with the
experimental poison to form an ever-expanding ring of death;
a toxic cloud rising up from below like some monstrous kraken.
Before the reaction was exhausted, the eastern coast of America

would choke on the deadly fumes. "Ironic, isn't it? We're about to give New York the ultimate liberty – the liberty of death. It's a real shame President Rickard couldn't see reason. One billion dollars is such a piddling little sum..."

The Ghost shifted, trying to break out of the ropes, and was rewarded with a stabbing pain in his side that made him wince. Venger's goons had really worked him over. He counted at least four broken ribs, not to mention the broken leg that he was going to have to heave around the place on crutches for God only knew how long. That was going to make fighting crime a real pain in the keister, and with his arms tied, it left him one good leg to save the country.

Why the hell hadn't he stuck to beating on gangsters?

"You're bluffing, Venger." *I hope.* "If that stuff does what you say it does, you'll die with the rest of us."

Venger looked wounded. "My dear Ghost – I have doctorate degrees in biology, virology and medicine. Do you really think me so stupid as to invent a deadly poison and not inoculate myself against it? When New Yorkers are gasping their lungs out like freshly-landed fish, I will be leading the squads of N.I.G.H.T.M.A.R.E. agents looting the east coast of its valuables. If we can't have our payday one way, we'll have it another. Perhaps our dear Prez will think twice before he bets against the greatest criminal organisation in the world."

The Ghost frowned. He'd fouled up on this one, these were international criminals operating on a massive scale. It was S.T.E.A.M. who should be fighting these guys, not some guy in a blue suit and a skinny tie whose biggest talent was taking a beating and coming back for more. Why the hell hadn't he turned the whole thing over to the big boys when he'd had the chance? The whole world was waiting for N.I.G.H.T.M.A.R.E.'s midnight deadline, and Jack Scorpio's high-faluting Special Taskforce was on a wild goose chase to Yellowstone Park. The only people in the world who knew Venger was here were him and Easton West – and who'd believe a ten-year-old kid?

The only thing he could do now was keep the nutball talking. As long as he was running his mouth, he wasn't emptying that poison vial into the water. "Got it all worked out, haven't you? How many people are you planning to kill for your kicks, you sick, twisted..." He trailed off. *Should I insult the guy, or not insult the guy? A slanging match would be pretty good – that'll keep this going a while – but not if he gets mad enough to toss that crap off the crown.*

Venger didn't seem overly offended. He just smiled his superior smile. "Judging by this wind, I think the poison cloud should blow inland for quite a distance. It may even reach the White House before it loses full potency. And even after... well, if you've ever breathed acid vapour, you know that even if it doesn't kill you, it will certainly sting. And this will be very similar, if you haven't had your inoculation jab. That's why I had my men bring you up here. I want to watch the effects on a human body up close. I hope you don't mind being part of my experiment."

"Sheesh. You scientists." The Ghost rolled his eyes behind his ever-present blue domino mask. "Just once, I'd like to meet a crazy world-conqueror who took drama. He could try and Shakespeare me to death."

"Hmm. Funny you should mention that." Venger smiled widely. "I did do a minor in drama at college – 'the man of a thousand voices', they called me. I could have been a star of the stage. Isn't it funny how things work out?"

"Never too late, pal. Lot of great plays get put on in prison. A little state's evidence and you wouldn't even see the inside. What do you say?" The Ghost was really hoping he'd actually go for this. If he didn't, he was out of options. A last-minute change of heart was about all the hope he had left.

For a moment, Venger almost seemed to consider it. "Hmmm..." Then he smiled. "No. But I do appreciate you trying to keep me talking. I wanted to allow the idiots at S.T.E.A.M. a false glimmer of hope before I showed them just how pitifully they'd failed." He smiled, lifting the bottle up into the air, theatrically removing the cork with his other hand. The air suddenly filled with the sickly smell of rotting lilacs –

– and then Doc Thunder landed on the Statue of Liberty, ringing it like a gong, the small Japanese boy clinging to his back hanging on for dear life.

"Easton!" yelled the Ghost, a note of triumph in his voice. "Great stuff, kid! Gimme a hand out of these ropes, huh?"

"I got help like you said, Mister Ghost Boss!" Easton yelled as he clambered off the big man's back. Having been unable to interest the police in his story, he'd done the next best thing and gone straight to the Doc's brownstone. Fortunately, Doc had been home.

"Put down the fluid, Venger. You don't want to do this." Thunder's eyes were a steely calm, and he spoke softly, carefully. If that solution should fall over the side... even one drop... "Listen to me. If you do this – if you allow this atrocity to happen – there'll be nowhere you can hide. You know that. Every law enforcement agency on the planet will be after your blood from now until the day you die. There will be no escape. Let it end, Venger – Anton. Let it go." He smiled, keeping his eyes on the other man's. He spoke softly, rationally, and he meant every word. You couldn't lie to these people, they could smell insincerity. How many times had he been talking to men with their fingers on the trigger, or the button, or the bomb? How many times had he failed to prevent them from destroying themselves?

For the sake of New York, he couldn't fail now. "I want to save you. I want to help you. If you come with me, we can... *I* can work with you. I can get to the bottom of your anti-social tendencies." The words set off warning bells in his own ears. They sounded fake – ridiculous and fake – and all of a sudden he knew that he'd lost this one. He couldn't pull it back.

Now he needed to get to Anton Venger before he dropped the fluid.

Anton shook his head, terror in his eyes. The West boy was still fumbling with the Blue Ghost's ropes, trying to free him without putting too much pressure on his ribs. Venger began to step back towards the edge, keeping his eyes on Thunder, holding the bottle of blue ooze protectively against his chest.

Doc Thunder knew that if he made a sudden move, Venger would hurl that bottle into the harbour. "Anton!" he breathed, trying to freeze him with his voice. It didn't work. Venger took another step back. Then another. Then another. Then –

– the Blue Ghost stuck his good leg out.

Venger gave a little scream, like a child, as he toppled backwards. But there was nothing little about the scream he let out as the blue liquid splashed out of the bottle and over his face, coating it, then eating into it, seeming to merge with it...

"Dear God..." breathed the Ghost, as Easton West buried his face in the powder-blue suit jacket, hiding from the terrible sight.

"None of it went in the water. We're safe." Doc Thunder breathed out. He hadn't even been aware he'd been holding his breath. "But... I don't know if he'll live through that."

The Ghost looked at the shrivelled, withered skin, once tanned, now a terrible bluish-white. The face which seemed to be melting, distorting as he watched. The agonised look in the man's grey eyes.

"I don't know if he'll want to."

"He didn't."

That was then, and this was now, and Doc Thunder and Maya were racing in a hansom carriage towards Saint Albert's Hospital. "He blamed me, of course. Oh, he hated the Ghost, and he hated N.I.G.H.T.M.A.R.E., I'm sure he hated himself. But most of all, he hated me. If I hadn't turned up when I did, he'd still have a face. All this was before your time..."

Maya smiled. "Very little is before my time. But I take your meaning. What on earth did you do for fun in that big lonely brownstone before Monk and I came along?"

Doc smiled, despite himself. "I played a lot of chess. Miles would come around for a game occasionally." He grew pensive again, shaking his head. "Miles. I can't believe I never saw it."

"You couldn't have–" Maya began, but Doc cut her off.

"Don't tell me I couldn't have known. I could have, I *should* have known, Maya. You might not have known how he got that way, but you knew what he could do. *I* knew what he could do." He shook his head, his face contorted in self-recrimination. "And when my oldest friend's personality changed, and he started favouring his left hand, and his face stopped registering emotion... I thought he'd grown cold. I thought he'd just stopped being a good guy. I thought that instinctive, gut-level dislike I felt whenever I met him... was *him*. And all the time..."

Anton Venger.

The Face Of Fear.

That blueish-white visage, once handsome, was now slack, shapeless, drooping like unfired clay. And like clay, it could be shaped. Molded. Given time, and a little makeup, it could be made to look like anyone in the world. Anton Venger was a skilled impersonator, and the madness that had claimed him after his terrible accident only increased his ability to take on the personalities of others, albeit as a dark reflection, with all of their weaknesses and insecurities given full life within this strange, twisted doppelganger.

As a member of N.I.G.H.T.M.A.R.E. he would have been invaluable, but his madness had led him to reject them, to strike out on his own, to make war against all of civilization, against a species he no longer felt any part of. When Anton Venger gazed upon the world, he saw no beauty, no joy, no hope, no love. All he saw was the chemical taint of his never ending hatred; a hatred that burned a cold white-blue.

A natural outsider, he'd found himself drawn over time to another outsider – to Lars Lomax, the most dangerous man in the world. The Lomax-Venger Team, as Lars had dubbed them in a moment of bonhomie, had almost been the end of everything a dozen times, but eventually, all things must pass.

"You weren't there when Venger died, were you?" as Doc Thunder spoke the words, he realised he hadn't spoken for several minutes, lost in his thoughts. "Not that he did die, as it turns out..."

Maya shook her head. "No. I was in Venice, trying to deal with the war between N.I.G.H.T.M.A.R.E. and E.R.A.M.T.H.G.I.N. along with Monk and Jack Scorpio. Of course, we didn't know that was just a distraction engineered by Lomax. We thought it was the main event." She sighed. "'Am us not men?' Whatever happened to them?"

"Warhol's dreampunk ideas are the new thing in the art world. Détournment is out. The futureheads that are clinging on to the movement are being co-opted by extremist groups. Which means

Untergang, of course. All roads of that nature eventually lead to Berlin." He shook his head. "E.R.A.M.T.H.G.I.N. will mutate into something else. Evolve. Or devolve. Pranksters and tricksters, nipping at the nose of culture – so long as there's a culture to nip at, we won't see the last of them. I hope we never do... I like the idea of a world where the worst thing I have to fight is somebody's joke."

Maya nodded. "Meanwhile, you were there for the final dissolution of the Lomax-Venger Team."

"I was." Doc gazed out of the window, remembering. "Paris. City of romance..."

"Mmmm... such a specimen. So very pretty-pretty-pretty..."

The voice seemed to melt, spilling over the tongue like rich liquid chocolate, as Doc Thunder found himself staring into eyes of brilliant gold, unblinking as a serpent's and possessed of a malevolent playfulness that sent a chill down his spine even as the long, perfectly painted fingernails brushed slowly over his naked chest.

He was bound, of course. Great steel anchor chains stretched from the ceiling of the ornate Parisian drawing-room to shackles that held his wrists, while his ankles were secured to the base of the strange contraption he'd been placed on – like a shaped metal saddle secured to a stout pole. It was an uncomfortable predicament, and more than a little humiliating, especially considering the Silken Dragon hadn't allowed him to keep his clothes.

She was like that.

She was the daughter of the Velvet Dragon, N.I.G.H.T.M.A.R.E.'s first leader, a cold, brilliant and debonair psychopath who had died attempting to hurl Jack Scorpio Senior from the top of the Eiffel Tower. He had raised her to think of the world as a plaything, a bauble to be toyed with and claimed as her own whenever she pleased, and all the creatures in it as her slaves. Anyone looking at her would only see the surface at first; a stunningly beautiful woman of mixed French and Oriental descent, possessed of a bountiful figure, which seemed always on the verge of spilling out of the shimmering golden corset she wore, and a luscious, oozing sexuality, a wickedly deviant mind that glittered in her golden eyes, a merciless confidence that revelled in breaking the strong and taming the weak. By the time they realised the true danger – the sheer, ruthless evil hidden beneath the perfume of her skin, an evil that thought nothing of taking the entire planet as a hostage – it was far too late.

"So pretty-pretty-pretty..." she purred, raking her nails once more down Thunder's sculpted abdominal muscles, brushing them lightly through the thicket of his–

"Stop right there." Maya frowned, irritated. "You were flirting with her, weren't you?"

"I wasn't *flirting,* she's an evil–"

"Oh, please! Like she's not your *type!* Chain you to a dungeon wall and you're anybody's, I should know. Let me guess – did you tell her that beneath her iridescent beauty her evil shone cold and hard as a diamond?"

"Well, I didn't say that *exactly...*"

– her tongue teased against his for a moment before their lips parted. "Am I not beautiful, my pretty-pretty-pretty? Am I not to be desired by all who look on me?"

"You're as beautiful and desirable as a diamond." Thunder breathed, eyes stern. "And like a diamond, you're cold, and hard... and flawed."

"You dare to call me flawed?" her voice grew icy as her teeth met at his earlobe, a serpentine hiss in his ear. "You will die for that, my pretty-pretty, inch by inch."

"Your evil is your flaw. And all of your beauty can't hide it." Thunder hissed, before another brutal, claiming kiss sealed his lips.

"Oh, good grief. You're incorrigible. I can't believe I fell for that line." Maya grew thoughtful for a moment. "She does sound interesting, though. It is a shame we couldn't have met her on a more informal –"

"It would have been harbouring an international fugitive. Sorry. Also, she was completely insane."

Maya sighed. "Well, you can tell me all about that part later. Skip to the relevant bit."

Doc frowned. "Lomax. And Venger."

"I HOPE I'M not interrupting..." Lomax smiled, walking into the drawing room with a Polish vodka-martini in one hand and a cigar in the other. "My God. You've actually wounded him. What is that?"

Silken Dragon smiled, twirling the barbed flogger in her hand lazily, before leaning to run her tongue along the bloody gashes she'd carved in Thunder's back. "My scientists developed it. An alloy that can actually pierce the good Doctor's skin. We call it inexorium. It makes torture so much more... enjoyable, when you can see the pretty pattern of scars form on the skin. So pretty-pretty-pretty..."

"Good Lord." His eyes widened, looking at the glittering metal as he took a long sip of the martini. "Tell me you've made a bullet with it. We can end this here and now."

"Where would the pleasure be in that? Anyway, inexorium is so very pricy, and so difficult to make. Just the barbs on the tips of this flogger cost me over a million dollars. And they're just tiny scraps of barbed metal... but so effective, aren't they? So wonderfully cruel." She pouted. "Am I very cruel, Lars?"

"You're as crazy as an outhouse rat is what you are, my dear, and quite frankly – I love it." Lomax grinned, puffing on the stogie before exhaling a cloud of smoke. "Tastes like victory, Thunder. You really should take up the habit."

Doc Thunder winced, testing his chains again. No weak link, but perhaps... "You don't need another bad habit, Lomax. You've got enough already – *aahh*!" He gritted his teeth, crying out as the barbed flogger struck across his back, criss-crossing the cuts it had already left.

"Bad pretty-pretty," the Silken Dragon hissed, her golden eyes dancing with a merciless delight. "Speaking is a privilege, not a right. Will I have to muzzle you, my new pet?"

Lomax waved his hand expansively. "Nonsense. It wouldn't be Thunder if he wasn't ready with a sanctimonious little quip, would it? Where's Maya, by the way? I was looking forward to a game of chess."

"Far away from you." Doc's eyes narrowed.

Lomax sighed. "You're still mad at me for kidnapping her the last time, aren't you? And you should be. I beat her five games to one. At one point she asked to switch to backgammon. Backgammon! Let me tell you, there was blood on the chessboard." He looked at Thunder's gaze for a moment. "Not literally. You know I'm never going to hurt her, Thunder. Never. She's off limits. Know why?"

Doc didn't say anything.

"I mean, I'm a sucker for the whole Lost City vibe, it's so... kitsch. And she's a great chess player. But the real reason I'd never lay a finger on her?" He smiled, blowing smoke in Doc's face. "One day she's going to hurt you, big man. She doesn't know it, but I can tell just by looking at her. She's got all the time in the world, and all the possibilities that gives her, and one day you're going to lie to her, or do something stupid, or just not be enough anymore, and she's going to go live her eternal life somewhere else. With somebody else. And that..." He grinned, knowing he'd struck home. "That's going to break your heart in two."

Doc scowled.

"You and Maya? Unsustainable. I'm going to love seeing her go back to her temple. That's going to crush you. I might send her a fruit basket after it happens with a little thank-you note. Neither of you know it, but she's on my team." He laughed, taking another long sip. "If I were you, I'd get ready for a fall, Thunder. But if I were you... well, I'd do a lot of things differently."

"You've got a poor opinion of love, Lomax – *aaahh*!" Another cruel blow to the flesh of his back. Silken Dragon laughed, softly.

Lomax smiled. "You think it's love. Cute. So where is she?"

"Busy dealing with the diversion you created in Venice."

"Ah, E.R.A.M.T.H.G.I.N.! Easily rooked and manipulated to help goad idiotic numbskulls... like Jack Scorpio and his collection of morons. Which reminds me, what does N.I.G.H.T.M.A.R.E. stand for?"

"Why, it stands for the total domination of the weak by the strong, of course. What else?" Silken Dragon flicked the whip against Thunder's hide again, making him jerk and the chains rattle.

"I'll drink to that." Lomax took a swig of his martini. "You know, I never really thought of myself as the mercenary type, but I really have enjoyed working with your organisation, Ms. Dragon. The pay is good, but the fringe benefits..." He took in Thunder's helpless, tortured body. "...they're something else."

"You have no idea." The golden eyes glittered.

"You're a little too rough for me, kid. Besides, I never mix business with pleasure. Apart from chess, of course. Fancy a game?"

"Why not?" she grinned. "I'll carve out a board on his chest and make the pieces from his finger-bones." She leant close, tasting the sweat on Doc Thunder's neck. "I will teach you to adore me, pretty-pretty-pretty. If it kills you, you will tell me how much you want to please me with your final breath."

"And if it doesn't... well, part of my fee is that I get to finish off whatever's left when she's bored of you. Not as direct as I'd like, but that's life in the rat race." He laughed. "And speaking of rats..."

Lomax walked to a speaking tube in the wall, flipping open the cover to yell into it. "Venger! Get up here! It's time to meet that business partner I talked about!" He turned back to Doc, smiling ruefully. "He'd never have agreed if he'd known I was in cahoots with N.I.G.H.T.M.A.R.E. He's still a little mad at them about his unfortunate condition. But we need him for the next phase." He checked his watch. "You see, right now, Jack Scorpio has a condition-red emergency to deal with in Venice, and he's under the mistaken impression that his old pal Doc Thunder is protecting the President. He's not aware that you're here, indulging your little predilection for the wronger side of the tracks." He chuckled, finishing the martini. "Nice work if you can get it. Meanwhile, thanks to a slight communications foul-up I may have arranged, our mutual acquaintance President Garner is expecting Jack Scorpio to bodyguard him during this time of international crisis... enter Anton."

Doc Thunder shook his head. "You seem like a third wheel on this one, Lars. This is the kind of thing Venger could have cooked up all by himself."

Lomax almost choked. "Anton Venger? The man's a pawn! God, you don't believe all this 'team' nonsense, do you? I just say that to make the ugly little weirdo feel better. Without my genius, he'd be one more freak at the circus–"

"What?"

The door to the room was open, and there Venger stood, his blank, sagging, blue-white face betraying no emotion, his voice a hoarse, rasping monotone. But in his eyes, there blazed a terrible, baleful hate.

Lomax smiled, throwing his arms wide. "Anton, Anton, Anton... "

"What is *she* doing here?" He turned, looking Lomax right in the eye. "She's the one who did this to me! You allied us with *her?*"

"Anton, baby–" Lomax's voice adopted the smooth, slick tone of a Broadway producer. "You change your mind about who did 'that' to you every day of the week. Eventually you're going to have to admit you just did it to yourself." He turned to the Silken Dragon, smiling reassuringly. "Tough love. Works wonders."

"No!" Venger backed away, the cry sounding all the more terrible for coming in his emotionless monotone, from a face that never seemed to change expression. "We're meant to be equals! Partners! A *team!* I – I thought we were – you *can't*–" His flesh seemed to bubble slightly, the only sign of his emotion. "You can't *do this!*"

"I already did it. Come on, Anton, old buddy. You've got to admit she brightens up the office a little."

"We're meant to be a *team!* The Lomax-Venger Team! *You betrayed me!*" His face was bubbling now, starting to melt and flow like hot wax. The sight was so unnerving that Doc Thunder found himself totally captivated by it – the sheer horror of seeing a man's tortured, disfigured soul displayed for all to see on his suppurating flesh.

"Well, if it was the Venger-Lomax Team I might have consulted you, but probably not." He turned to Thunder and mouthed the words *prima donna.* "Look, are you going to impersonate Jack Scorpio or not?"

"Never! Never for her!" Even his scream was a monotone.

"Well, we can't do it without you, pal. Why, I'd have to make an incredibly convincing mask using skin cultures I'd grown from samples of your hideous fizzog that I'd secretly taken while you slept!" He paused. "Oh wait, I did! Looks like you're expendable, old pal. Ciao for now."

He took the cigar out of his mouth and squeezed it lightly, sending a dart bursting out of the lit end and into Venger's neck. The man with the Face Of Fear gasped, eyes wide, took a couple of steps forward and then collapsed.

"How about that?" Lomax grinned. "I guess these really are bad for your health. Plan B, Thunder. Never leave home without it."

"You're a monster, Lomax." Thunder growled, the chains clinking as he strained on them again. "That man needed psychological help."

"Yeah, yeah. Wait until you see Plan C. It'll knock you sideways." Lomax surreptitiously watched Silken Dragon's legs as her high heels clicked across the wooden floor and she bent at the waist to take Venger's pulse.

"Quite dead. Do you have any more of those cigars, Lars?"

"I've got more insurance, if that's what you're saying, so no funny business. If you want a box of your own – I'll trade it for the recipe for that inexorium you were talking about."

Silken Dragon smirked. "Not at that price. Perhaps in lieu of your fee for the President's assassination."

"It's a thought." Lomax motioned towards the body. "Bring that thing to my lab. I'll harvest the face and throw the rest away."

"Proud of yourself, Lars?" Doc Thunder's voice was acid.

"As a matter of fact, I am. I'll leave you to the tender mercies of my lovely employer, shall I?"

"Mmmmm..." Silken Dragon purred, licking her full lips. "Such a shame I have none, pretty-pretty-pretty. I will take you to the depths of Hell, and there you will learn that I own you. And when I am bored of my plaything, I will ask my wonderful new friend Lars to slit your throat, so that I may bathe my perfect body in your blood. And you... as the life drains from you into my ornate bathtub... you will thank me."

"Sounds like a charming evening. But I have plans. Raincheck?" Doc Thunder flexed again, the veins on his muscles standing out as he gritted his teeth, putting all his strength into pulling on the massive chains. The beautiful, merciless woman in front of him only laughed.

"Oh, my wonderful toy, you will never break free. Those chains could hold an elephant. My foolish pretty-pretty-pretty."

Doc grinned, and the grin was savage.

"Who said anything about the chains?"

A piece of plaster fell from the ceiling.

"THEY HADN'T REINFORCED the room. The ends of the chains on my wrists were bolted to the ceiling, but the ceiling itself was the weak point. So, suddenly, I had two big chunks of plaster and concrete on the ends of free-swinging chains. Two giant maces..."

Maya laughed. "I remember you telling me about that part. Lomax ended up with a skull fracture. Six months in the prison hospital."

Doc nodded, and sighed. "They both escaped, of course, but I really thought Venger was dead. I checked the body myself. No pulse. And five years after that, Lomax died, and Miles Hamilton changed so completely that our friendship couldn't survive. He became left-handed, emotionless..." He slammed a fist into his palm. "It's so obvious now... why didn't I see it?"

"Because people don't come back from the dead." Maya said, and Doc laughed, mirthlessly.

"Donner did. And Venger makes two. That's two in two days, and that worries me. Because Silken Dragon's supposed to be dead, too..."

He shook his head, looking off into the distance.

"And, unlike Lars Lomax, we never found the body."

CHAPTER NINE

The Case of The Red Mask

MARLENE LANG LAY on the couch in her apartment, sipping a Brandy Alexander in her nightgown and waiting for the phone to ring.

She had no doubt it would. Rarely did an evening go by without a gentleman caller, and she'd built up quite a stable of admirers.

It might be David, begging her to come around for another shoot, proclaiming in his broken tones that she was the only model who could possibly do, telling her that he understood that he'd been in the wrong. In which case she would smile sweetly, tell him that she was dreadfully busy this evening, and then go and take a long, luxurious bath. David had to learn not to sulk.

It might be Jack – lovely Jack, her one-eyed sailor, her grizzled soldier, back from Uzbekistan or Antarctica or London, catching a night between one delightfully top secret mission and another to ravish her expertly on the balcony, treat her to oysters and champagne in bed and then fly off on a cavorite wing-pack like something out of a radio serial. Jack called rarely, but his brief visits always left her drifting in a pink haze for weeks.

It might be Easton, cool, calm and collected Easton, asking her out to a sushi bar in Japantown to drink cheap sake and help him forget some tragedy. She loved the way he looked at her; that mixture of need, sorrow and contempt, like she was an addiction he couldn't shake, a poison he didn't want a cure for. It was all so wonderfully *noir*.

It might be Timothy – gentle Timothy, living in his moldy, fetid bedsit in the Village, occasionally slipping out to O'Malley's bar, terrified of the police. Sleeping with him was like charity, like slumming with an underclass of one, and yet there was something in him, a fire that sparked and possessed him; all the fire and spine and strength that David lacked. Dear Timothy Larson, her most secret lover.

It might be Parker, of course. Parker wasn't quite as exciting as Jack or Easton or even David – who had the most wonderfully wicked imagination if not the spine to match – but he had a cruel streak and hidden depths underneath the frosty surface. She enjoyed their verbal jousting, the sexual tension, and most of all his air of cold amusement, as if there was something he knew that she didn't, a secret all his own beyond the ones they shared. Also, she had to admit – and the thought made her instinctively flex her bottom – it had been rather an awfully long time since she had been properly spanked.

New York had the most interesting men of any city in the world, and she was building up rather a varied set.

And of course, there was the other one.

The most interesting of them all.

As if in answer to her thoughts, the phone rang. She smiled as she picked up the earpiece, a thrilling premonition dancing its way down her spine.

She was not disappointed.

"Ms. Lang... you're needed." A click, and the line went dead. Tonight, it seemed, the Blood-Spider was in no mood to mince words.

Enjoying the secret shiver of anticipation building inside her, Marlene stood, unhooked the nightgown and let it puddle around her feet, and then went to the wardrobe where the sleek black uniform waited for her.

* * *

LESS THAN FORTY minutes later, her body caressed and hugged by the tight leather of her chauffeur's costume, her long legs flexing as she pressed her foot down on the accelerator, she guided the Silver Ghost through the twisting traffic of New York City.

The Blood-Spider was quiet in the passenger seat – more so than usual. His expressionless lenses stared straight ahead, and aside from a curt mention of their destination there had not even been the slightest word to her as she powered through the streets in the purring machine, startling horses and rickshaw drivers and astonishing passers-by.

"What's the matter?" she heard herself say.

A pause. So long that she assumed he was simply ignoring her. Finally, he spoke.

"We have... urgent business. Business that cannot be ignored."

"What kind of business?" she asked, before she could stop herself. She was on dangerous ground here, she knew. He was obviously in no mood to talk. And yet, something in her could not help but poke and pick at his looming, oppressive silence.

Again, a long pause. Then he turned his head, staring at her with those unreadable, blank lenses.

"Perhaps... the end of the Blood-Spider."

THE ROOF OF the hospital was flat and barren, in large part taken up by a large metallic structure, a lattice of steel and copper that looked like an Eiffel Tower in miniature. It was designed to absorb lightning strikes and bring them harmlessly to earth, so neighbouring structures were not damaged. Occasionally, the staff of the hospital would come up here to smoke. The hospital was a good ten stories high, and the view, while not spectacular, was certainly worth the trip from the lower floors. On a night like tonight, however – with the setting sun shrouded in dark cloud and a fierce rain already descending – there was nobody who would bother making the long trek up the maintenance stairs.

Almost nobody.

The maintenance exit leading onto the roof opened with a creak, and the man who for the past two-and-a-bit years had answered to the name Doctor Miles Hamilton shuffled out. He leant on his cane, turning his head and checking the roof was quite empty. Then he stood straight, taking the weight fully on his legs, the years seeming to fall from him in an instant. The rain was falling heavily now, but he didn't seem to notice.

Events were moving towards the endgame. Parker Crane would be on his way, and everything he'd worked for the past three years would be set into motion. Had he been capable of it, he would have smiled. Instead, his face shifted and bubbled as the rain fell from above, lashing at his skin, washing away the expertly-applied makeup that so perfectly duplicated the skin tone of Doctor Hamilton and leaving in its place a sickening bluish whiteness, like the flesh of some corpse-fish from the ocean's deepest trench. The dye washed from his hair in a grey river, leaving it pure white, and his emotionless mask began to slacken, the features sliding and slackening, until the face staring out over the city resembled nothing more than a wax sculpture that had been left close to a furnace. A sickening parody of a face, made all the more horrible by the utter absence of any recognisable expression.

As the man without a face gazed over the city, he emitted a series of short, wheezing exhalations, akin to a man doing violent exercises – stomach crunches, perhaps. "Hhh! Hnnhh! Hhh!" Short little gasps, barely audible against the drumming of the rain on the roof.

Anton Venger was attempting to laugh.

He heard the creak of the maintenance door, and turned, speaking in the rasping monotone that was his natural voice once all pretence had been stripped away. "Mister Crane. I'm sorry to have contacted you at such short notice–"

He froze.

The man who'd just entered through the maintenance door laughed, his eyes dancing behind his blood-red mask, and Venger felt an icy chill in the marrow of his bones.

"No problem, amigo. Only too happy to be here." El Sombra said.

He smiled.

Venger gripped the handle of his cane tightly, pressing a concealed button with his thumb. A three-inch blade popped from the very tip of it, glistening slickly with some foul unguent. "A deadly poison, extracted from the Amazonian tree frog. One cut and you'll die slowly and in the most hideous agony the mind could possibly conceive."

El Sombra drew his sword from his belt. "I don't know any tree frogs, amigo, but one cut from this and you'll die fast, I guarantee. Mostly because I'm going to cut off that ugly head of yours and sculpt it into a gargoyle. Or maybe a vase for flowers."

Venger's top lip twitched, and a pulsation ran across his quivering, pallid flesh. On another man, it would have been a smirk. "You can try..."

There was a low rumble of thunder.

"WE'RE HERE."

Marlene frowned, applying the brakes and bringing the Silver Ghost to a halt. The Blood-Spider opened the door and stepped out, walking purposefully into an alleyway near the hospital.

"You can't just leave it at that! The end of the Blood-Spider?" She could not keep the anxiety out of her voice. She realised that she had childishly assumed that this would be forever, or at least until she got bored of it and moved on to something else. To have the end of all of it dangled so casually in her face like this was more than she could stand.

The Spider turned, his mask betraying not the slightest hint of emotion. Again, the lenses gazed into her, seemingly reading her slightest thought. *"Go home, Ms. Lang."*

Marlene pouted. "Damn you! You can't just dismiss me like–"

"For your own protection. Take the car, go home, and pack a suitcase with essentials."

She fell silent. Suddenly, she realised how seriously she should have been taking this. "What happened?" Her voice sounded small and frightened.

"Up on that roof, there is a man who knows my secrets. Perhaps all of them. Perhaps all of yours. If I do not contact you

by midnight... leave this city. Find somewhere to hide, and pray you can hide well. I will contact you in good time." The hiss of his voice sounded almost compassionate.

Marlene swallowed, her heart beating in her ears. "What... what if you don't?"

"Then the Blood-Spider is dead."

He turned and walked into the darkness of the alley, and was gone.

ON THE ROOF, El Sombra's sword clashed against Venger's cane as lightning arced across the sky.

Anton Venger had been an accomplished swordsman before his disfigurement, and the poison cane had been a favourite trick of his during his days as N.I.G.H.T.M.A.R.E.'s top undercover agent. He'd lost none of his skills in the intervening years. If anything, the madness that had infected his brain after the loss of his good looks had only added an extra dimension to his prowess. The tiny blade at the end of the cane flashed and darted, each time coming less than an inch from piercing the flesh of his half-naked opponent with a deadly sting.

But if any man knew about the subtle art of madness used as a weapon, it was El Sombra.

Once upon a time, he had been Djego the poet, a shiftless layabout hiding behind a tissue-thin veneer of pretension. Then the bastards – the Nazis – had come to his little town, razing it to the ground and rebuilding it as a clockwork nightmare, a grotesque experiment designed to create a strain of human robots. Djego's mind had fractured under the stress of losing everyone he had ever loved, as well as the influence of a strain of unknown psychedelic he had encountered in the desert after fleeing the scene of the massacre. Out of that madness had emerged his second personality – the Saint Of Ghosts, El Sombra, the shadow-self that existed to perform a single task: to take revenge on all who had wronged him.

Mostly, that revenge consisted of a quest to murder as many Nazis as humanly possible on a bloody trail that would lead to the king of them all – the insane brain of Adolf Hitler, now housed inside a gigantic steam-powered robot deep within a secret chamber at the very heart of Berlin.

He'd heard, on his travels, about North America's infestation by Untergang; the destabilisation agency put in place by Hitler himself, experimenting in 'asymmetrical warfare', after his doomed Russian campaign. Nobody could prove that the terrorist organisation was run via orders from the Fatherland, and Germany denied everything, of course. El Sombra had decided it was worth looking into.

He'd found out a number of things already. Interrogating – some would say torturing – his way up the ladder of command had led him to Heinrich Donner, the organisation's disgraced ex-chief. But the real find had been the secret journal in Donner's bedroom.

The one that explained everything.

Well, not quite everything – who explains *everything* to themselves in their diary? – but enough. More than enough.

It had led him to the Jameson Club, and while investigating to see just how that fitted into the puzzle, he'd overheard Parker Crane and his telegram. And that had brought him here, to clash a razor-sharp sword against a deadly poison cane, battling for his life against a man with a molten face and crazed, wild eyes, dangerously close to a huge lightning rod in the midst of a raging storm.

Sometimes, life was good.

"So what brings you here, amigo?" Again, the sword and the cane clashed together, the sword-hilt locking with the cane's head as El Sombra leaned close for a moment before pirouetting back and slashing in a wide arc, only to have the blow parried expertly by the other man. Neither of them seemed to blink.

"The reason why?" Venger laughed again – that peculiar expulsion of air in short, guttural bursts – and then lunged, the point of his blade barely missing El Sombra's abdominals. Then his eyes, the only part of him capable of expression, grew hard and cold, like two small stones in a sea of shapeless clay. "My ugly. My disease. My love... and all my lover's revenge."

"You and me could write a bad romance, my friend." El Sombra murmured, blade flashing, clashing, deflecting the poison point as it sought out the weakness in his defence, the eye of the needle that would send the Saint Of Ghosts prematurely to the kingdom of heaven. As the dance of sword and cane went on, the two men circled, feet shifting warily. El Sombra did not realise his back was to the huge lightning conductor until it was too late.

"I don't want to be *friends!*" Venger lunged forward suddenly, the deadly point of the blade aimed right for El Sombra's heart, putting him on the defensive and forcing him to take a step back. But he had nowhere to go. His only option was to clamber backwards up onto the metal structure.

Now, he mused, he had the advantage of height. The advantage of height, and also the advantage of being fried like a strip of bacon at any moment.

The thunder roared in his ears.

Doc Thunder and Maya burst through the front doors of the hospital, looking at the bustling activity. It was the second night in a row he'd entered like this, and the staff instinctively looked to see if he was holding any dying people in his arms. When they saw his hands were empty, they breathed sighs of relief.

"Can I help you, Sir?" the receptionist said, doing her best to smile.

"Maya, go and check on Monk." murmured Doc, before turning his attention to the woman sitting in front of him. "Hamilton. Doctor Miles Hamilton. I need to see him urgently." He thought for a moment. He couldn't let Venger suspect, and he needed an excuse that would bring him running... "I want to donate more blood."

The receptionist smiled. "All right, sir. He's on a break at the moment. I think he's gone up to the roof." Doc turned, walking towards the exit. "Sir, I can send an orderly to fetch him."

"It's all right, I'll go see him myself." Doc smiled, tightly.

"But the stairs to the roof are that way."

"Oh, I'm not taking the stairs." Doc smiled again, stepping out into the street. "I'm going to take the quick way."

Then he jumped.

*　　*　　*

THE BLOOD-SPIDER climbed slowly up the side of the rain-slicked wall, looking like nothing so much as a human spider slowly closing in on the fly at the centre of the web. Despite the rain, the suction cups held fast, as he knew they would. He'd done this before, many times, and it was the last thing Doctor Hamilton would expect.

His plan could be summed up in one word – fear.

The Doctor would be waiting on the roof, watching the maintenance door. When the Blood-Spider appeared behind him, seemingly from nowhere, he'd be much more inclined to talk about exactly how he'd discovered the Spider's true identity, and what that strange 'other interest' comment in the telegram meant. Blackmail, perhaps? Was the good Doctor intending to sell the Blood-Spider's darkest secrets to the highest bidder?

If so, he would learn to his cost that there was far more to the Spider than he could possibly suspect... before he died screaming for mercy.

The eyes behind the implacable lenses narrowed as the Blood-Spider climbed higher. There could be no mercy offered in this matter. To have his secrets revealed would jeopardise the cause – his holy quest to cleanse New York of the inhumans. The criminals. His trigger fingers burned again, the itch nagging at him under his gloves. It had been a very long time since he'd shot anyone.

He was close to the rooftop now, and suddenly, between the cracks of thunder filling the raging sky, he could hear the clang of steel on steel. The clash of swords.

Carefully, he peered over the edge of the rooftop.

There were two men on the roof, one with a sword, the other with some sort of trick cane. The one with a cane had a face bleached blue-white, sagging like unfired clay, a grotesque monster by any reckoning. And yet it was the other who caught the Spider's eye; the man with the sword. A half-naked Mexican man, dressed only in black tuxedo pants, with a red sash tied around his face, forming a mask over his eyes.

The sword killer. The vigilante who'd been such a thorn in Untergang's side. Was this the murderer of Heinrich Donner?

What was he doing here? How was he involved?

The Blood-Spider watched, fascinated, as the swordsman leapt off the metal structure, somersaulting over his enemy just as a bolt of lightning crashed into the metal attractor, missing him by inches and lighting up the whole rooftop in brilliant white electric light. In the light, the Spider realised that the man with the half-melted face was wearing Doctor Hamilton's uniform. Had he stolen it? No, that *was* the Doctor, or the Doctor was that, had been that thing, all along. How and why?

There would be time to answer such questions later. For now, all the Blood-Spider saw was the killer he had been hunting and the man who had attempted to blackmail him in a life-and-death struggle, with a crackling lightning conductor on one side and a ten-story drop on the other.

Supporting himself with the suction cups on his toes, he drew one of his automatic pistols, removing a silencer from his belt with the other hand. Then he began screwing it in place.

It was only a question of who to kill first.

EL SOMBRA TURNED, deflecting the deadly cane as it sailed within a millimetre of his throat. He'd managed to score a couple of hits on his enemy – he'd slashed Venger's long white hospital coat open, and even drawn blood with a light scratch on his arm – but he was nowhere close to ending this fight. Venger was simply too skilful. And, unlike El Sombra's non-poisoned sword, his cane only needed to strike once. The smallest scratch would kill him. He couldn't afford to be distracted for a single second.

So it was unfortunate that Doc Thunder chose that exact moment to land on the hospital's roof.

His immense body landed with a crash that shook the whole roof, distracting El Sombra for a single, vital second – enough time for Venger to lunge forward, the point of the cane-dagger slashing across the masked man's cheek. Instantly, El Sombra felt a wave of weakness as the poison rushed into his bloodstream. He staggered.

"You're too late, Thunder," Venger spat in his cold, cruel monotone. "I don't know how you found out about this little meeting, but you're too late to save your friend. My poison is even now working through his bloodstream. Within moments, he'll die. Die in unendurable pain."

El Sombra fell to his knees, the pain already beginning. But there was no sympathy in the Doc's eyes. That piercing blue was as cold as steel.

"He's no friend of mine, Venger. This is the man who left someone very important to me downstairs in that hospital with four bullets in him."

El Sombra opened his mouth, trying to speak, trying to shake his head. *Bullets?*

Doc Thunder scowled. "I honestly don't care if this piece of trash lives or dies."

CHAPTER TEN

Doc Thunder and The Saint of Ghosts

"THIS IS THE man who left someone very important to me downstairs in that hospital with four bullets in him. I honestly don't care if this piece of trash lives or dies."

Yes, it was him, all right. Red mask, crazy eyes. This was the man who'd done his damnedest to murder his best friend. No doubt about it, this was who Monk had been talking about. And yet...

"How is Monk, but the way, Venger? You being his doctor and all. I'd think very carefully about how you answer that question, if I were you."

Venger chuckled, another expulsion of short barks, unrecognisable as laughter to the untrained ear. "Oh, of course. Your monkey-boy bum-chum. He's stable, don't you worry. Off the critical list. I do know rather a lot about medicine, you know. Probably even more than your other friend, Doctor Hamilton." Suddenly, his teeth gritted, and his eyes assumed once more that intense, hateful gaze. "I'm not a complete monster. I've got nothing against the ape-man. It wasn't *him* who gave me this face, was it? It was you. You and that pathetic masochist in the blue suit."

Doc nodded, taking a step forward. "Danny Coltrane, the Blue Ghost. Was it you who made him disappear? The way you disappeared Hamilton so you could take his place?"

Venger's mouth fell open, flopping like the mouth of a fish. On a normal man, it would have been a delighted grin. "You don't know *anything,* do you? You don't have the slightest clue–"

He was interrupted by El Sombra, whose gut spasmed at that moment, sending a tidal wave of vomit out of his belly and onto the wet roof. His skin was a jaundiced yellow now, his eyes unfocussed, and great drops of cold sweat were rolling down his skin, indistinguishable from the raindrops. The poison was doing its work. He was in the final stages now.

Venger laughed. "Are you sure you don't want to do anything for him? I know you say he tried to execute one corner of your little love triangle, but look at him! I got that poison from a tree frog, you know. It works directly on the brain's pain receptors. It must feel as though he's boiling alive. I wonder why he doesn't scream?"

Doc Thunder didn't speak. He was staring contemplatively at the writhing masked man, pulling a strange face, almost wincing. Venger cocked his head. "No compassion for such a terrible fate? I thought you were supposed to be the hero of decency and fairness? The great progressive setting an example for all us common-or-garden proles? You're almost acting like the Blood-Spider!" He laughed again, another little machine-gun burst of gasps from his sagging lips, then shouted. "I wish he were here to see it!"

On his perch, the Blood-Spider frowned. It was almost as if Venger wanted to be rescued.

He was out of luck. The only reason he hadn't been shot yet was because of Thunder's timely arrival. The Blood-Spider hadn't expected him.

The silencer on the barrel might mask the shot from human ears, but from Thunder's? Could he risk it? He didn't want a battle with the man.

Not just yet...

"YOU'RE RIGHT, OF course," murmured Doc Thunder. "I have to do something for him."

With that, he grabbed El Sombra by the throat, lifting him up to stare into his eyes. After a moment, he spat into the dying man's face.

Then he let him drop.

"Satisfied?"

Venger lifted a finger to his face, physically raising one of his eyebrows and then the other, pantomiming a look of surprise. "Note my expression." Another staccato rattle of gasps, as his flesh bubbled and relaxed, returning to its standard emotionless cast. "You've gone rather... *badass* all of a sudden, haven't you, old man? Am I supposed to be impressed?"

"My turn to ask the questions." Doc Thunder's voice was low, menacing. He took another step towards Venger. "You'll find that little pigsticker of yours has a hard time penetrating my skin. And whatever you've smeared on it won't even give me a rash. Unless you've gotten a sudden urge to take a swan dive from this rooftop, I suggest you start telling me exactly what I want to know. Question one – what *did* you do to Miles Hamilton?"

"You'll never guess." His eyes were mocking, dancing with glee. "Or maybe you will. A fifty-fifty chance."

Doc Thunder raised an eyebrow. *Fifty fifty? What does that mean?* "Tell me."

Another rattle of gasps. Even if you knew it was laughter, it would still seem incongruous coming from the slack, half-melted features. "I did to him what you did to me. Or rather, I did worse. A version of the same compound that caused my face to become this... travesty. Except somewhat more potent, of course. I injected him with it... and then I watched him melt. The terrified look on his face as it slowly lost cohesion, the awful scream as his jaw slid off and burst like a water balloon as it hit the ground, his eyes trickling down his face like a pair of maraschino cherries sliding off a melting ice cream sundae..." He sniggered, or made a sound that could have been a snigger. "Yum yum. Deee-licious."

Thunder's eyes narrowed.

Venger reached up and formed his mouth into a pantomime frown. "Oh dear, have I upset you? How sad. You should learn not to ask questions you don't want the answers to. If it's any consolation, I had nothing against him, any more that I have anything against the big ape downstairs. But unlike your friend the Gorilla Reporter... he was in the way."

Carefully, he began to move sideways, away from Doc, keeping his cane-dagger pointed at the lightning bolt in the centre of Doc's chest as his feet padded softly on the rain-slick rooftop.

Doc followed. "You were wrong earlier, Venger. You are a monster. I'm not going to rest until you've been locked away for the rest of your unnatural life. Now put that contraption down before I twist it around your scrawny neck."

All of his attention was on Venger. Venger had made sure of that himself, made sure Thunder wasn't paying attention to his surroundings. If he had been, he might have noticed that Venger's movements had put Doc between him and the lightning conductor.

The storm was directly over their heads. Just a matter of time...

Venger pressed the stud on the head of his cane once again. The tip of the dagger flew out of the end like a dart, gleaming with the deadly poison it had been coated with, before it bounced harmlessly back, clattering on the rooftop, the point broken.

"You don't listen, Venger. I told you that wasn't going to work on me." Doc frowned. "You were masquerading as my personal physician for years. You know I'm bulletproof, never mind dagger-proof. And even if you could afford an inexorium blade, my blood would just negate any poison you can think of. So tell me –" His voice was thick with contempt. "– what was the point of that?"

Venger chuckled. "I have to eject the dagger before I can trigger this." He pushed the stud again – and a compressed steel net shot out of the cane's tip, expanding as it left, wrapping around Doc

Thunder's body, tangling him up. Venger ran forward, kicking hard at his chest while he was off-balance and struggling with the net, and sending him staggering backwards to slam against the conductor –

– and then a bolt of lightning sizzled down from directly overhead.

Doc Thunder screamed, the lightning crackling off his wet skin as it shot through his body. It felt almost like the Omega Machine, but a thousand times more intense, wilder, more agonising. He'd never felt quite this much pain. Although the lightning strike itself only lasted a second, it felt as though the fire was still crackling through his every nerve ending even after he crashed forward onto the rooftop.

He tried to strain, to break out of the steel netting, but there was no way. He couldn't even move. Dimly, he saw Anton Venger standing over him.

"Good timing, eh? I've always been lucky that way."

Thunder tried to speak. A small trickle of blood slid out of the corner of his mouth. Venger blinked. If he could have appeared shocked, he would have.

"Goodness me. That did hit you hard, didn't it? It actually made you bleed."

Thunder twitched, shaking his head. "Nuh. No." He sucked in a deep breath. "Did this to myself earlier. Bit... bit my cheek. Got the blood flowing."

He smiled.

Venger paused for a moment, thinking about that. When would he have...

Then realisation dawned.

"...oh my God."

El Sombra appeared behind him, suddenly, grabbing hold of Venger's face hard enough to leave handprints in the clay-like flesh. Then he twisted.

Venger howled, and the sound was horrific, never changing in pitch, a flat, unreal burst of noise. A scream without emotion. El Sombra twisted again, and something popped in Anton Venger's neck. His body went limp.

El Sombra began to drag the body to the edge of the roof.

"Wait..." Doc Thunder said, before lapsing into a coughing fit. El Sombra smiled, hauled it over the side, and dropped it off. Doc Thunder shook his head, feeling impotent. "That... that was murder..."

"Whoops." the masked man smiled, holding up his limp wrist and slapping it with the other hand. "Bad vigilante! Very naughty. Although – and I don't know about you, amigo, you might not agree – I thought that story about how he dissolved a guy was a little bit worse." He lifted his sword, aiming the point towards Thunder's eye. "Thanks for spitting in my face, by the way, amigo. That really made me feel like saving your life. In fact, why don't you give me one really solid reason why I shouldn't poke this through your eye and into your brain?"

"Because spitting on you is what *saved* your life." Doc swallowed, then began straining against the steel net, struggling inside it in an attempt to work his arms together in front of him. From there, he could start trying to tear his way out of it when his full strength returned. "My blood has certain... healing properties. It's what makes me what I am. Even if you're not a blood match, spitting it into your wound should have been enough to negate the poison."

El Sombra frowned, touching his fingertips against the fresh wound. It was true. As soon as Thunder had spat on him, the fever had dissipated. "So you're Spit Jesus. Congratulations. What do you want, a medal?"

"I expect an honest answer to an honest question, that's all. Although if you think you can kill me, you're welcome to give it a try. I can just as easily get answers from you in Rackham Prison hospital." He smiled, winding his fingers around the steel mesh and then pulling. One by one, the links in the netting began to break.

"What the hell, amigo, I'm in a conversational mood. Just lay off the net for a moment, eh?" El Sombra laid the tip of his sword just below Thunder's eye. Thunder didn't blink. "Ask your question."

"Did you shoot a man last night in the penthouse suite of Atlas apartments?"

El Sombra blinked, eyes widening. "Huh. Right place, amigo, wrong crime. I don't use guns. No idea how they work. The only thing I need is this." He pressed the tip of the sword against Thunder's cheek. The skin didn't break. Neither did Doc's gaze.

"So you had nothing to do with the shooting of my assistant? No, of course not." His eyes flicked to the left, considering. "You'd have shot Venger long before he could have stuck you with that cane. You'd probably have shot me – people do. You're not lying when you say you don't use guns." He looked back at El Sombra, evaluating. "But you did kill Heinrich Donner."

El Sombra smiled, grimly. "That's right. I got a hot tip and some incontrovertible evidence leading right to his evil terrorist wrinkly bastard ass, and then I broke into his fancy penthouse and I stabbed him in the back. Thrust the point of my sword right through his stinking, evil heart. Should I apologise?"

Doc Thunder paused. "Why?" He said it softly, quietly. El Sombra's smile widened.

"Why didn't you?"

THE BLOOD-SPIDER listened closely from his perch on the edge of the rooftop. His gun was still trained on El Sombra's head. He was trying to work out whether or not to fire.

On the one hand, he'd heard all he needed to – a full confession. On the other hand, Doc Thunder was there.

He wondered if it wouldn't be better to shoot now, while Thunder was trapped in that steel net. Shoot him and run. Right now.

His trigger finger began to itch.

"I WANTED TO bring Donner to trial. I wanted the world to see–"

El Sombra laughed. "Why? You knew he was guilty, amigo. You knew just what he was guilty *of*. Why not just do it? I'd have done it, a dozen times. Or were you holding back because you didn't want people to know about *your* little secret?"

Doc Thunder froze, looking warily at the masked man. "What do you mean?" It was a question he already knew the answer to.

El Sombra leaned close, looking the other man right in the eye. "I know who you are, amigo. I know *what* you are. I read Donner's–"

Doc's eyes narrowed. Enough.

The Blood Spider's eyes narrowed. Enough stalling.

Kill him.

Now.

As the Spider's finger tightened on the trigger, Doc Thunder moved. The masked man had made the mistake of taking the point of the sword away from his eyeball for half a second, and then he'd leaned in close to give Doc an extra-intimidating stare. Presumably he'd learned that one in some chapbook about scary banter.

Bad move.

Doc snapped his head forward suddenly, viciously delivering a brutal head butt to El Sombra's nose, smashing it and sending him flying back in an arc, trailing blood from the crushed cartilage.

Thunder didn't feel the bullet that passed within a few inches of his face, through the air where El Sombra's head had been, or hear the silenced gunshot. So he never knew that he'd saved the masked man's life. Neither did El Sombra.

It probably wouldn't have changed much if they had.

"That's what they call a Bronx kiss, masked man." Doc growled, tugging at the netting hard, ripping it away from him so he could stand up. "Welcome to New York City. We've got a nice hotel waiting for you; it's called Rackham Penitentiary. You'll like it there. Bare nipples are in vogue." He smiled, grimly. "Get up. And don't think about using that sword. It's going to take more than that to cut my skin."

El Sombra rose, shaking his head groggily. For a moment, he gripped his sword tightly, then he lifted it up above his head, opening his hands and shaking his head slowly. "Fine, amigo. You've got me. Put the cuffs on."

Doc took a few steps closer, reaching out for El Sombra's wrists. "I don't actually carry –"

El Sombra moved quickly, bringing the sword around in a circle, swinging it as hard as he could, aiming the edge of the blade between Doc's legs. As it slammed home, Doc gave a strangled scream, dropping to his knees immediately. El Sombra grinned.

"Maybe you do have an indestructible nutsack, amigo, but I think that's going to leave a dent, right? Want me to do the other ball? Or maybe I should put this in your brain and put you right out of your misery once and for all, eh? It wouldn't be like killing a real human, would it?" He snarled. "Come on, tell me why I shouldn't. All I'd be killing is a monster built by monsters –"

"Stop right there."

Maya stood in the doorway leading into the building, holding a pistol at her hip. Her eyes were hard as stone. A man in a red mask, standing over a man she loved. She raised the gun, aiming between El Sombra's eyes.

"*Dios mio!*" the masked man breathed. "Tell me, *chiquita*, has anybody ever written you a poem? I know somebody who writes great poems. He's really improved a lot. They rhyme now." Inspiration seemed to strike him. "Or I could rescue you from a giant robot! That often works."

"Shut up." Maya cocked her pistol. She was in no mood to mince words. "No, don't. You can tell me why I shouldn't kill *you*."

El Sombra smiled. "Because I've never slept with a woman." Doc Thunder blinked at him. "What? It's true."

Doc Thunder sighed. "It's not him, Maya. He didn't try to kill Monk. And he saved my life. And..." He swallowed. "We need to talk. About Donner. About what you read in that journal of his."

Maya scowled, lowering the gun and turning to Doc Thunder. "Something about a monster created by monsters. Want to explain that one, Doc?"

Doc winced, covering his eyes. "Not now, Maya. Right now we need to consult with... what's your name?" He looked up. "Hello?"

The rooftop was empty, but for the two of them.

*   *   *

THE BLOOD-SPIDER frowned, putting away his pistol. He'd almost fired, several times, but... it wasn't the time. He'd seen the masked man leap from the rooftop while Thunder and his princess were distracted. Doubtless he had a means prepared to break his fall and ensure a quick getaway. And the man was quick, the Spider had to give him that.

But not quick enough.

I have you, murderer, the Spider thought to himself, beginning his descent. *I will find you, devil, no matter where you choose to hide, to revel in the sins you've committed in the name of your own inhumanity. For where all inhuman devils revel in their sins...*

...the Blood-Spider spins!

"HOW DID HE do that? We only took our eyes off him for a second."

"You've got worse problems." Maya cut off Doc's train of thought, looking stern. "I checked in on Monk on the way up here."

Doc's blood ran cold. "No. Venger said he hadn't hurt him."

"He hadn't." Maya smiled, humourlessly. "His impression of Doctor Hamilton stretched to doing no harm. But he didn't help him, either. Monk got just enough of your blood to get him stable and put him on the mend. He's on a saline solution now. He's still sleeping, probably will be for some time."

Doc frowned. "So where..."

"I don't know. None of the doctors seemed to be able to tell me where the sample you gave ended up. We checked the hospital's cold room. Not a sign."

Doc felt that chill again, seizing his heart. "That's why Venger pretended to be Doctor Hamilton, so he could steal my blood. Why didn't I see it?" He shook his head. There was a lot he hadn't seen, thoughts that had been dancing in and out of his mind like puzzle pieces ever since the Omega Machine. He felt as if he was right on the edge of putting the whole jigsaw together. "You're right, Maya. I think we have got problems."

Maya looked away. "I didn't say 'we', Doc. I said 'you'." She looked back at him, a deep weariness in her eyes.

"I'm leaving you, Doc."

Doc Thunder looked at her – looked at her properly for the first time since she'd brought him that paper the morning before. Suddenly he couldn't think of anything else. "Maya –"

"I'm going back to Zor-Ek-Narr."

CHAPTER ELEVEN

The Case of The Secret Scientist

THE BLOOD-SPIDER'S feet touched down on the floor of the alley by the hospital, and he took a moment to look around and check for any clues. To actually catch the Sword Killer was perhaps too much to hope for, at least immediately, but there was the slim chance that he'd find a hint as to which direction he'd taken. The important thing was that he knew who had murdered Heinrich Donner - clearly an inhuman killer.

Inhumanity would not be tolerated. Could not be tolerated. Such was the mission of the Blood-Spider.

As the Spider looked around, his ears caught a sound from nearby; a soft, wheezing moan, like the air escaping from a tyre. He turned, drawing his silenced pistol in a flash of movement.

It was Anton Venger. He had landed in a dumpster.

Perhaps it was due to the pliable nature of his flesh, but the snapping of his neck had not killed him, although he seemed unable to move, and his head now lolled at a grotesque angle. Most of his bones seemed to be broken, and blood leaked from his nose. The Blood-Spider was disgusted, but not entirely surprised, to note that the blood of Anton Venger was not red, but a light, sickly blue. His eyes flickered towards him, imploring, and he attempted to move his lips to speak. Even in such pain and fear as he was in, his face retained only the emotions he gave it. As such, he looked sanguine and unconcerned about his own death.

"Crane?" he breathed, weakly. "Help... help me."

"Help you?" The Blood-Spider looked at him through the implacable lenses. His voice was a cold hiss, like escaping steam – in its own way, just as emotionless as Venger's. A passer-by would have been mystified by the apparent ennui with which they greeted the situation.

Or terrified, perhaps.

"Help you." the Spider repeated, as though contemplating the question. Venger's body twitched, shuddering like a cockroach pinned to a board. *"You sent Crane a telegram."*

"Yes. I sent you a telegram." His eyes widened as the Blood-Spider lifted his automatic, pointing the barrel of the gun squarely between his eyes.

"Crane."

"Wh... what...?" Venger was breathing heavily, a constant rasp from his damaged lungs. He was clearly terrified, and in great pain.

That was good.

"You sent Crane a telegram. Crane. If I were you, I wouldn't become confused on that point again."

Venger twitched again, trying to nod. "Fine! Fine! I sent Crane a telegram. I – I have something for you. For Crane. It's in my coat pocket. The vial's very thick, it won't have broken. It's, ah... for our mutual friend." He swallowed, and his lips twitched and bubbled, as if he was attempting a smile. "Our friend Fifty fifty. Heh."

"Fifty fifty. What does that mean?"

Venger blinked. "It's the code. Fifty fifty. You know." He swallowed. His face still did not change, but his eyes grew glassy, the pupils dilating with terror. "You don't know... oh God, he said you knew! He said you were working for him! You must be working for him! You *must* be! Fifty fifty! Fifty fifty! *Fifty fifty!* Crane, for the love of God, you *have* to know–"

The automatic spat a single, silent bullet, and a blue flower bloomed in the centre of Anton Venger's forehead as his brain matter, the colour of delicate Japanese pottery, exploded out into the garbage.

"I told you not to become confused."

He hadn't meant to pull the trigger – there was so much more to learn – but to have Venger screaming his name, his real name, where anyone walking by could have heard him... better he was silenced. The Blood-Spider had no doubt that whoever this mysterious 'Fifty fifty' was, he would be hearing from him soon enough.

And if his hunch was correct, so would Doc Thunder.

Working quickly, the Spider searched through Venger's pockets. Inside one of them there was a thick vial, still stoppered and sealed, undamaged by the fall from the roof.

It was full of blood.

The best part of a pint, unclotted, still cool from the cold room of the hospital. Wound around the neck, there was a slip of paper reading 50/50 – DOC THUNDER.

Doc Thunder's blood.

The Blood-Spider nodded once, grimly, and slid the vial into the inside pocket of his coat. Then he turned and walked deeper into the pooling shadows of the alley.

By the time the police found the body of Anton Venger, he was long gone.

MARLENE LANG PICKED up the phone on the first ring.

She'd only just managed to get in the door of her apartment, after securing the Silver Ghost in its usual hiding place in her private garage, behind a false wall in the side of the apartment building. The Blood-Spider owned the building under an alias – he was the only other person who knew it was there. Even Parker didn't know about it.

She reacted instinctively, but froze once she'd lifted the receiver out of the cradle. What if this wasn't him? What if it was whoever he'd gone to meet – whoever his 'business' had been with? What if he (she didn't consider that it might be a she) had killed the Spider and was now coming to do the same to her?

"H-hello?" Her voice trembled, uncertain.

"Ms. Lang."

She let out the breath she'd been holding. She hadn't expected a call the moment she'd come in. If he'd needed her that urgently, he would have asked her to keep the engine running, surely? For a quick getaway. But then, he'd wanted to protect her. She was surprised at how that thought made her feel.

"Do I still need to pack the suitcase?" Her voice shook, no matter how much she willed it to stop. His tone seemed almost amused, but still compassionate, inasmuch as it ever seemed to be anything at all. How much was there, and how much was she reading into it?

"You may still need it. But right now... you're needed. Meet me at pickup point C."

She nodded. That one was near the corner of first and thirty-fifth, not far from the hospital. He must have called from the kiosk there. "I'll come right away, Sir." she said, blushing at how the *sir* slipped out. He hung up, leaving her with the dial tone and her whirling thoughts.

As Marlene turned to leave, she caught a glimpse of herself in the full-length mirror that hung by the door. Usually, she thought of the outfit the Blood-Spider had chosen, for reasons of his own, to dress her in as being risqué – daring, even. But now she realised it actually looked rather smart. Professional.

All of a sudden, she mused, she had a new understanding of what she was doing. She had come face to face with just how serious this could all get, and rather than shrink from it, or ask to be relieved of her duty, her first instinct was to throw herself in even deeper. And suddenly, she realised, it *was* a duty. Not a lark for a bored rich girl with expensive and naughty tastes, but a solemn appointment.

She was the Blood-Spider's driver, and that meant something.

She smiled at herself, then stepped confidently out of the door. Time was of the essence, after all.

And the war on crime was not about to wait.

* * *

THE BLOOD-SPIDER said nothing as the two of them sped through the streets, heading for the location in the East Village he'd specified. She hadn't been there yet – he'd never mentioned the place. But she knew better than to ask questions now. Indeed, she was rather enjoying this new feeling of quiet, sober professionalism, even subservience – of being a cog in a well-oiled machine. What was it she'd said to Parker?

"The most fabulous thing to do now is to believe in something utterly and completely, without restraint."

How true. How very true.

She opened up the throttle, a smile crossing her lips as she weaved expertly between two horse-drawn carriages, the horses rearing as she left them in the rear view mirror, rounding the next corner in a screech of tyres. Eventually, the Blood-Spider nodded, and she braked smoothly to a halt and triggered the passenger door release, with all the quiet deference of a British automaton.

"Very good, Ms. Lang. Pick me up on this spot in twenty minutes."

He turned and vanished into an alley, and she gunned the engine and eased the Silver Ghost onto the night streets.

A compliment! Perhaps her first from him. It felt rather like coaxing a climax from another man.

"Yes, quite the most fabulous thing." She murmured to herself, and began to cruise slowly around the block, keeping one eye out for crime. Her mind drifted back to that long weekend in Geneva with Jack, when he'd taken her to the shooting range to impress her and she'd ended up impressing him with a perfect grouping. She had a lot of additional skills to bring to the war, she knew.

Perhaps if she was awfully good, the Blood-Spider would let her have a gun.

THE DOOR WAS nondescript – a flat rectangle of metal halfway down an alley between a chapbook store and a long-forgotten dance club. The wall nearby was marked by freshly-chalked graffiti: DON'T PUSH ME 'CAUSE I'M CLOSE TO THE EDGE. A breaker slogan. Indeed, The Blood-Spider could see one of the squares of cardboard they littered their chosen alleys with scattered on the ground. He was glad none of them were here now. Littering was a crime, after all. And it would be so terrible to have any unpleasantness.

His trigger fingers were itching again.

At the end of the alley, he could see a homeless man, covered up by a thick, filth-covered blanket, his head buried in his lap, a mass of greasy black hair hiding his features. The Spider wondered for a moment whether or not he should simply put a bullet in the man's head... but no. Best not to invite trouble.

It was missing the masked man on the hospital roof that had done it, put him in this mood. He'd been so close – so very close – to putting an end to Donner's murderer once and for all, and now the strange Mexican had slipped through his fingers. That was unacceptable. Not only was he Donner's killer, he had been spending the brief time since he entered the city on a rampage that had ended with the deaths of nearly a dozen men.

While the irony was not lost on the Blood-Spider, the simple truth was that there was no room for two vigilantes in a town as small as New York. Even Doc Thunder, the saviour of Manhattan, America's Greatest Hero – even he made the place feel... crowded.

But then, that was why he'd come to Professor Timothy Larson.

Looking around to make sure nobody was watching, he knocked on the door in the pre-arranged pattern. After a moment, it was answered by a rail-thin man with a mop of shaggy, dirty blonde hair and a ratty beard, who looked at him with red-rimmed eyes. This was Timothy Larson.

"Come in out of the rain, man. I was, uh, writing a lecture."

Larson was a strange one. He'd apparently been part of the original futurehead movement as a young twenty-something man when it had started off in the seventies as a group of merry pranksters, before it rejected itself, becoming obsessed with détournment and anarchy, mutating into its current form as a thing to be feared, a tapestry of taboos that were allegedly made safe but all too often held all their old power and more. 'No future' had once been a challenge to authority rather than an acknowledgement of the status quo.

Larson let the Blood-Spider into the small bedsit he'd installed him in – a gloomy little cave, lit by a single oil lamp, encrusted in dust and filth. There was a door in the back that led to a toilet that hadn't been cleaned in months, but the rest of the room was all one thing; kitchen, bedroom and bathroom in one –a criminally small tin bath leaning in the corner, a mattress on the floor, a small camping stove and a sink against one wall. The rest of the space was taken up with workbenches and tables covered with beakers, test tubes, Bunsen burners and the stains of a thousand spilled chemicals. The whole place stank, and the Spider found himself grateful for the mask he wore. Larson grabbed a sheaf of notes off one of the tables.

"Dig this, man – 'if the truth can be *told,* so as to be *understood,* it *will* be believed,'" Larson said, reading from a sheet of lined paper while the Blood-Spider entered and locked the steel door behind him. "'The emphasis – in breaker music and the street dance culture – on physiologically compatible rhythms is really the rediscovery of the art of natural magic with sound, that, uh, *sound,* properly understood, especially *percussive* sound, can actually change neurological *states–*'"

The Blood-Spider cut him off. *"Breaker music is a weakness rotting this city and it needs to be stamped out, Professor Larson. For your sake, don't let me find out that you've been taking part in the criminality going on outside."* He reached into his coat. *"It would not be... healthy for you."*

Larson pouted. "It's just a lecture, man. Actually, I was going to have some breakers perform during it. Kind of a performance piece, you know?"

Of all the members of the Spider's Web, Larson was the most secret, and the most secretive. He had good reason to distrust the police. Apparently, they had never forgiven him for attempting to synthesise an artificial opium as a means of opening what he called the 'doors of perception' within the human mind, or for attempting to pour this opiate into the water supply in order to force the city into delirium. A prank gone too far, some would say. The Blood-Spider, on tracking him down – or had Larson simply stumbled into his path? – had been impressed enough with the man's genius to provide him with new, state-of-the-art equipment and the latest findings on a variety of subjects. It had been a worthwhile expense. Larson was perhaps the most brilliant scientist the Spider had ever met.

He was also the only one who treated the Blood-Spider as he would treat anyone else in the world. He was neither terrified, like Stacey, or fascinated, like Marlene, or deferential, like Jonah - he simply treated the Spider as a perfectly ordinary person, no different from anyone he might meet at the theatre or the bakery. In turn, the Blood-Spider found him to be a fascinating and occasionally quite charismatic, if often irritating individual - he was continually grateful to the fates for making Larson far too useful to execute for his opium-related crimes when they had first met. It would be a shame not to have known the man.

That said, it was always best to let him know where he stood.

The Blood-Spider grabbed hold of the collar of Larson's shirt, lifting him up by it, before slamming him against one wall hard enough to knock the breath out of him.

"Remember who owns you, Professor Larson. You work for the Blood-Spider. The rest of your nonsense can wait."

Larson nodded, eyes wide. "Sure thing! Of course! I - I just wanted to, you know... get your *opinion...*" He swallowed, readjusting his collar as the Spider let him go. "You, uh, don't like breaker music?"

The Blood-Spider removed his hand from his coat, showing Larson the vial. Larson's eyes almost popped out of his head when he saw the label. "Holy crap! Is this Doc Thunder's real blood? Like, out of his body and everything?" He shook his head slowly, as if not quite able to believe what he held in his hands. "We need to get this cold before it congeals..." He looked up suddenly, puzzled. "What's this mean - fifty-fifty? Is it diluted?"

Blood-Spider shook his head. *"Quite pure. Apparently that refers to a specific person somewhere in this city... someone I'd like to meet."* Larson frowned, turning the vial over and over in his hands. *"Any idea who it might be?"*

"Someone who's not one thing or another?" He shrugged, shaking his head. "Or half with you and half against you - like a cop moonlighting as a criminal. Know anybody like that?" He laughed. "Or somebody who's around you a lot when you're, you know..." He gestured at the mask. "Not *you*... but, like, while you're off, y'know, being *you*, they're... being *them*. Fifty-fifty split. Does that make sense?"

"It raises some interesting possibilities. Much like that vial of blood. Perhaps you could tell me more about it, given time. I saw him use it to cure a man of a rare poison..." He scowled under his concealing helmet, irritated by the memory. Venger had deserved to die for his incompetence alone.

Larson chuckled. "So we know it's got some kind of healing mojo – that's cool. I'll bet with a little study we could find out just where Doc gets his whole whammy from. Actually, you know what? That last batch of notes you got me, that seemed to be headed in that direction already..." He chuckled, then stopped, looking sideways at the Blood-Spider. The grin on his face turned sly. "That's why you brought this to me, right? You want some of that for yourself. Aw man, you *dog*, you must have *planned* for this."

The Blood-Spider stared back at him, the eight lenses impassive.

"I plan for everything. I'll expect results swiftly, Professor. Do you understand? Within the week."

"Sure thing," Larson grinned. "You're the boss, babe. I'll find you what you need. Reverse-engineer what's in this and get it into you. Sound good?"

The Blood-Spider looked at him for a moment, then turned to the door, unlocking and opening it with a creak.

"Not a word, Larson. If you value your life. The Spider's vengeance is swifter than any venom."

"Sure, sure." Larson smiled as he closed the door, examining the vial of blood in his hands. "See you soon, man..."

Outside, the Blood-Spider turned to take another look at the homeless man, as if reconsidering his earlier impulse to simply kill him and be done with it. But no. To bring the police down on Larson while he was engaged in such important work on the Spider's behalf would not do. Better to leave him be.

Besides, he had to reconvene with Marlene. There would be other times.

As he turned and walked back towards his rendezvous with the Silver Ghost, the homeless man raised his head, lifting a strip of red cloth from under the blanket and tying it securely over his face.

El Sombra liked automobiles. The wonderful thing about them was that people who owned a fast one seemed to be under the impression they couldn't be followed. But a man who ran across the rooftops and through the tight alleys could easily keep pace with the fastest car, so long as it spent a good portion of its time in New York traffic. And Marlene wasn't quite as speedy a driver as either of them thought.

"Later, amigo." He grinned, before lifting a thick brown volume from underneath his blanket, with the word *Tagebuch* inscribed in gold lettering on the front.

He had a little revision to do.

IT WAS GETTING on for one in the morning when Parker Crane finally returned to the Jameson Club.

"Welcome back, Master Parker," murmured Jonah as he opened the front door and ushered Crane into the sanctuary of the Lower Library, before any of those members still plodding around the club, in the manner of ruminants plodding around a lush green field, could ask any awkward questions. "And may I say," he said, after the door had been securely locked, "What a pleasure it is to find you still alive."

"Thank you, Jonah," Crane half-smiled as he handed over the briefcase containing the Spider's mask and the uniform that he'd worn to the hospital. "That will need cleaning."

He settled into one of the soft leather armchairs, closing his eyes for a moment and breathing deeply, the half-smile widening slightly. "What a wonderfully interesting evening I've had. You'll be happy to know I solved the mystery of Heinrich Donner's death, although other mysteries present themselves." He sighed, the smile dropping from his face. "Still, the night was remarkably free from dangers – to me, at least. The suction cups Larson invented for me helped enormously with that. Where would the Spider be without the ability to crawl up the sheerest wall, Jonah?"

Jonah sniffed. He did not approve of Timothy Larson. "He is a... surprisingly beneficial resource, Sir."

"Oh, I have a feeling we haven't seen the half of it." He took hold of the chilled vodka martini that had materialised on the tray suddenly in Jonah's hand, sipping slowly. "Thank you." He was well used by now to Jonah's habit of knowing exactly what was needed when it was needed.

"Tell me..." Crane stared into the distance, his grey eyes focussing on some unseen point that existed only in his mind. "What would you do if all the power of Doc Thunder could be yours? The power to bend steel, in your grasp? The ability to withstand a speeding bullet fired at point blank range. To win a tug of war with a locomotive at full steam. To jump to the roof of a tall building in a single bound, all of that. What would you do with it all?"

Jonah considered for a moment. "Such a question requires a leap of imagination as to how one might acquire such powers, Master Parker."

Crane chuckled. "Let's just say they're closer to being acquired than they have been in quite some time. What would you do?"

Jonah frowned. "I would venture to suggest, Sir, that my answer would be... 'better'."

Crane nodded. "Quite. No more mollycoddling society's worst elements. No more allowing the criminals, the inhuman scum, to roam free and unchecked. No more collusion and collaboration with Presidents like Bartlet or worse, that little thug Rickard; people who undermine this great country. Real justice, achieved by real power. Think of it, Jonah."

Jonah allowed himself a tight smile. "Removing that second 'S' from the country, you mean, Sir? I'll admit I've never felt all that comfortable living in the United Socialist States Of America. I've never felt comfortable with socialism as a concept at all."

"Well, not this kind." Crane chuckled, dryly. "A coup, then. President Crane. I rather like that."

Jonah nodded. "It was always going to be on the agenda eventually, Sir. You can hardly have a war on crime unless you are the one defining what a crime is. Otherwise you find yourself on such slippery ground..." His face grew thoughtful as Crane finished the martini. "Of course – assuming this is not some idle fantasy – that leaves the problem of another man with all the powers of Doc Thunder."

"That being Doc Thunder. I knew a battle with him was on the horizon as soon as I put four and a half bullets into his ape. Ah well, it's not as if I could have allowed him to live. Many would say he's lived far too long already." Crane frowned as he finished his drink, setting aside the empty glass. "This only moves his death slightly up the schedule."

Jonah bowed. "Very good, Sir. Shall I fetch the special ammunition?"

"Yes... but we must spin the web before we catch the fly." He looked over at the grandfather clock that ticked ominously in the corner of the room. "A little after one. The newspaper offices will still be open and busy. I believe I have time to place an advertisement."

Jonah raised an eyebrow. "Calling him out, Sir? Rather a risky strategy, if I may say so."

Crane leaned forward. "You may not. The telephone, Jonah. And another martini. And... yes, a Spanish dictionary."

Jonah bowed again, and returned in a few moments with the telephone – the one connected to an untraceable line – and a small, locked box that had been stored carefully in the club's impregnable safe. The members were not short of valuables, and many used the club as an unofficial bank vault; in the giant walk-in safe next to the wine cellar there were furs, jewellery, gold krugerrands, securities and bonds, and even the negatives of occasional blackmail photos which the members had paid through the nose for. There was nothing remotely as expensive as the contents of the ebony box, however. The contents of that box represented an expenditure of more than seventy million dollars, paid to a black marketer with a line on arms and equipment remaining from N.I.G.H.T.M.A.R.E.'s end at the hands of Doc Thunder.

It rattled.

Picking up the phone, Crane threw a handkerchief over the mouthpiece, then spoke. "Operator? *The Daily Bugle...* whoever's in charge of placing the advertisements. I'll wait." He turned to Jonah, who was returning with the dictionary and drink, and smiled slyly. "This isn't a challenge, Jonah. This is a lure."

He turned back to the telephone. "Ah yes, Mr... Robertson? Yes, I have an advertisement I'd like to place. I'll be sending a cashier's check via courier shortly. When? Tomorrow morning, the early edition. Yes. Yes... Mr. Robertson, the check in question will be for five thousand dollars. Yes, I thought that would change things. The text of the advertisement?"

He opened the dictionary, leafing through to the correct page. "El... *Sustantivo*. We need to talk about your blood. Meet me in Grand Central Station at sunset. Your friend in the red mask." He smiled. "No, no, Mr. Robertson. Thank *you*." He put the phone down.

"Grand Central Station, Sir?" Jonah's face betrayed a look of unease. "Won't that be a little crowded at that time of day?"

"Ah, but it has to be a public place or he'll smell a rat. Besides, with all those people around, he can hardly cut loose, can he?" He grinned, almost feral. "I, on the other hand – well, if some unlucky commuter should wander into the path of a bullet, I won't lose too much in the way of sleep. The first rule of the war on crime, Jonah: everyone in this country is guilty of something."

Jonah nodded, and left silently to fetch a third martini to serve as a nightcap, while Parker Crane unlocked the ebony box with the tiny key he kept constantly on his person. The light of the gas lamp lit the six bullets inside with a soft gleam. They were not made of lead, as his normal ammunition was, but forged from something that shone like silver and shimmered like mercury, and was far more valuable – and more deadly than either.

Inexorium.

CHAPTER TWELVE

Doc Thunder and How He Came to Be

TWO SUNS SHONE in the sky.

The roc swooped down from between them, and Maya twisted, tugging at the chains that bound her, spread-eagled on her back, turning her face away from the sight. The altar was curved, like the shell of a river turtle, leaving her oiled body arched invitingly, a meal for the monster. The giant bird had fed on traitors and criminals before, and she knew that unless she could work free of the shackles, that terrible curved beak would tear into her belly as if she were any other offering. A chill of fear ran down her spine as the bird circled, toying with her, and she suppressed it with an iron effort of will. If she were to die here, after so many long centuries, then she would die like a Goddess.

"You will pay for this treachery, Zarnos!" she hissed, her emerald eyes blazing with rage.

Her treacherous high priest laughed as he lounged on her own throne, flanked by two of her own leopard warriors, their cat-like eyes glassy, dazzled by the hypnotic effects of the Gem Of

A Thousand Desires; that pernicious stone with which Krato, leader of the Scorpion Cult, had attempted to dampen her will and seduce her mind – before she had rewarded his blasphemous intentions with a dagger to the heart, and scattered his dark order to the four corners of Zor-Ek-Narr. The Gem glittered and shone with devil's magic, as befit something cast and consecrated during the Age Of Woe, before light had entered the world. How such a forbidden object had found its way into Zarnos' ringed hands, she knew not, but he had used it to slowly but surely take control of her kingdom, while she had been distracted by the arrival of the Stranger into her land.

She cursed herself. If only Zarnos had not ordered the Stranger banished to the darkest depths of the Vault Of the Serpent God, the sinister labyrinth from whence none had ever returned. If the Stranger did not starve to death in its winding, lightless pathways, leagues away from succour, he would be hunted and torn apart by the legendary Gorgorex, half-snake and half-bull, the fearsome guardian of the secret of the maze, whose horns could pierce stone and whose venom could slay legions. And even if he somehow survived the Vault, why would he come for her after all she'd done to him?

Zarnos' laughter grew louder, ringing in her ears.

The roc swooped once again, for the final time, razor sharp talons glinting in the light of the suns–

– and the Stranger leapt from his hiding place in the rocks, shirt torn to blue rags, aiming a fist like a hammer into the giant bird's skull, snapping it to the side an instant before the great beak would have closed about her glistening, naked form. The sound was like a boulder cracking in two, and the roc spiralled down, fluttering from the heights of the Sacrificial Eyrie down to the valley far below.

The Stranger rubbed his knuckles. "Sorry for making you wait. But that's the kind of thing you only get one shot at."

The he smiled, and in that moment her heart was his.

"Blasphemer! Slay him, my Leopard Men!" Zarnos cried, standing up from the throne he had so sacrilegiously stolen, and pointing one long, bony finger at the Stranger. Their wills vanished into the depths of the Gem Of A Thousand Desires, the leopard warriors were helpless to do anything but obey. Their tails twitched from side to side as they lowered their spears, advancing towards the Stranger with fangs bared.

"They're not your Leopard Men, Zarnos. And I suggest you think twice before trying to use a spear on me." The Stranger crossed his arms and simply waited as the two warriors thrust their spears forward, only to see the honed flint points shatter and crack against his bare skin. He smiled grimly. "I have to say... I don't appreciate being poked."

He was more gentle with the leopard warriors than he had been with the roc – merely swatting them to one side with enough force to stun – and while Maya felt a chill of fear close about her once more as Zarnos raised the Gem to shine its malevolent light into the Stranger's eyes, he kept them covered, seeking out the corrupt vizier by the sound of his desperate, wheedling voice. "You will obey me! You will obey the will of Zarnos! All must obey my will!" He carried on screaming the words shrilly even after the Stranger had reached out and crushed the dangling gem between his mighty fingers, scattering the fragments at his feet.

Zarnos backed away, his eyes widening in terror. "You are no man! You are a monster! A devil from the Age Of Woe, where no light shone! Keep back, fiend, you will not feed on Zarnos' spirit!" he was babbling, not seeing where his frenzied, backwards steps were taking him.

"Zarnos, you fool, stay still!" The Stranger hissed, reaching out a hand. *The cliff edge –"*

But it was too late. Zarnos, self-styled Emperor Of All That Was, stumbled back, his feet treading air before he plunged with a shrill scream into the valley below; a scream ending in death.

"Poor devil," the Stranger murmured, shaking his head as he walked back towards the altar, and the Goddess chained to it. "He should have known. Sooner or later, the path of evil will always lead to a long, lonely fall. Like Icarus, Zarnos flew too close to the sun in his blind thirst for power, and the only way to go was down." He looked up, shielding his eyes, watching the twin suns beginning to dip down towards the horizon. "Suns,

I mean... I'm still puzzled about that. Back home we only have the one."

Maya laughed, stretching out on the curved stone, relaxing fully for the first time in days. "According to my astronomers, there is only one sun. The doubling effect is produced by something in the air around my kingdom. Residue of some sort from the simmering heart of the Mountain Of Eternal Flame."

The Stranger nodded. "An optical illusion – light refracting off crystal deposits in the air. Presumably those same crystals account for the strange mutations among the people and animals in the region..." He tailed off, staring at the suns. "It's very beautiful."

Maya smiled. "As beautiful as evil?" He laughed, looking down at her, his eyes roaming for a second before meeting her own. "We call it the Dreaming Sun." She purred. "They say that praying to it can make a dream come true. Care to make a wish?"

The Stranger laughed again, and then leaned close. "Let's get those chains off you."

"No." Her eyes glinted darkly. "Leave them as they are."

He raised an eyebrow, then smiled, bending to kiss her belly. "If you insist."

She purred, enjoying the feel of his lips and the soft rubbing of his beard, listening to him breathing in her scent, feeling his strong hands closing about her waist, seeming to restrain her more than the taut chains. "Tell me, Stranger." she breathed, "Tell me your true name."

He looked up, his blue eyes piercing.

"Doc Thunder."

"You lied to me."

Maya spoke the words without emotion, without anger or sadness. She simply stated a fact.

"No, I didn't." Doc Thunder sat in his lab, surrounded by all his equipment, all his experiments, all his useless junk. His voice was lost, haunted, and so very, very tired. For the first time in his life, he had no idea what to do, what to say.

How had it come to this?

She'd slept in the bedroom, alone, and he'd stayed down here, pretending to work, doing nothing but fiddling, keeping his fingers busy and trying not to feel that emptiness, the black despair yawning inside him.

He hadn't realised what it would feel like to lose her. He hadn't realised he could.

Wasn't he America's Greatest Hero? Hadn't he killed a giant roc, escaped a maze of death, fought leopard men and made love to her on a heathen altar in the light of two setting suns?

How could it all come to nothing after that?

As dawn had broken over the city, Marcel had entered, bringing coffee, the morning paper and a bacon sandwich. Doc had smiled, made some strained, fractious joke about the devil that he instantly regretted. Marcel had only half-smiled, sadly, and placed a hand on his great, slumped shoulder.

"Sometimes it is only us, monsieur. Sometimes it is only us."

He ate the sandwich in silence, and didn't taste it. The coffee went untouched after a few sips. He didn't open the paper.

Eventually, he'd heard Maya rising, early, bustling around the bedroom, then walking down the stairs, past the empty gym. He heard her saying a brief hello to Marcel. Then she'd walked into the lab, wearing the long white ceremonial robe she'd worn when he first laid eyes on her, and told him that he'd lied to her.

"You lied to me." She said it once again, shaking her head, not looking at him. "I asked you for your true name and you gave me an alias. A pretend name. Your parents weren't Mr and Mrs Thunder. They didn't name you 'Doc'."

Doc sighed, shaking his head, feeling the length and depth of the chasm that had opened up so suddenly between them.

He loved her. He loved her for her wit, for her beauty, for the way her eyes changed colour in the sunlight from hard emerald to ocean water, for the things she said in restaurants, for the way she looked when she was asleep, for the way she walked through the city like a cat and was not touched by it, for a thousand thousand reasons and more every day.

He loved her, and the thought of her leaving him hurt. If he'd been given the choice, he'd have taken the lightning again. He'd have reached out and grabbed that conductor and held it like a long-lost friend, if it meant avoiding this for one more day.

He tried to think of something to say that would make her change her mind, and he couldn't think of anything. Finally, he spoke. "We don't always get our true names from our parents..." It sounded hollow. He let the words trail off and stared at the coffee going cold on the worktop.

Maya shrugged. She didn't consider that much of an explanation.

Nobody said anything for a long time after that. Idly, Doc played with a steel spanner, bending it this way and that with his fingers. He couldn't bring himself to look at her.

Eventually, Maya spoke. "I don't love you."

Doc nodded.

Maya sighed, sitting down on a stool next to a workbench piled high with hydraulics and copper tubes, spare parts from something long forgotten. "Maybe I don't love. I never did before I came here. It wasn't something I was ever asked to do." She shrugged. "Why should it be? Love is a relatively modern invention even in your world of a single sun. In Zor-Ek-Narr, we had other things to occupy our time."

Doc swallowed, shaking his head, feeling stung deep inside. "But you felt something for me."

Maya shook her head. "I felt something for Doc Thunder – something like what I assumed love must be. But it was easy to love Doc Thunder. It was like loving a picture of a man. A perfect fiction. And Doc Thunder was a wonderfully perfect fiction, because he never made any mistakes. That was the point of him." She sighed, tracing her finger through the dust on the bench. "And that's not you anymore, is it? The moment you heard Donner's name, you made error after error. And now it turns out you've been making terrible mistakes for as long as I've known you." She looked over her shoulder at him, and her voice was bitter. "How does it go? Your job is to be the example for the little guy? If one man looks at you and thinks he can try just a little bit harder, blah blah, and so on? And there you are, letting all your friends die and letting monsters take their place while you walk away."

She grimaced, not even wanting to look at him. "I don't know if I can trust you anymore, Stranger. How can I love you? You'll only break my heart."

Doc reached for his coffee. "What about Monk? Do you care about him, or have you changed your mind about that as well?" He could hear the bitterness in his own words.

Maya paused. "He made my heart laugh."

"Me too." He sighed, then scowled. "*Makes*. Damn it, he's not *gone*, Maya. He's stable, he's out of danger and the second he can be moved, I'm bringing him back to the brownstone. And then I'm going to give him a direct transfusion – supervise it myself. He'll be better than new."

Maya frowned, suddenly deep in thought. "Your blood. You think Venger managed to spirit it away before he died? You think he's responsible for what happened to Monk?"

Doc rubbed his temples. He didn't want to think about this now. "No. He was waiting for his chance. He's seen me give transfusions in the past to get people off the critical list, people with my blood type. He knew Monk and I were a match. It was a matter of time." He frowned. Something Venger had said – and something he'd remembered in the Omega Machine. He was having trouble putting the pieces together.

"Why would he want it?" Maya was looking at him, curiously, as if seeing him for the first time.

"The same reason Donner did." He shook his head, rubbing his eyes with a finger and thumb. He'd never felt quite so defeated.

"And why did Donner want it?" Maya turned, looking him straight in the eye. "Tell me, Stranger." She said it mockingly, her eyes looking deep into his. "If you can. Tell me your true name."

Doc looked at her for a long moment.

"My name is Donner. Hugo Donner. Heinrich Donner was my father."

Maya blinked. "But..."

"You need to hear it all. Everything I've been hiding my whole life. Then..." He stood up, looking down at her. "Then I'll help you pack your bags."

*   *   *

MY STORY BEGINS in 1935. Hitler had been Chancellor of Germany for two years. He was chafing against the restrictions placed on him by Victoria, as he has been ever since. At the time, he was already planning an expansion to the east – his doomed attempt to conquer Russia – but the plan was always to move on to America. They were the enemy. Karl Marx had fled to America to escape the dark arts of the Tsars, the trade deal with Japan was making New York one of the most multicultural cities in the world, and President Grimm was speaking out against Hitler as early as 1931. Hitler needed Russia, he was willing to deal with China while it suited him, but he wanted us.

Of course, it didn't take a strategist like Rommel to figure out that as soon as he'd done the hard work of taking Russia, Victoria would swoop in from the west and hammer him while he was weakest. Then she'd get everything, and deal with a diplomatic thorn in her side into the bargain. He needed a strong military – much stronger than anything he had – so he could take Russia, hold it, and still be strong enough to stay on the bargaining table against the Empire.

He needed soldiers who wouldn't tire, who could see for miles, who could hear a pin drop fifty feet away. He needed soldiers immune to bullets and shells. Soldiers who could kill with their bare hands, travel in leaps of a quarter of a mile or more, punch out a traction engine.

Sound familiar?

That was Project Gladiator. The transformation of ordinary German soldiers into supermen capable of winning wars on as many fronts as he needed. He'd had people working on this since before he was elected, and by 1935 he finally had a serum – albeit one that had to be injected *in utero,* into the amniotic fluid, while the foetus was growing. It was the only way Professor Strucker could get it to work on the rats, and they weren't about to start injecting that stuff into prisoners. They needed a human test subject, and one loyal to the Fuhrer.

Which was where Heinrich Donner came in.

My mother's name was Anna, and she was two months pregnant with me when Donner decided that giving his unborn child up for medical experimentation was a good way to rise in the party machine. Anna didn't agree; not until he made it clear that if she went through with the birth without getting the injection, he'd strangle me in my swaddling clothes, cook me and make her eat me.

Yes, really.

She went through with it.

Things didn't work out too well. Strucker had a massive heart attack right after injecting my mother. It turns out the only copy of the formula was in his head, because, like most people in the Reich, he was worried that if he stopped being useful for ten seconds, they'd kill him. Still, no problem. They could reverse-engineer the serum from my blood as soon as I was born, maybe even make a version that worked on adults. It would have bonded to my bloodstream. I was just the test animal they were looking for.

Heinrich Donner volunteered to slit my throat himself.

That was enough for Mother.

Don't ask me how she managed to get away from him – she never did tell me the details – but she was in the Netherlands before the week was out. Four months later, she was coming into New York city on a fishing trawler and she thought she was finally safe. She never did contact the authorities, she just disappeared into a tenement on the lower East Side.

That's where I was born.

I wasn't the only kid on my street with a German name, but my build marked me out early. I grew like a weed and tore through books like a woodworm. By the time I was ten, I was as tall as a boy of fifteen and twice as broad, and I could pass tests college kids failed. Eventually, mother had to tell me why I was so different. That's how I first learned about Donner, my father. What he did. I asked her why she didn't change our name when she got here. She said it was because she hoped he might still come around. She was willing to forgive him, even after everything he'd done and threatened.

"He was a good man, before the Reich. A good man." she used to say that with a little wistful smile on her face. I never did understand it.

Especially not once he found her.

While I was growing up, Hitler was trying to take Russia, and we all know how that turned out. When he finally threw in the towel in 1945, after a year of bloody stalemate just trying to keep his own borders from being overrun by every horror you couldn't imagine – and I've fought a few things from that region, I know what he was up against – the whole idea of taking on Victoria at her own game via conventional means was over.

It was Donner who suggested the unconventional.

Untergang. A criminal organisation with total deniability, sponsored under the table by Germany via black budget, but in such a way nobody could ever possibly prove it. A destabilisation tactic. A way to harry local law enforcement, strike out against the government, disseminate propaganda and perform covert assassinations and sabotage, while Uncle Adolf tut-tutted at the preponderance of crime in America and held up his clean, clean hands. Asymmetrical warfare. Terrorism on a massive scale.

Since it was Heinrich Donner's idea, he was sent over as the organisation's leader. Oh, he had a cover in place, and a decoy to take the blame for him, but it was him behind everything.

And he hadn't forgotten the promise he'd made to the Führer.

On my eleventh birthday, I came back from school to find my mother had been murdered by a group of four Untergang black-ops specialists. They'd dragged her to the bed and suffocated her with a pillow, before rigging the apartment with incendiary explosives to cover their tracks. Then they'd waited for me to return. Their plan was to stage an armed ambush and take me down as quickly as possible. They had intelligence reports about how strong and quick I was - the same ones that had verified my mother's identity - and they were confident that, between the four of them, they could incapacitate me without difficulty. If it became necessary, they would simply kill me as they had my mother.

Following which, they would steal the blood either from my unconscious body or my corpse.

They thought they could surprise me, but they'd forgotten my hearing. I could hear them moving around, I knew something was wrong, and... well, I came through the wall. Just crashed right through it. That's how I got the first one; he was leaning against it. The others didn't last much longer.

The apartment – my home for the first eleven years of my life – didn't survive the battle. My mother's body went up in the flames, along with every remnant of my life up until that point. I lived on the streets for a year, dodging attacks from Untergang agents who literally wanted my blood.

Eventually, I fell in with the police – Commissioner Coltrane was in charge back then. Danny's grandfather. I wish I'd thought to lie about my age, but we managed to work something out anyway.

That was the last time anybody called me Hugo Donner. I wanted nothing to do with that name. I remember the desk sergeant – a guy called Bud O'Malley – asking me what my name was, and one word boiling up in my head...

"Thunder," I told him.

"Kid Thunder."

MAYA BLINKED. *"KID Thunder?"*

Doc shrugged, embarrassed. "Well, I didn't get my first doctorate until I was sixteen. Anyway, that's the story. Even after my skin got as tough as it is now, Donner still wanted my blood, and he was still willing to do anything he could to to get hold of it. And now... well, he's got it. After all these years. Much good may it do him."

Maya reached to grip his shoulder, gently. "You really think it was him? A scheme he didn't live to see completed?"

Doc shook his head. "I don't know." He looked up at her, and she saw the weariness in his eyes. "I don't know, Maya. I don't know the answers. I thought Donner was the only person who knew who I was or how I came to be, so... but I'm probably wrong. I don't know."

He paused, then sat down, reaching for the cold coffee. He took a sip and grimaced. "And I don't know about you and me, either. I don't know if you can trust me – if you want to trust me to never make a mistake again, you can't do that. You can't trust me not to fail." He turned and looked at her. "But I need you anyway. I need you for this. Because I don't know what the hell I'm going to do next, Maya."

She stared at him for a moment, frowning coldly at him. "No, Doc Thunder doesn't know. I think Doc Thunder's about run his course." Then she broke into a half-smile. "But I think you do."

He looked at her for a long moment, then spoke. "Find out who's got my blood, if anyone has. That's priority one–" He was interrupted by the door to the lab opening.

Marcel entered, carrying a try with two cups of hot, steaming coffee, prepared perfectly. "Monsieur, Madame. Everything is worked out, I trust?"

Maya smiled. "Not nearly. But I think we've made a start."

Marcel nodded. "*Très bien!*" He noticed the unopened paper. "Ah, Monsieur – you may want to look in the classified section today." He smiled, opening the paper to the correct page and thrusting it under Thunder's nose.

"What am I looking for?"

"*El Sustantivo* – just there, in the bottom left hand corner."

Doc nodded. "Hmmm. Looks like our friend from last night wants to contact me. Or somebody." He raised an eyebrow at Maya. "About my stolen blood, too. Very convenient."

"You think it could be a trap?" Maya frowned, peeking over his shoulder.

"It's in Grand Central Station. That's a very public place, at least. Still..." He frowned, folding the paper and tossing it onto the workbench. "I think keeping that appointment might prove to be a very big mistake."

Maya nodded. "So. What are you going to do?"

Doc Thunder looked at her.

"Make it."

CHAPTER THIRTEEN

The Case of The Quisling of Crime

"Wuxtry, wuxtry! All the news, all the time, for a dime! Doc Thunder in battle with the Face Of Fear! Don't ask, just buy it. Red Mask sighted on hospital rooftop during deadly affray! Anton Venger returns from grave only to die a second time! Read all about the riddle of the missing doctor and the murdered master of disguise. Face it, true believer, this is the one! It's the pulse-pounding front page scoop we just had to call: 'IF DOOM BE HIS DESTINY!' Wuxtry, wuxtry! All in colour for a dime!"

The paperboy's shrill cries echoed through the bustling station, competing with the grizzled old hot dog vendor –

"One dollar five! Guaranteed unhealthy! C'mon, you assholes wanna live forever?"

– and the sushi vendor ten feet away, trying to keep the stench of frying onions out of his fish –

"Nigiri, fifty cents! Roll, sixty cents! We got tuna, we got eel, we got crunchy katsu pork! Just like mama makes!"

– and the pencil-thin young man with his pencil-thin moustache, selling costume jewellery from a cheap suitcase –

"Gen-yoo-wine fake diamonds! Gen-you-wine necklaces, chokers, bracelets, earrings made from real glass! Three dollars – can you say no, folks? Hand 'em over by candlelight, you can always run in the morning!"

– and the slick, sharp-dressed breaker kids, taking off their zoot jackets to windmill on a flat sheet of card, two more playing the toms and freestyling over the top while a pair of bulls watched and tapped their feet –

"– I'm the c-a-s an' the o-v-a an' the rest is f-l-y –"

– and the porters calling the trains, and the passengers calling each other, and the luggage trolleys rumbling over the tiled floor, and the sounds of a thousand pairs of moving feet, echoing back and forth from one wall to the other and back.

Grand Central Station at night.

All human life was here – the housewife running from her abusive husband to her sister in Schenectady, the banker who couldn't face his wife's cooking without a couple of tonkatsu pork rolls inside him, the cops on the beat arguing about whether Warhol had finally lost it with all this dreampunk crap, the kid sleeping rough on the streets who'd wandered in to get out of the rain, the British tourists pointing and gawping at everyone else in between looking at their map and wondering how to walk to the Statue Of Liberty...

...and up above them, up, up in the shadowy arches of the station, where the gaslight didn't reach, there was a man in a pitch-black coat and a metallic, blood-red mask with eight glittering lenses, who carried a pair of automatic pistols, and he watched them all.

Watched and waited.

Occasionally, he glanced at the clock that told the bustling crowds how late they were for the trains they could never hope to catch now. Eight fifty-nine, and fifty seconds, fifty-one, fifty-two... he watched, his fingers on the triggers itching, buzzing, yearning, as the second hand passed the top of the arc and began a new circuit around the dial.

Nine o'clock. No sign of him.

The Blood-Spider hissed irritably into his mask.

How typical of Doc Thunder to be late for his own funeral.

"I DO SO wish you'd reconsider this course of action, Master Parker."

Three hours before, Jonah had expressed his misgivings about the whole venture. It had come very close to ruining an otherwise excellent dinner of roast quail and asparagus tips.

"Surely it would be safer to wait until you had, ah, acquired abilities commensurate to the good Doctor before embarking on a campaign against him?" Jonah swallowed, unused to this sort of confrontation. Crane only smiled.

"Jonah, if I suddenly turn up being able to bend steel and leap the height of a decent-sized office building, he'll put two and two together. He knows *somebody* stole his blood. No, better to pick him off now before he suspects my involvement. Who knows, maybe I'll get lucky and Donner's murderer will turn up as well – warn him of the trap. Two birds with one stone." He lifted a forkful of quail to his lips, chewing meditatively for a moment. "And consider the larger picture, Jonah. America's Greatest Hero, gunned down in public! In the panic and tumult, the question goes up; who will replace him? His friends either die in mysterious circumstances or sail away to their forbidden cities, if they know what's good for them. And then..."

He leaned back, smiling expansively. "A new Doc Thunder, for new times. The Blood Thunder." He laughed. "Blood and thunder! That's rather good, isn't it?"

Jonah swallowed. "Master Parker, please. Remember the cause. The war." He laid his hand gently on Crane's shoulder. "You're taking a terrible risk. You seem to be becoming... unstable. Remember, Sir, that while you do have great power, you also have a grave responsibility."

Crane shook his hand off. "I'll decide what my responsibilities are, Jonah. And I say this is the best chance to further the cause we've had yet. Doc Thunder dead, all his power in my hands... and total war with the inhuman elements of our society. War to the death!"

Jonah looked at him for a long moment, and it was impossible to tell if what lay behind his eyes was reproach or pity. "I see. In that case, I will leave you to prepare, Sir." He began to clear away Crane's meal, then took a look around the dusty confines of the Lower Library. "One more thing, though, Sir, if I may."

"Get on with it."

"Sir –" Jonah took a deep breath. "– you are spending rather a worrying amount of time down here, in this room, sequestered away from the other Jameson Club members. There are other rooms in the club where you may take an early supper without raising quite so many eyebrows."

Crane snorted. "And are there other rooms in the club where I may openly discuss the murder of such a prominent celebrity? With ammunition secured from the ashes of a known terrorist organisation? Hmm? Dry up, Jonah."

"Sir, please –"

"I said dry up!" Crane bellowed the words. "I'm the leader of this particular organisation, Jonah. Do you understand me? I decide what our strategy is! I decide who to *kill!* And I decide whether or not to leave my comfortable little nook here and spend my valuable time with those *overstuffed blowhards* up *there!*" His voice rose, uncaring, until it was almost a shriek.

Jonah looked at him in horror.

"Soundproof walls, Jonah." Crane smiled, his grey eyes mischievous. "Now, tell me again how you'd rather I said all that upstairs in the smoking room while passing out cigars."

Jonah blinked, the look of shock still palpable on his face, and turned to leave. He did not say a word.

"Oh, and Jonah – telephone. I'm going to need Ms. Lang tonight, I think. *She* at least knows how to obey an order."

Nine o' clock.

Marlene Lang waited patiently. Back straight in the leather seat, cap pulled down over blonde hair styled in a very severe bun, mirrored sunglasses. Hands in the ten and two position, unmoving. Lips frowning in an icy pout.

She'd held the position for fifteen minutes, and fully intended to hold it until the Blood-Spider's business in the station was concluded, whatever it might be. At which point, he would make his way to the Silver Ghost, parked in a dark alley two blocks away, and they would drive to a safe location which he would make known to her at that time, and not before. It was all deliciously professional.

Professionalism was her new watchword, she had decided.

David had called earlier in the day, and she had told him, in what she felt was a very reasonable tone, that she would no longer be modelling for him at his studio. She'd let him have his say, quietly enduring his wheedling, passive-aggressive tone as he'd begged her to reconsider, his voice echoing tinnily over the receiver as he told her that without her as his muse he had no reason to create his art, that his talent needed her beauty as its essential focus – lies of that nature. She had sighed, like a schoolmistress lecturing a petulant child.

"David, it's very simple. I just have better things to do with my time."

And with that, she'd hung up on him. She would probably have done the same if Jack had called, or Easton. Even Parker – her fellow crime-fighter – would find her closed for anything other than the most pressing business. Since the trouble of the previous night, she'd found herself infused with an almost religious fervour for the cause. It had been the first time she had fully entertained the possibility, which she surmised was still quite real, that the Blood-Spider could be exposed or killed at any moment, and might even end up dragging her down with him. Faced with a choice between dealing herself out of the game before things escalated further and throwing herself into the whole dangerous enterprise wholeheartedly and without restraint, she had chosen the latter. Well, of course she had.

Any other choice would simply have been too dreary for words.

She idly checked her eyeshadow in the rear view mirror. Professionalism was the new watchword in all things, and that meant keeping herself immaculate.

When her eyes looked forward again, there was a man standing in front of the auto.

He was a well-built man, of Latin descent, handsome apart from a freshly broken nose and the wet, bedraggled state of his hair. Although that was somewhat made up for by his wearing nothing but a pair of tuxedo trousers and red sash tied around his face with two holes in it. In his right hand, he was holding a very dangerous looking sword.

"Nice wheels."

She stared at him for a long moment, then went for the pistol she'd hidden under her seat, ducking her head for a moment and grabbing the handle of the gun in a practiced motion, bringing it up to fire at – nothing.

The man was gone, as suddenly as he'd appeared.

She blinked, looking up and down the alley for any sign of him. Nothing. He'd simply vanished. Uneasily, she fingered the safety on the pistol, then laid it on the seat next to her. She wanted to be ready if that strange man – whoever he turned out to be – should appear again.

She wondered why his hair had been wet.

Two blocks away, Doc Thunder walked into Grand Central Station.

For a moment, he simply stood on the balcony overlooking the main concourse, closed his eyes and breathed it all in; the smell of roasting onions, hot dogs, sticky rice, shoe polish, perfume, honest sweat. The soft, insistent buzz of conversation, the shuffle of feet, the yell of station announcements, the tapping-out of the beat of a pair of toms, the whistle of the trains on their distant platforms.

Humanity, in all its glory.

When he opened his eyes, the crowd was looking back at him.

One by one, they'd turned to look at the big man in the blue t-shirt, the man who'd fought back against the Hidden Empire when all seemed lost, who'd stopped Untergang, N.I.G.H.T.M.A.R.E., Lars Lomax, Anton Venger, Professor Zeppelin, the steam-powered giant robot ape Titanicus, Mordus Madgrave and his army of the risen dead, Captain Death and the Pirates of Wall Street, the Orchestra Of Fear, Jason Satan and so many others. A rogue's gallery of maniacs, mutants, monsters and madmen. For fifty years, while others had come and gone, he'd stood firm against them all.

America's Greatest Hero.

A few people figured that deserved a round of applause.

The sound rippled through the crowd, commuters and breakers, hot dog vendors and police, even the tourists, all of them stopping where they stood and putting their hands together for the man who'd saved them all. The sound built, echoing off the ceiling, bouncing from one pillar to another, escaping onto the platforms where the arriving passengers wondered what all the fuss was about.

Up on his perch in the high darkness, the Blood-Spider listened to it all and waited for his moment to fire.

Doc blinked, surprised and a little embarrassed despite himself. It wasn't the first time he'd been greeted like that, but every time was a shock. He smiled, raising a hand. "Thank you. Thank you all, very much. It means a lot." And it did.

Then his expression grew more serious. "But... I'm going to have to ask you to clear the concourse. I have reason to believe there's someone here who wants me dead, and he's not going to worry about collateral damage. If you could all clear the station in an orderly manner – thank you, that's great..."

The cheers and applause changed slowly to worried murmurs, as the crowd began to break at the edges, some moving onto the platforms, most filing out through the main exits. Within a few minutes, the concourse was completely empty.

"Alone at last," Doc smiled, seemingly to nobody in particular.

Above, the Blood-Spider waited. Did he have police outside? Had he come here alone? Was it too late to get out without being seen? So many variables. He was safe up in the darkness, he knew. So long as he remained hidden, he had a choice.

"The newspaper announcement just didn't ring true, I'm afraid. Last time I saw 'my friend in the red mask', I smashed his face in with my forehead, although that was after he'd threatened to stab me through the eye. Not too friendly, really. Oh, and *sustantivo...* that's not the Spanish for thunder." Doc smiled. "It actually means 'noun'. I take it you used a dictionary for that one?" He paused for a moment, listening. "Not telling? Well, if it is you, my 'friend' in the mask, I'll apologise and accept the title of 'Mister Noun' without a murmur. Just step out and let me get a good look at you."

He turned, looking up at the ceiling. For a moment, the Blood-Spider froze. Thunder was looking right at him - no, he couldn't be. The shadows up here were pitch black. Just stay still...

"No? Well, I suppose there's only one other person it can be, then. I don't think we've actually met, but I've been following your career with interest. A good friend of mine - Easton West? - was hoping I'd find you eventually. You killed a young gang member in Japantown a few days ago, I don't know if you remember..." An edge crept into his voice. "You kill so many."

The Blood-Spider narrowed his eyes, behind his strange mask with its eight glittering lenses. Below him, Thunder reached into his pocket, taking out a small business card. He read the inscription slowly:

> *Where all inhuman*
> *Devils revel in their sins –*
> *The Blood-Spider spins!*

"That's very good. That's a haiku, isn't it? I'm sure Hisoka's family appreciated that little touch of home." He slipped the card back in his pocket. "His name was Hisoka. The boy you murdered. Inspector West wanted you to know his name."

Up in the thick darkness above, the Blood-Spider's hand was shaking. *He knows.* His finger was sweaty inside the black glove. *He knows. Fire. Kill him.*

Why couldn't he fire?

"I ran into him at the hospital, actually – while I was looking in on Monk. He's still not out of his coma. Still, it could have been a lot worse. If I hadn't got there in time..." He shook his head. "A close-run thing. Anyway, the Inspector told me that the bullets they dug out of his body matched the ones they dug out of Hisoka. Same calibre, same manufacturer... and guns leave marks. Every gun leaves its own personal signature on the bullets it fires. So it strikes me that you might want to use a different gun for pleasure than the one you use for business..."

The Blood-Spider's hands shook. *Fire! Kill him!*

He knows!

He tried to will himself to pull the trigger, but his finger wouldn't move. *Every gun leaves a signature.* But not on inexorium, surely? But what if it did? And the calibre would be the same... It would be the end of the Blood-Spider for all time. Could he risk that?

Could he still get away?

OUTSIDE, MARLENE DRUMMED her fingers impatiently on the wheel. She'd seen the crowds coming from the station. Something was happening there, something that wasn't included in the plan. She frowned, worrying her lip. More than ever, it was vital the Spider had a quick getaway from whatever he intended to do in there.

She had a nagging feeling that something was terribly wrong.

She wished she had a way of signalling him. He needed to know about the masked man. What had he been doing there, any –

– her eyes were suddenly drawn to the dials.

There was an array of dials on the dashboard; temperature of the internal furnace, water pressure for the hydraulics, steam pressure, and of course the speedometer. They were all over the place. The temperature of the internal furnace was way over normal, water pressure was at zero. And the pressure of the steam on the internal turbines was getting very–

– there was a grinding noise, and she felt the whirr of the turbines stop. Her heart froze in her chest. The Silver Ghost never stalled. Other autos stalled, all the time, but the Silver Ghost was special. The maze of fine hydraulic tubes underneath the car meant that there was always...

Oh God!

Heart thundering, she opened the driver's side door and stepped out – and the high heels of her black pumps splashed into a huge puddle of water, spreading slowly out from underneath the car. Wincing, she got down on her hands and knees, her cap tumbling off her head and splashing into the growing pool as she peered underneath the machine.

The Silver Ghost was armoured so well that a machine-gun couldn't scratch it.

But only from the top. Underneath, it seemed, it was very vulnerable indeed.

Before he even made himself known to her, the masked man had crawled under her auto, without being seen, and used that sword to disconnect every pipe he could find. Since then, all the water had been draining out of the machine, until now there was nothing left for steam. And without steam, the auto wouldn't move a single inch.

The Silver Ghost was dead.

"THERE'S ONE THING that puzzled me. I'm assuming you investigated Donner's murder at the same time Monk did, and he ran into you. But Monk Olsen... well, he's a celebrity in this town. Moreover, he's unique. There's literally no mistaking him for anyone else." Doc frowned.

"Now, the bullet in the kneecap... I can put that down to shock. Maybe the first one in the lung. Even the one that glanced off his skull. I'm a reasonable man." Slowly, he lay his fist in his hand, cracking one massive knuckle. It sounded like a gunshot.

"But."

Another knuckle. Another gunshot.

"He was down. He was no threat. You knew who he was. And then you fired a bullet into his gut – that's a slow death – and then another into his chest. Why? The thrill of the kill? Simple sadism? Just not thinking straight? Or is it something else?"

And another.

"Something occurred to me, a moment ago."

The Blood-Spider kept his gun trained on Doc Thunder's head. *He can't see me. I can still get away. Or...* His hand was shaking so badly he didn't even know if he'd hit his target if he fired. What was the matter with him? Why couldn't he just fire?

"You see, once I knew it was you who tried to kill Monk, I

took a look at your other killings. And there's something rather strange about them."

The Blood-Spider felt a chill rush through him. *Does he know?*

Doc smiled, humourlessly, his footsteps echoing on the tiled floor of the station, walking slowly around like a teacher in the world's largest classroom.

"There's not a single white, straight person among them. Well, apart from Anton Venger – you were the one who shot Anton Venger, weren't you? – and I'm not even one hundred per cent sure about him. I'm fairly sure he and Lomax were more than just colleagues. But anyway, everyone else you've killed has been... well, there's no other way to say it, is there?"

Doc's smile vanished.

"Non-Aryan."

He turned, looking up into the shadows. "And as I said, something occurred to me. The last piece of the puzzle. The crowd, giving me that little ovation. I'm going to put false modesty aside for a moment here and admit that, yes, I am loved. Perhaps not by everybody, but the people of this city do seem to hold me in very high regard. An outsider – someone who studied at this city without actually living here – would probably say it's because I fight crime. Now, did you see what happened when I asked them to clear the station? Grand Central Station, nine o' clock at night – cleared. No complaints. Not a murmur. Even the police went without a word. In fact, nobody else has come in here, so I'd go as far as to suggest they're outside right now, making themselves useful and spreading the word that I've put the main concourse of Grand Central Station off-limits."

He smiled. "It's a good thing I don't let power go to my head, isn't it?"

The smile vanished, and he turned on his heel, wandering into the dead centre of the concourse.

He's daring me to shoot, thought the Spider. *To give away my position. Why don't I shoot?* He cursed, silently. *I could drop him like a stone from this position! He'd never even hear the bullet!* But he continued to wait, fingers slick with sweat inside his gloves, trying to control the trembling of his hands. He had to be sure. Absolutely sure. Doc Thunder had just demonstrated that he was, to all intents and purposed, the King of New York City.

And if you shoot at a king, you have to kill him.

"Now!" Doc shouted, turning around again, as if lecturing an invisible audience, "Let's say I walked in here with a big bomb and yelled 'clear the station or I destroy us all'! Complete chaos! Mass panic! Oh, it'd clear the station, probably, after a shoot-out with the cops. But it's such a messy way to achieve my goals." He shrugged. "Or to put it another way; President Bartlet refuses to negotiate with terrorists. But I've got his direct line. At the end of the day, you get more by being loved than by being feared."

"Which brings us to Untergang."

All of a sudden, the Blood-Spider's hand stopped trembling.

"We've stopped hearing from them. Not because I finally beat them, the way I did N.I.G.H.T.M.A.R.E... they just went away. Vanished into the ether. Right about the time you turned up, in fact. Which makes me wonder... what if there's a new leader of Untergang? What if that leader wanted to try a new tactic? Rebranding the organisation. Making them loved rather than feared. Having them fight crime, or the right kind of crime, at least. What if the Führer agreed to a trial of this new strategy? What if the new leader of Untergang created a persona designed to appeal to the worst in people, to bring the citizens of New York around to his cause, his war on crime, which would, of course, then become a war against 'urban crime'. Or some other little euphemism." Doc smiled. "'Inhuman', for example. Sounds a lot more relatable than *sub*human, doesn't it? Comes to the same thing, though. Anyway, what if there *is* a new leader of Untergang, masquerading as a faceless, fearless crime-killer in order to sway public opinion towards fascism?

"And what if it's you?"

He knows.

The Blood-Spider raised his gun. Suddenly he was completely calm. There were no more choices now, no more chances. *He knows. One bullet, that's all it will take. He has to go.*

Doc Thunder must die.

And then Doc Thunder turned around and looked him right in

the face.

"People get so worked up about the bulletproof skin and the bending steel that they always forget about my eyes. I can read small print from a hundred feet away. And I can see in the dark." He smiled, and cracked another knuckle.

"Hello, Blood-Spider."

Then he cocked his head, suddenly puzzled. "Wait. You know I'm –"

Under his mask, the Blood-Spider smiled –

– aimed his gun full of magic bullets straight at Doc's heart –

– and fired.

CHAPTER FOURTEEN

Doc Thunder Must Die

Doc HAD SPOTTED the Blood-Spider as soon as he'd walked into the station.

He figured he'd get rid of the civilians before making his move, so the Spider couldn't use them against him. That was when he'd had the revelation about the Blood-Spider's true identity. He was so busy connecting those dots in his mind, he failed to ask the obvious question.

Namely, if nothing less than a bursting shell could penetrate Doc Thunder's skin...

...why was the Blood-Spider bringing a gun to a mortar fight?

It was a question that didn't occur to him until he was staring down the barrel of the Blood-Spider's gun – the one he'd assumed was harmless as far as he was concerned. If the Spider had fired earlier, rather than waiting until he had an almost point-blank shot, Doc would have died instantly as the inexorium bullet tore through his heart.

As it was, he was able to realise his error in time and throw himself to the side – enough for the bullet to smash his left shoulder instead of hitting his chest. He went down hard, trying to roll back onto his feet, to keep moving.

Inexorium bullets. Unbelievable. Evidently taking N.I.G.H.T.M.A.R.E. out of commission had led to a lot of their technology being released onto the black market. Presumably he could expect a rematch with Titanicus any day now.

And that was the possibility that would let him sleep at night. Because that would mean N.I.G.H.T.M.A.R.E. was really gone. That they weren't wrapped up in this somehow, behind it all, puppet-masters pulling the strings.

He'd never found Silken Dragon's body.

He put that thought out of his mind – right now, he needed to concentrate on survival. The only advantage he had in this open space was that inexorium bullets were so prohibitively expensive. The Spider would not have too many. One hit near his feet, chewing into the tile and concrete and spitting up fragments. Unlike an ordinary bullet, it would not distort on impact, like the one that had passed so effortlessly through this shoulder, that one could be recycled if someone dug it up.

And if there was a moral to the last few days, it was that nothing ever stayed buried.

Doc hurled himself behind the abandoned sushi stall – a massive thing the size of a car and normally staffed by two smiling brothers from Kyoto – seconds before a third bullet plowed through the wasabi tray and out of the back, missing him by inches.

I've got to keep him on the high ground, Doc thought. *If he's firing those things into the ground, that's one thing. If he fires them horizontally through a wall, people in the street outside are going to start losing major organs.* He waited for another shot – nothing came. The Spider was waiting for him to make a break. *With the price of magic bullets these days, he can't afford to waste them. How many does he have left?*

His shoulder was already clotting, but it'd be useless for at least a day, maybe two. He'd probably have to rebreak the bone so it regenerated properly. He thought of Miles Hamilton then, of how he'd supervised such operations in the past, and frowned. "Spider!"

"I have nothing to say to you, Thunder. We're past conversation at this point."

"You set this up." He rubbed his wounded shoulder with his free hand. "You told Venger to get my blood, didn't you? He was acting on your orders!"

The Blood-Spider laughed, that terrible laugh from some ultimate circle of Hell. *"Don't be a fool!"*

"It makes too much sense to be coincidence!" Thunder roared. "You shot Monk because you knew how I'd react! You knew I'd do anything to save him! And you had your pet, Venger, waiting!"

Another echoing laugh.

"I thought you were a scientist, Thunder. Don't fudge the evidence to fit your hypothesis. Venger was working for another player. Someone Untergang would dearly like to meet. Tell me, Doctor, before I end your life, do you have any idea what 'fifty fifty' could mean? Venger kept repeating it."

Doc shook his head. Venger had mentioned it during their conversation on the hospital roof, almost as a taunt. Fifty fifty. Equal odds. Six of one, half a dozen of the other. What did it mean?

"I'm afraid my Nazi party membership seems to have lapsed, Spider. So as much as I'd like to help you bring your fascist insanity to my town, I'm afraid you're right – we're beyond conversation."

"Then die!"

Another bullet chewed through a tray of cucumber rolls, then the wood and metal of the trolley, and finally tore denim, grazing Doc Thunder's leg and leaving him with a red, burning line of agony against his thigh. Another shot would probably puncture his belly. And again, there was that cruel, murderous laugh, echoing with pure, uncontrollable evil.

Doc Thunder wondered how long the Blood-Spider had been mad.

"Give it up, Doctor. I'll make it quick for you. Come on, there's no way you can win! Look at the mathematics! I've got bullets

that can blow through anything you hide behind like it was tissue paper, and what have you got? Nothing!"

"I beg to differ."

Doc grabbed hold of the bottom of the sushi cart, testing its weight. Slightly under three quarters of a ton. He took a firm grip on it–

–and then he stood up.

Behind the implacable lenses of his mask, the Blood-Spider's eyes widened. *"No. It can't be! It can't be!"*

Doc Thunder stood, one arm hanging limp at his side, the other raised above his head, three quarters of a ton of metal and wood sat in his palm as if it were a Frisbee, slivers of raw fish and rice and glittering chips of ice tumbling from the trays balanced precariously on top of the massive cart. "Oh yes it can."

He grinned a wolfish grin.

"Heads up."

With his one good arm, he threw the cart like a baseball, aiming it straight at the Blood-Spider's head. The Spider reacted instantly, hurling himself from his high perch up on the arches as the cart exploded into matchwood where he'd been standing just a moment before.

He turned in the air, reaching out with his free hand to touch the smooth pillar, and Doc noticed for the first time that upon the Blood-Spider's gloves and the soles of his boots were dozens of tiny suction cups. He watched, fascinated, as these devices allowed the Blood-Spider to slow his fall, skidding down the smooth marble pillar with a squeal of rubber on stone, turning a fall which would surely have shattered his shinbones into splinters into something which he could walk away from.

Doc Thunder did not intend to let him walk away.

He charged forward, pulling back his good hand, balling it into a fist. The Blood-Spider reacted instinctively, leaping off the pillar and going into a tuck and roll just as Thunder's massive fist crashed into the pillar where he had been, smashing a huge chunk out of the ornate stone. Another man might have broken his hand. Doc Thunder barely even skinned his knuckles.

The Blood-Spider rolled back onto his feet, the automatic in his hand spitting another of the deadly inexorium bullets through the meat of Thunder's thigh. Thunder cried out through gritted teeth, sinking down onto one knee, clutching at the wound, trying to staunch the flow from his femoral artery long enough for it to clot.

Too bad the mysterious Mr. Fifty isn't around to take my blood now, he thought. *There's a pint or three here he could soak up, if he brought a sponge...*

Something about that nagged at him. Fifty fifty...

Behind him, the Blood-Spider rose to his full height.

"It's a wound that would probably kill a normal man, unless it was treated instantly. All you have to do is keep yourself from losing too much blood, and you'll be fine. It does mean you can't move your leg, or move your hands away from your leg. You're as helpless as a kitten until the flow stops... but that's a small price to pay, isn't it? You'd probably be able to stand on that leg in a few minutes... if you had a few minutes."

Doc winced. The Spider had a point. If he took his hand off the wound, he'd be dead in seconds, his own superhuman heart forcing the blood out of him like a water cannon. There was no way he could reach and disarm him without dying.

The Blood-Spider examined his automatic, taking his time. *"One bullet left. It's a shame, really, Donner. Just think, if not for Strucker's unfortunate little heart problem, you might have been the leader of a new race of Nazi Supermen. Something to think about on your road to the grave."*

He raised the gun, aiming the barrel directly at Thunder's head.

"Goodbye, Doc Thunder –"

A sword spun out of the darkness above, whirring around and around like the twirled baton in a marching band, the razor point of it slicing across the Blood-Spider's forearm, leaving a deep gash and causing his wrist to jerk, sending the fatal bullet off course to lodge inside the thick marble pillar behind Thunder's head. The sword clanged against the marble floor, bounced in a shivering arc, then slid a few more feet, slowly spinning, and came to a gentle stop.

The Blood-Spider screamed, roaring both with the pain of his slashed forearm and the rage of knowing that he had missed his last chance to kill Doc Thunder. He looked at the sword, the eyes behind the lenses narrowed in furious agony, then threw his gun to one side and reached for it, a trickle of blood coursing down his wounded arm and onto the blade.

He could still kill Thunder. There were weak points – the eyes, the mouth, anywhere one of his bullets had already pierced flesh and the wound had not closed. He would thrust the sword through the eye and into the brain, or through the shoulder wound and down into the heart, quickly, before Thunder could react. And if he raised his hand to prevent it, if he took his hand away from the torn artery that threatened to release his life's blood onto the marbled floor – that would also kill him.

The Spider gripped the sword's hilt. He could still do this. He could still –

"Amigo... that's *my* sword."

The voice came from the darkness above them, where the gaslight did not reach. The Spider's blood ran cold for a long moment, and then he grabbed hold of his other gun, tearing it from its holster and raising it to fire a volley of bullets into the darkness. *"Where are you? Show yourself!"* he hissed, turning in place, the gun raised to fire at the slightest sound or movement.

"You're not the only one who can hide in the shadows, my friend. I've got very good at it, over the years."

The Spider whirled around and fired off another three shots, aiming where he thought the voice might have come from, expecting a cry of pain, a falling body, but only hearing the sounds of lead impacting against the plaster of the roof and the sound of his shell casings tinkling against the echoing marble floor. *"Where are you? WHERE ARE YOU?"* Suddenly his mask felt hot, constricting. He could smell his own sweat in it, feel it pressing against his cheeks, his forehead. *"No. No, no, no..."*

"Old man Donner was right about you, amigo. Right about the other you, I mean. Parker Crane."

"Shut up! That's not my name!" the Spider screamed, helplessly, shrieking it into the darkness. *"Show yourself!"* Another volley

of shots, with no result. Was he throwing his voice? Was he everywhere at once? Was he a shadow himself? A ghost?

The voice echoed from another place now, continuing his speech exactly where he had left off. "He said you were crazy, and under pressure you were going to crack up. Okay, that's *all* he said about you, but that was enough. That told me you were worth watching."

"Shut up!" Another volley of shots into the darkness, and now the gun was light in his hand and the floor was littered with the cases of wasted shells. And still that mocking voice echoed from the shadows above.

"See, I didn't know if you were a good guy or a bad guy. I mean, sure, you killed people, and you were kind of a dick about it, you know? But I didn't know if you were one of the bastards. I didn't know if you needed to die or not, amigo."

"I said shut –" The Spider whirled, aiming the gun and pulling the trigger, sending another bullet screaming off at nothing–

– and then the gun clicked empty.

He was out of bullets.

He turned, looking at Doc Thunder, and saw him take his hand away from his leg, revealing a pulsing red scab. In another moment, maybe two, he'd be able to stand.

He turned again, and there was the man in the red mask. Just standing there, in the middle of the concourse. His smile didn't look human. And his *eyes*. Oh, his terrible eyes...

"Stay back." The Spider whispered, and his voice sounded in his ears like a frightened, animal thing, waiting to curl up and die in its hole.

The man in the red mask only laughed. A rich, deep, joyous laugh, a laugh that echoed and filled the whole station, bouncing from pillar to pillar, careening through the great vaulted arches. Such a laugh!

Then the laughter stopped, and he fixed the Blood-Spider with a look that would freeze the fires of Hell.

"My sword. Don't make me ask again."

And suddenly – quite suddenly – there was no Blood-Spider.

There was only Parker Crane, the Nazi. Parker Crane, the traitor. Parker Crane, who thought he could destroy America, and only managed to destroy himself.

Parker Crane. Just a man wearing a mask.

He ran, and left the sword behind him.

Doc Thunder watched, bemused, as the Spider – what was his name? Crane? – hurled the sword away from him and bolted from the concourse. "Nice trick," he murmured, turning to the masked man. "Throwing your sword from up on the balcony – good aim, by the way – then throwing your voice and a little mental suggestion to make him think you were up in the arches where he'd been. My hat's off. Where did you learn that?"

The masked man shrugged, lifting up his weapon, checking that the impact against the marble floor hadn't damaged it. "In the desert. You can learn a lot in the desert, if you put your mind to it."

"Good psychology, too." Doc nodded, gently prodding the healing wound. He could feel the muscles knitting together. Not long now. "Although I think whatever you did there might have pushed him over the edge of whatever mental breakdown he was heading towards..."

"Just my latin charm, amigo," shrugged the masked man, looking at the wound slowly healing in Thunder's leg. "Ouch. You need a doctor?"

Doc Thunder blinked. *Latin.* He shook his head. "Give me a second." He gritted his teeth, and put his weight on the damaged leg. It wasn't too agonising. Slowly, he stood. "I think I'm good to go. We need to get after him before he loses himself. He's a danger to the general public, and besides, he needs to pay for what he did to Monk." He turned to the masked man, putting out his hand, smiling ruefully. "I owe you an apology, by the way. I was wrong to accuse you."

The masked man laughed. "Well, maybe I was wrong to call you a monster, hey? Nobody gets to choose their parents, my friend." His palm slapped against Thunder's, and they shook.

"I don't think I caught your name, by the way." Doc Thunder smiled.

"El Sombra." said El Sombra.

And then two highly trained police officers burst into Grand Central Station and began shooting at him.

A MINUTE EARLIER, Crane pulled off his mask, quickly folding the leather part flat and sliding it into his inside coat-pocket, and dove into the crowd outside the station. A cop grabbed his shoulder, and another leant into his face, scowling. "Hey, buddy, don't you know nobody gets to go in there? Doc Thunder's orders!"

"I –" Crane's face was a mass of sweat and raw panic. "I went to the toilet. When I came out, it was all happening! A man in a mask... I think he's an illegal alien! He's trying to kill Doc Thunder!" The cops looked at each other, then tore into the station, guns drawn.

Like sheep, Crane thought. *Tell them to herd, and they herd.* He snarled, his contempt rising like bile, then ran towards the meeting place where Marlene would be waiting. Faithful Marlene, who had taken to the cause like a duck to water...

Water. His feet were splashing in it.

His eyes widened as he took in the sight – the Silver Ghost with its bonnet open, water trickling from the underside, and Marlene, bent over like a salacious pinup as she tinkered with the engine, desperately trying to bring back life to a machine that was now dead forever. She looked up as he approached.

"Parker? What are you doing here–" Her eyes widened as she saw what he was wearing. "You...?" She blinked, taking a step back.

"What happened?" He barked at her, eyes blazing. "I gave you one duty! One responsibility! One! And you – oh, you stupid little *whore!*"

"Parker, you can't talk to me that–" She was interrupted by a slap from his open palm that sent her to the ground, blood trickling from a split lip. She looked up at him, eyes wide with shock. "You – you *hit* me!"

His eyes blazed at her. "You can think yourself damned lucky I didn't shoot you!"

She shook her head, eyes gazing at him in - was that astonishment? Or disgust? Or both? "But you're supposed to be the *Blood-Spider* -"

He looked back, staring down at her in impotent fury, then reached into his coat, pulling out the mask and hurling it at her. "There's your precious Blood-Spider," he muttered. Then he turned, rushing out into the street, leaving her where she lay.

"Cab! Damn you, cab! *Cab!*"

Picking herself up, Marlene watched as Parker pulled himself into a hansom cab, yelled a tirade of obscenities at the driver, and sped off in the direction of the East Village. That was the Blood-Spider, then. Nothing but Parker. Parker, wearing a mask and in over his head. And Parker, her debonair, dashing Parker - *he* was nothing but a vicious little thug when the chips were down.

Dimly, she realised that her life as she knew it was over. Whatever Parker had been up to, there would be repercussions. Easton would want her to make some dreadful statements to the police. Jack would probably call her a traitor. After all, Doc Thunder was a national resource, and hadn't she known, deep down, that Parker was trying to kill him? She just hadn't wanted to believe it. Or perhaps she'd wanted to believe that he actually had a chance.

Time for that suitcase, she mused.

What hurt the most wasn't the slap, or the growing horror of having to leave her whole life behind her. It was the disappointment of knowing that, at the end of it all, the great Blood-Spider was just another man.

But did he have to be?

She picked up the mask, looking into those eight implacable lenses, thinking about the war on crime, and her own words. *The most fabulous thing is to believe in something utterly and completely, without restraint.*

When she walked away from the dead auto, into the darkness of the alley, she was wearing it.

*   *   *

"...WELL, THANKS FOR the prompt response, all the same." Doc sighed to the sheepish Officer Rawls, as he examined the fresh bullet holes in his blue shirt. Sooner or later, he was going to run out of these.

Fortunately, he'd managed to shield El Sombra with his body, but the masked man had reacted immediately, delivering a brutal kick into the face of Officer Valchek – who was still unconscious – and very nearly running the other one through before Thunder could stop him.

He turned to El Sombra, frowning. "Impetuous, aren't you? Which reminds me, we're going to have to have a talk after all this is over about the number of bodies you've left behind you."

El Sombra raised an eyebrow behind his mask. "What, you've never had a few deaths on your conscience? At least I only get the bad guys killed, hey?"

"And having beaten up two police officers, you're now trying to start a fight with me. Wonderful." Doc Thunder sighed, rubbing his shoulder. The bone was starting to heal, but he wasn't going to be able to lift that arm properly any time soon. He'd have to fight with one. "More of that latin charm, I take it?"

He never heard El Sombra's reply.

Latin.

"Oh God," he breathed. "How could I have..."

"...do you have any idea what 'fifty-fifty' could mean?..."

"...wait until you see Plan C..."

"...want him out of my hair for a while..."

"...if I were you... I'd do a lot of things differently..."

"...I thought he'd never get here..."

...El Sombra was waving his hand in front of Doc's face.

"Hey, amigo – you okay?"

"Fifty-fifty." Doc said, slowly. "I knew it. I knew there was someone behind all this. Nothing ever stays buried." He swallowed. "But I was looking in the wrong place. Latin numerals, you see?"

El Sombra gave him a puzzled look. "Amigo... what the hell are you talking about?"

"In the Latin language, the numbers are represented by letters. I for one, X for ten. And for fifty... L. So fifty-fifty... is L.L." He stared off into the distance.

"I think we may already be too late."

CRANE HAMMERED HIS fist on the metal door, yelling for Timothy Larson to let him in. Eventually, the door opened.

"Whoa... Parker Crane, out of sight! What brings you here?" Larson smiled, taking a long sip from a freshly brewed mug of coffee. "Listen, let me get you some java–"

"I don't need your damned java!" Crane hissed, grabbing hold of the lapels of his shirt and slamming him against the wall. "I need the blood! Tell me you've got something–"

"Hey, easy..." Larson frowned, pushing Parker gently away and then closing the door with a small clang. "Listen, you need to just chill out for a second, okay? Just relax. Everything's going to be fine, you know?" He smiled, putting a hand gently on Crane's shoulder. "I know some great meditation exercises you could try."

Crane slapped his hand away. "Shut up! I need to know what you've found in that blood, and I need it now! Don't you understand, Doc Thunder knows everything! He's probably on his way here now–" Crane suddenly froze. "Wait, how do you know my –"

Larson smiled. "Well, I've got good news and bad news. The good news is, I got the big secret Untergang's been after all these years. A serum that'll give Doc Thunder's brand of the right stuff to any adult who takes it." He raised his hands. "I know, I know, I'm a genius. No applause, just throw money. That's my motto."

Crane took a step back. Suddenly, Larson seemed like a completely different person. "I – I only ever spoke to you as the Blood-Spider. How do you even know who Parker Crane is?"

"No flies on you, Parker! That's what I like about you, you're smart. Smart enough to think you're the smartest guy in the world, which is my *favourite* level of smart, because there's only *one* smartest guy in the world and he likes people to underestimate him. Anyway, the bad news – there was only enough serum for one, and I didn't feel like sharing. Sorry 'bout that. Guess you don't get to be President after all, but that's politics." Larson grinned, reaching and tearing away his moustache and beard, then rubbing his chin. "Any makeup glue left? I want to look my best for company."

Crane shook his head, his eyes wide, sweat beading on his face. "What... what are you talking about? How do you know about Untergang? About my plan..."

Larson lifted off his shaggy wig, revealing a gleaming bald pate. "*My* plan. You were just a useful tool, Parker, but now that I'm packed full of that serum – and let's just test that out–" He calmly picked up a steel test tube rack, and Crane watched in horror as he slowly twisted it into a double helix, as easily as twisting a wire coat hanger. "Huh! Wasn't sure that'd work. Anyway, Parker, I've got a spot for a dogsbody, but that's about it. So unless you want to be test number two of my amazing new Thunder Serum..." His eyes narrowed. "I'd lay off the attitude when you talk to me."

Crane's mouth was dry. "Who are you?" He whispered.

The bald man grinned. "Why, I'm the most dangerous man in the world, kid. Timothy Larson Lomax, at your service."

He stuck out his hand.

"But everybody calls me Lars."

CHAPTER FIFTEEN

The Last Case

"So, I UNDERSTAND you were wondering who killed Heinrich Donner?"

Lars Lomax sipped his coffee. He'd asked Crane to make it for him, with a cold, hard inflection in his voice that made it clear he wasn't asking at all. Now Crane shrank up against the wall, as if trying to escape through it. Lomax was between him and the door and, if he wanted to, he could put down that coffee, reach out with his hand and twist off Crane's head. He could do it as easily as scratch his own.

And he was mad. Quite mad. Crane was certain of it.

"It was me. My bad." Lomax smiled, waggling his eyebrows. "I mean, I didn't pull the trigger – or, you know, shove the sword in him – but I've got to take the credit. It's kind of a complicated story, though..." He frowned, then drained the last of his coffee, setting the cup back down with a shake of his head. "I don't know if you want to hear it. I mean, this is... on the scale of intricate master plans, this is about a nine. I'd have to be some kind of egomaniac to start boring you with the full thing. Let me tell you, it gets pret-ty crazy in places. You sure you want to hear the whole enchilada?"

Crane shook his head. "Just... just let me go." He shook his head, voice wheedling. "You've got what you want."

"Of course you do! Atta boy!" Lomax laughed, clapping Crane on the shoulder hard enough to knock him sideways to the floor. "And I've got to admit, I love this part. Seriously, it's burning a hole in me. I've got to tell *somebody* how I did it, and I can't tell Thunder, because that's the part where he usually escapes and kicks my ass. I figure this time I'll get it out of the way early and kick *his* instead. So why don't you pull up some floor there and I'll tell you the true story of how Lars Lomax died and was born again after a thousand and one nights to ascend to exalted glory? Kind of like Jesus meets the Arabian Nights." He shook his head, chuckling, and pulled up a chair, which creaked under his weight. His shirt was already starting to bulge as the muscles underneath began to expand. Every time Crane looked at him, he seemed larger, more menacing.

Hands shaking, Crane poured another coffee.

"I guess it all started when I realised what Anton Venger's big problem was."

He smiled, closing his eyes and breathing in the steam from the cup. Crane eyed the door. Could he reach it before...?

"Anton Venger and me, we made a good team." Lomax looked up, his brown eyes boring into Crane's. "Well, from his point of view, it was more than a team. That business with his face... he was desperate for any kind of affection after that, you know? He latched onto it like a remora. Show the slightest pretence of kindness and he'd follow you anywhere, especially if you happened to hate the same people. So... well, he might have seen our relationship as being something more intimate than just being business partners." He sipped his coffee, then shrugged. "I mean, okay, I'm not saying I never took advantage. He could look like anybody, you know? Put a poncho on him and it was like getting blown by Marilyn Monroe. I'm not proud." He took another swallow. "What's in this? Hazelnut?"

Crane jerked, as if stung. "N-no, I –"

"Or cyanide? I did leave some lying around." He grinned, looking Crane in the eye, and suddenly the rich brown of his eyes was a bright, piercing red. He offered the cup to Crane, who shrank back, pressing back against the wall of the little room. "What's the matter? Don't want any?"

Crane shook his head, too afraid to speak. Lomax was perhaps six inches taller now than when he'd come in, and the seams of his clothes were starting to come apart under the pressure of his expanding form.

Lomax grinned, and something was wrong with his teeth.

"Sure? I could make you drink it. Might teach you a lesson." He drained the cup, then passed it to Crane. "More. And this time go easy on the poison. Just half a spoon for flavour."

He leaned back, the chair creaking in protest. "Anyway, me and Venger were a team. He was crazy about me – literally – and I strung him along because he was about the most useful guy you could imagine. Except." He sighed, flexing his fingers, watching them thicken. "If you know there's a master of disguise running around who can't do emotions, then suddenly your master of disguise isn't that useful any more. Hey! There's a guy who doesn't smile and speaks in a monotone! It must be Anton Venger! Get the cuffs!"

He looked off into the distance. "God, that voice was creepy. That monotone voice singing 'Happy Birthday, Mister President...' I didn't ask him to do that again." He shook his head, as if shaking off the memory. "Anyway, it occurred to me that things would run a lot more smoothly if he was dead. If the world knew Anton Venger was dead – if Doc Thunder had told them so – well, everybody would stop looking for him, right?"

He stretched, and the shirt burst off his back, splitting right down the middle. Crane started, making a little whimper. Lomax just smiled.

"It was a great plan. Team up with N.I.G.H.T.M.A.R.E., have a very public falling-out with Venger, dose him with something I invented that'll slow down his life signs to the point of death, then – while Thunder's being tortured to death, which is a nice little bonus – go rat Silken Dragon out to S.T.E.A.M. and hole up somewhere until the fireworks are all done with. I already had people in place to fake the autopsy and ship the body to a secure location..." He took the fresh coffee from Crane, taking a sip. "No cyanide at all in this one! What did I tell you?"

"I – I thought you were joking." Crane looked at the door again. Only a few feet away. If he ran now–

"I never joke about coffee. You're starting to get on my last nerve, Parker. Maybe I'll pop your head like a zit and see what comes out." He followed Crane's line of sight. "Don't look at the door, Parker. You'll never reach it in time. You don't mind me calling you Parker, do you, Parker? I figure after all these fun times we had together – you know, you pushing me around, treating me like a joke, like your pet science gimp – I figured we'd be on first name terms by now. I never kill people I'm on first name terms with. Are we on first name terms, Parker?"

Crane swallowed, hard. He couldn't look away from Lomax now. Every few seconds, a new muscle would pop up on his shoulders, like a bubble coming to the surface of a lake. A lake of skin. The veins on his arms were starting to pulse a livid purple.

He didn't look like Doc Thunder at all.

He looked stronger.

"Parker! Focus!" Lomax yelled, and his voice was a deep, angry growl.

"Yes." Crane whispered. "Yes... Lars."

"Actually, my first name's Timothy, but nobody calls me that. Even my parents called me Happy." Lomax laughed. "And believe you me, I'm happy now. Anyway... the plan. The big plan to rehabilitate Anton Venger as a productive corpse. It all went off without a hitch, unless you count Thunder breaking out early and clocking me upside the head with a big chunk of masonry. By the time I broke out of prison, Venger had spent six months in a packing crate in a state of living death." He shrugged. "Didn't do a lot for his personality, frankly. He was even more devoted to me when I got him out, on account of how he thought I'd saved his life. The plain fact of the matter is I could have left him in there a lot longer and I kind of wish I had..." He paused, looking at the way the thick red hairs were growing on the back of his hand.

"Anyway, I needed to keep him sweet, give him some kind of

reward for all the time he spent in that crate. So I figured we'd go kill the Blue Ghost. He was getting old, getting slow. He was basically just a mascot for that bike gang his foster kid formed, so I figured, okay, we'll knock him off, give Anton something to keep him from going completely off the rails." Lomax looked at Crane, eyes steely. "Only we were too late, weren't we? Why don't you pick up the story from here, Parker?"

Crane shook his head. "I don't know what you –"

"Oh, *please.* You were the fresh new head of Untergang after whatever old coot that replaced Donner finally retired. You had a lot of big, sexy plans. Not as sexy as mine, but pretty big and sexy nonetheless. You took a look at the Blue Ghost – mysterious masked avenger, operatives all over the place, big fan-following with the working classes, and you figured... we need one of those. Just take away the Japanese orphan kid and replace him with a foxy Aryan chick – and how's Marlene doing, anyway?"

Crane spluttered. "How do you know about –"

"Wouldn't you like to know? Anyway, give your brand new Blue Ghost some guns so he's not getting beaten up all the time, package it all up to appeal to Untergang's core voters... I've got to hand it to you, Parker, I know a winning strategy when I see one. There was just one thing wrong, wasn't there?" Crane shook his head, unable to meet Lomax's eyes. They were entirely red now, the white of the eye subsumed, the pupils two black dots in a bloody sea.

Lomax laughed. Crane didn't dare to look.

He had fangs.

"You needed a vacancy! There's no point being the all-new, all-Nazi Blue Ghost if the old Ghost's still around, right? So you strangled him with your own two hands and dropped his body off a pier, and poor little Easton West's been trying to solve the murder ever since! I felt for the guy, I can tell you. And poor Anton! That was all he'd been thinking about for months in his box, and you got there first. Shame on you!" Lomax shook his head, the red eyes burning with mock indignation.

"He wanted to do away with you there and then. In fact, he was all for killing you and taking your place. Running Untergang for our own concerns. I thought about it, I'll admit..." Lomax stood, rubbing the base of his spine. His head almost banged against the ceiling of the room, three feet above Crane's head. "But... that was a little too obvious. I wanted all the benefits of taking over your whole organisation without any of the downsides of actually having to run it. I mean, who wants to run Untergang? Not even *you* want to run Untergang! You've driven it into the ground while you lived out your crazy vigilante fantasy!"

He smiled, turning to Crane and leaning down. Crane thought he smelled brimstone on the monster's breath.

"So *that's* when I came up with the *real* plan. Get ready, Parker."

He loosened his belt enough for the tail that was growing out of his spine to poke over it.

"This is where it gets *weird.*"

"...THAT'S RIGHT." Doc Thunder nodded, as the bike cop put another quarter into the payphone and wound the clockwork handle on the side. Doc gave him a brief thumbs-up and continued talking into the mouthpiece. "I've got El Sombra with me. Yes, the man with the sword, Donner's killer. No, he hasn't put a shirt on. Look, we're going to go try to catch Lomax before he gets away, but I need you to call Jack Scorpio and co-ordinate with S.T.E.A.M. If Lomax has done what I think he's done, the army might not be enough." He listened for a moment, then broke in. "Okay. If I don't come back inside six hours... well, you know. Bye." He put the phone down and sighed.

"Trouble with the missus?" the cop asked. Doc blinked.

"You're very perceptive, Officer... McNulty, was it?"

McNulty nodded. "The way you ended your call. Listen, last time me and the wife had some trouble, you know what I got her? A baby pig."

"A baby pig." Doc rubbed his forehead. "Officer–"

"Mr. Porkins, we call him." The cop smiled brightly. "'Course, he's a little bigger now, and it's hell hiding him from the building super, but as soon as Joanie saw his cute little nose wrinkle it up, she forgot all about the whores."

Doc sighed. "Thanks, Officer. I'll bear that in mind." He turned to see El Sombra walking out of the station, cleaning marble fragments off his sword. "What took you so long?"

"Just a hunch, amigo. Who knows, it might end up paying off, hey? Could make all the difference." The masked man patted the pocket of his suit trousers.

Doc rubbed his temples again, shaking his head gently. "Fine. Get up on my back, and hold tight – hook an arm through the back of my shirt. This is going to get bumpy. You remember where we're going? East Village, right?"

El Sombra looked sideways at him. "What, you're going to fly there?"

Doc nodded. "Close enough. Let's go."

He jumped.

LOMAX PACED SLOWLY around the boxy, closed-in room, his tail twitching and swishing to and fro like a cat's.

"First of all, Anton Venger needed to take Miles Hamilton's place. If I wanted to get Thunder's blood, that was the best way to do it. Get Venger undercover and wait for him to get his personal physician to supervise a blood transfusion. Bound to happen within a year, two at the most." He laughed, sourly. "Ha! Well, the best laid plans, and so on. Anyway, I couldn't send Hamilton in if I was still on the loose. Thunder would smell a rat. He'd probably smell a rat anyway. *And* I needed a way to get in with your people, so I'd have access to all your equipment and knowhow. If I tried extracting the serum from Thunder's blood on my own, well, I'd probably end up giving myself nut cancer. But standing on the shoulders of your giants..." He turned, giving another hideous, fanged grin. "How am I doing? Better than the real thing, right?" He flexed his immense hands, marvelling at the carpet of red hair that now reached from his back all the way down each arm.

"The answer? Combine it all into one. Kidnap Hamilton, hand him over to Venger's tender mercies – and Venger had a lot of frustration to take out by this point, let me tell you – and then play the whole thing out with Venger in Hamilton's place."

"P-play what out?" Crane was slumped in a corner by this time, clutching at his head, staring at the thing Lomax was becoming, step by awful step, in front of him.

"My death, of course! My beautiful death! Torturing Hamilton in front of Doc's lovely assistant! I'd kidnapped her for the purpose of leaving Doc some obvious clues. All on a big balloon filled with enough hydrogen to set the whole damn place on fire when I fired a bullet through it! Except for the nose, of course – fireproof, crashproof, loaded with supplies for an unscheduled stopover in the Amazon rainforest, and also loaded with Hamilton's skeleton, de-fleshed and pre-charred to take my place. I do my big torture scene, and of course with Venger's squishy face it doesn't do more than tickle, then in comes Thunder, we fight, *bang* goes the gun! Fire everywhere!" Lomax gleefully acted it out, his huge muscled arms sending tables filled with equipment flying, glass shattering against the walls and floor. The tables were solid oak, but to the thing Lomax had become, there were as light and flimsy as paper.

Crane felt his bladder let go.

"Thunder rescues his steady – rescues 'Hamilton'–" The creature held up crooked fingers to make the quotation marks. "–and I crash into the rainforest, ejecting my skeletal stand-in into the flaming wreckage before taking off to hide out in the deepest darkest jungle for a while. Needless to say, poor old Doc's too distracted by the flame-grilled crispy death of his number one foe to look too closely at Venger. And even if he wasn't, what's he going to say? Hamilton's not acting like himself? The guy just got through being tortured! And even if Doc does think Hamilton's gone weird, he's not going to think 'oh no, Anton Venger', since he saw Anton Venger die and all... I mean, it's perfect–" He stopped, sniffing the air.

"*Christ*, Parker! Do you know how that smells through these nostrils? I thought you were meant to be a dark avenger of the night?" Lomax leaned down, the vertebrae on his back pushing up through his skin, making small popping sounds. "Seriously, haven't you ever seen a man turning into a monster before?"

"The serum." Crane croaked. "It doesn't work properly. This – this is too much –"

Lomax laughed. "Says you. It's underperforming as far as I'm concerned. I wanted devil horns." He rubbed his temples experimentally. "Nope, nothing yet. Seriously, Parker, do you honestly think I wanted to be as good as Thunder? What's the point of that? He'll just call in S.T.E.A.M. or Maya's Leopard Warriors Of The Something-Something or, I don't know, that British guy, what's his name? Troy Mercury? Perseus Quicklime? You know who I mean, Untergang must have a file on him a foot thick." He shrugged. "Whatever. I need to be big enough to beat them *all*, Parker. Everybody in his little black book, one at a time or all together." He paused, scratching his chin. "My thinking's getting a little random, though, I'll admit. I keep getting this craving for raw meat. Where did I get up to?"

Crane shook his head, despairing. "You faked your death."

"I faked my death! Slimmed down on the trek back from the rainforest, invested in a wig and a beard and came back as Professor Timothy Larson, harmless opium proponent and total freak. Just the kind of guy you need to do work for you – criminal record, doesn't like cops, pro social justice, which is I think how you sold the whole 'war on crime' bill of goods to me... I was just what you needed. A top-flight scientist with no Untergang connections. A nice clean pair of hands."

Crane looked up at the monster. All terror had left him, for the moment. He only felt numb. Disconnected. "I thought Timothy Larson was real. We did background checks. That business with the opium in the water..."

Lomax laughed. "That's what makes it such a great alias! It *was* me. Just a different me, that's all." He cocked his head at Crane's mystified look. "Fine, the short version. I was born Timothy Larson Lomax, in Brooklyn. Willy – my dad – was an asshole, a pathetic little salesman, a phony little fake. All big dreams with no payoff. He died the way he lived, a failure. My big brother was headed the same way, too. Well, not me. I got out, went to college, got my professorship – as Timothy Larson. I didn't want to use Dad's name. Not back then."

"You know the rest. Big in the early futurehead movement, the merry prankster version. Friends with Warhol. A big proponent of the opium culture. I actually did talk like that back then. Like, don't you think you should say hello to a tree today, maaaan? It's so, like, beautiful." He grinned, his new fangs prominent in his mouth, sharp and cruel. His head was starting to bump against the ceiling, leaving dents in the plaster, and small spurs of bone were pushing out through the backs of his ankles. "I got busted for trying to put an opium derivative in the water supply, trying to turn everybody in New York on at once. The first big plan. And you know what? I liked it. The rush of knowing that a whole city could start dancing to your tune – the power trip. It was a one-hit addiction, Parker, my boy. I wanted to do that kind of thing full-time. I wanted to remake society into what I wanted it to be. And I kind of figured I owed it to my Dad to make Lomax the name the whole world feared. I don't know if he'd have wanted it that way, but... well, I thought it was funny anyway. Professor Tim Larson died, and Lars Lomax was born. "

Crane slumped back against the wall, staring listlessly at the black crust forming on the soles of Lomax's feet. "And when Lars Lomax died..."

"Re-enter Timothy Larson. So now I had my man in place to grab the blood, and all the equipment and notes to become the beautiful creature of God you see before you today." Lomax sat on one of the heavy tables, crushing the glass bottles and tubes resting there under him. As the table creaked under his weight, a hissing stream of acid ran from the smashed equipment, gouging a deep crevice in the thick wood before dripping off the table-top and onto the back of his leg.

He didn't seem to notice.

"And then nothing happened. Nobody needed a transfusion. A year went by. Two. Your little scheme went plodding along pretty much as I expected, in that it was an excuse for you to play vigilante and bone hot chicks on Der Fuehrer's dime. Venger was getting restless, and he'd managed to alienate Thunder completely, what with all his clumsy attempts to get that blood. I mean, he was pretty much asking Thunder to approve a private fascist militia made up of supermen. *Nice work Anton.* So there was pretty much no chance he'd go to him unless it was a total emergency. I tried setting up a couple of those, but no go. Nobody ever got hurt badly enough. My big plan was a washout. And then..."

He smiled, licking his fangs. "...El Sombra hit town."

Crane blinked. "Who?"

Lomax slammed his fist into the wall, leaving a crater in the concrete. "That's what I mean about you! You're the head of Untergang. Act like it! Call home! Daddy Hitler's got a file on this guy he could use as a doorstop!" He shook his head in disgust. "He's the half-naked guy with the sword, okay? He kills Nazis. That's all he does. It's his entire shtick. Seriously, one phone call would have saved hours of hanging around hissing like a broken kettle. Anyway, when he hit town and the small-time creeps and Untergangsters – all the ones who were sitting around on their keisters because you weren't using them – when they started dropping like flies, I saw an opportunity. I set up a meet and told him all about Donner."

Crane went white. "You dare–"

Lomax laughed. "What are you gonna do about it, tough guy?" Crane sank back to his slumped position on the floor, staring between his shoes, not daring to lift his eyes. Lomax chuckled, his tail thumping against the sagging table like a dog's. "See, once you'd let me into your little clique, it made it easy to find things out. I drop your name, get some tidbits, then drop those tidbits to the right people and they think I'm on the level and give me bigger stuff... pretty soon I knew all about Donner's little exile. Hell, I had the memo from that time he killed a hooker. *'Mein fuehrer, we hast ein little problem...'* El Sombra loved that, I'll tell you."

Crane shook his head, not speaking.

"So he killed the guy stone dead, and a couple of days later the papers had a field day with it, pretty much like I knew they would. 'Wuxtry, wuxtry! Dead man dies again!' Face it, tiger, this is the *one!*" He laughed like an earthquake. "I knew that'd bring you running, and I knew Thunder was going to send his top clue-hunting guy to the murder scene, on account of that whole thing they had going on in the forties. And Thunder's top man just happens to be a big bisexual deformed guy. Just the kind of subhuman – sorry, *in*human – the Blood-Spider likes to shoot whenever he gets an excuse, right?" The table began to crack under Lomax's weight, and he stood, the top of his head cracking into the ceiling and bringing down a flurry of plaster.

"Damn! Where the hell am I getting all this *mass* from? I have to study this later. So, Parker, are you all up to speed?"

Crane scowled. "Why didn't Venger give you the blood directly? Why that nonsense with the telegram?"

"Not nonsense. Deniability. If Venger goes to me with the one thing Untergang have wanted since they started out, that kind of blows my cover. Plus, I wanted him dead." Crane looked at Lomax in astonishment. "Oh, what? You honestly want a psychopath who knows how to melt people running around thinking he's in love with you? Because that's a great recipe for a long and healthy life. Don't make me the bad guy here, okay? He had to go. So, I told him you worked for me, not the other way around, and he should contact you once he had the blood. I figured I could trust you to do what you do with Venger and then bring the blood back to me, because where else would it go?"

"Straight to Germany." Crane muttered. "That's the protocol."

Lomax smiled. "You're in New York, Parker Crane. Protocol went out the window the second you arrived. This isn't a protocol kind of town. This is a town that breeds monsters and heroes, geniuses and madmen. This town makes gods, Parker." He shook his head, a look of amused pity on his distorted face, as the hue of his skin deepened and turned a rich, livid crimson. "And heaven help you, you wanted to be one of us."

He laughed, and the sound was like stone falling on stone.

"You wanted to kick it with the Gods of Manhattan. How's that working out for you?"

Before Crane could answer, there was a sound of thunder and the room shook, as if in an earthquake. "What was that?" Crane gasped, looking up at Lomax in renewed terror. "A bomb?"

"A landing." Lomax grinned. He flexed one massive hand, then the other, and the bones of his knuckles popped through the skin like a set of brutal spikes. When he looked back at the cowering Crane, his eyes seemed to glow. He chuckled, deep in his monster's throat, and spoke a single word.

"Showtime."

CHAPTER SIXTEEN

Doc Thunder and The Ultimate Foe

"THIS IS THE place?"

As Doc stepped out of the crater he'd made on the sidewalk from his landing, El Sombra took a long look around at his surroundings. A wide street, almost deserted, with only the occasional hansom cab and bicycle passing through. A small dead zone in the middle of New York's life. From this failed street, lined with businesses either closed for the day or closed forever, smaller alleys extended, crusted with grime and filth – and down one alley, nestled tightly between a shuttered, long-empty breaker bar on one side and a cheap chapbook store on the other, he could see a metal door. The same metal door he'd seen the Blood-Spider walk into after the battle on the hospital roof. "This is it, amigo. What say we go knock on that door and end this?"

Doc shook his head.

"He won't use the door."

From somewhere down the alley, there was a massive explosion, a destructive crash like a wrecking ball tearing through masonry.

The empty chapbook store seemed to shake. Then another crash. Louder this time. Closer.

"Brace yourself." Doc murmured, his eyes cold, focussed. Almost unconsciously, he adopted a ready stance, his feet planted, braced against the coming impact.

Another crash, and the window of the chapbook store cracked, a single line splitting the big, friendly window from top to bottom. A couple of chapbooks shivered and fell off the shelves.

El Sombra took a couple of steps back and drew his sword. Gently, he reached down and touched the small, hard object in his pocket, wondering.

Another crash. Louder still.

Doc breathed in. A single drop of sweat formed on his brow, reflecting the gaslight.

And then something terrifying smashed through the brick and plaster forming the back wall of the chapbook store, running through wooden shelves loaded with chapbooks and shattering them to matchwood with a swipe of its hand, the air clouded for a moment by the bright, primary-coloured pages before whatever it was burst out of the front window in a cascade of exploding glass, aiming right at Doc Thunder with a punch that took him off his feet and sent him careening through space into the brick wall on the other side.

The thing that had once been Lars Lomax roared.

It was fully ten feet of muscle, bone and sinew; its back, arms and legs covered with thick, red, shaggy hair, the great bony dome of its head bare apart from the thick eyebrows that sprouted from the protuberance of its brow. Spurs of thick, rock-like bone poked from knuckles, elbows, kneecaps and the backs of ankles. Its skin was a livid crimson, stretched taut over a tapestry of muscles upon muscles, a terrifying parody of anatomy that constantly flexed and shifted with the beast's every breath. Its eyes almost glowed, a rich bloody red, and instead of human teeth it possessed great murderous fangs, huge and sharp. Strangest of all – stranger even than the toes that had fused together, the soles of the feet replaced by a black, hoof-like carapace – was the thick tail of flesh that swished and swiped, back and forth, growing from the small of its back, just above the ruined remains of a pair of tan slacks.

There was nothing in it that would be recognisable as human, never mind as Lars Lomax. In fact, it looked like nothing so much as Satan himself, come to earth to feed on the sins of mankind. And yet, there was something in its bearing, in its inhuman, arrogant confidence, in the way its eyes blazed with mocking hatred at the fallen Thunder, as if daring him to get up and take further punishment - something that said that this was indeed the enemy of the Earth, the most dangerous man alive, the one man Doc Thunder could never truly defeat, not so long as he lived.

The Lomax-thing stared down at El Sombra, and El Sombra stared back, his sword raised. He'd dealt with monsters before. He'd faced human devils, battled killer machines, flying snipers and armoured tanks, stared down the armed might of Hitler's war machine. But this...

"El Sombra, right? We've met, sort of." The voice was like a cathedral collapsing into rubble. "I was the guy who put you onto Donner. I couldn't have done it without you." He grinned, his tongue licking over those razor-sharp teeth. "I owe you a lot, pal, so here's a warning. Try and use that little toothpick on me and you'll just ruin it. And then..." He smirked, and the muscles in his chest and back flexed obscenely. "Then, I'll ruin you. Seriously, if I get pissed at you, I can turn you into hamburger as easily as tapping my toes. I'll make you eat that sword sideways and crap it out the same way, pal."

He turned, looking down at Doc Thunder, who was picking himself up from the shattered remains of the shopfront he'd been punched into. "Go for the eyes," Doc coughed, wiping a trickle of blood from his mouth. "The rest of his skin's too tough to cut, but his eyes might be–"

Lomax grabbed hold of Doc's head, lifting him up and then slamming him down, face-first into the sidewalk, before placing the ball of a black foot on the back of his hated enemy's head, grinding him into the smashed concrete. El Sombra raised his sword, and Lomax shook his head, turning his terrible red-eyed gaze full on the masked man. "Bad idea." he growled. "Listen,

El Crazy, I'm as tolerant as the next guy but I'm on the verge of losing my temper. There's a perfectly good Nazi back there – leader of Untergang, remember? That criminal organisation you don't like? Why don't you go finish him off and leave me alone?"

El Sombra looked at him for a long moment, then walked towards the ruined chapbook store, climbing through the shattered window and then through the hole Lomax had made in the wall.

Lomax watched him go, and then turned back to Doc, squirming underneath the sole of his foot. "Looks like you just can't get the help these days. So, Thunder, who's coming to save you next? Maya? I'd hate to burst her head like a melon, but I can't have her beat me at chess again. Monk Olsen? Oh, wait, he's in that coma, my bad. I'll drop by the hospital later for some intensive chiropractics, fold him into an origami bird or something, how's that? Who does that leave... your cook? Easton West, everybody's favourite tough cop? The man rides a bike and smokes, sometimes both at once! I'm shaking – ooh, wait! Jack Scorpio, agent of S.T.E.A.M.! God, I've wanted to take care of that old blowhard for *years!*"

From behind, there was the thunder of hooves; a policeman on horseback, alerted by the commotion. At the sight of what Lomax had become, he drew his .38 and opened fire, to no avail. The bullets bounced harmlessly off Lomax's back as if they were raindrops. Snarling, the monstrosity turned around, reaching out and grabbing hold of the horse's neck. Then – with the terrible crack of fracturing vertebrae - he swung the beast upwards, killing it instantly and sending the rider tumbling off its back and onto the glass-covered tarmac. Laughing monstrously, Lomax swung the dead beast around his head, then brought it down, using it like a bludgeon on the stunned policeman. Horse and rider smashed together, the creature bursting open, sending a tide of blood and horse-offal spilling out into the road. The cop, crushed and suffocated beneath the weight of his own dead animal, managed to stay conscious for a few moments before surrendering to oblivion.

Doc felt the pressure of Lomax's foot ease for a micro-second as he swung the beast through the air, and he took his chance, Pressing his flat palms against the concrete of the sidewalk with all his strength, he managed to lift himself up just enough to squirm out from underneath, rolling clear before the man-monster could grab hold of him again.

"I don't need anybody else to fight my battles, Lomax," he muttered as he staggered to his feet, a stream of blood coursing from a broken nose. "I don't care what you've done to yourself. You've committed too many crimes to be allowed to walk free." His eyes narrowed. "It ends here."

Lomax raised one massive, shaggy eyebrow, then looked at the horse, still shuddering in its final convulsions, the policeman having already gone still. "Cruelty to animals. That always was one of your buttons." He chuckled, raising his fists, the spurs of bone at his knuckles jutting out toward Thunder like stone-age knives. "You realise no prison on the planet is going to hold me now, don't you? I mean, I was hard enough to keep locked away before. But now, they couldn't even keep me in custody for an hour. Not for a minute, not a *second!*" His brutal, inhuman laugh roared out under the night sky. "So are you going to kill me this time? Is the great Doc Thunder, the man who wants to save everybody in the whole wide world, going to get his hands a little bloody?"

Doc looked Lomax right in his eye, the blue piercing gaze duelling with eyes more at home in hell. "If I have to. I'm not proud of it, and I'm not happy about it, and if there's a way to contain and cure you, I'm going to find it. But a lot of people have died because of you and me, because I always underestimate just how wrong you are in that head of yours. And I can't stomach any more."

Lomax stared back at him. "It was a trick question, dummy. You're not going to kill me, and it's not because of any principles or moral imperatives or compassion or any of your usual high-minded bullcrap. It's because you physically can't do it. You *can't* kill me." He grinned, showing his teeth. "But I can kill you. And I'm going to make it *slow.*"

Then he charged.

Sᴡᴏʀᴅ ʀᴀɪsᴇᴅ, Eʟ Sombra crept into the tiny cell that had, for almost three years, been the home of the man calling himself

Timothy Larson. He wrinkled his nose in disgust. The place stank.

It stank of the noxious chemicals that had spilled from the dozens of ruined beakers and shattered test tubes that lay among the debris of the furniture. It stank of the fresh piss of the man who still sat trembling in one corner. It stank of the sweat that clung to the never-changed sheets on the filthy mattress. It stank faintly of opium, smoked late at night, half to keep up the illusion and half to alleviate the boredom that came with waiting endlessly for a chance that never came.

And underneath it all, it stank of madness.

El Sombra knew what it was to hate, to hate so hard and so long that you knew nothing else, to hate so strongly that it crossed that line into something beyond reason. He knew what it was to try to bring a government to its knees, to plan the end of a nation at the hands of a single man. He recognised something in Lars Lomax, some twisted reflection of his own feelings. If Doc Thunder had been a child of the Ultimate Reich – and El Sombra had an idea of how close Thunder had come to being just that – El Sombra would never have rested until he was dead, no matter what it took. He wondered what had happened to Lomax to make him what he was. Was it similar to that apocalyptic day of fire and nightmare and eternal shame that had created him? One massive explosion that had fractured his personality for good? Or had it been a constant drip, drip, drip of a thousand tiny incidents, eroding the rock of his sanity until finally it wore down to nothing?

El Sombra shook his head. It didn't matter. Perhaps Lomax had spared his life through some recognition of their similarities, but El Sombra wasn't about to make the same mistake. El Sombra had never deliberately killed anyone who wasn't a Nazi before, but there were exceptions to every rule. And speaking of which–

Crane made a whimpering sound in the depths of his throat as the masked man turned to face him. Tears coursed down his cheeks, and he clutched his legs, rocking gently in place. "Please." He sniffed, shaking his head. "Please don't let him find me."

El Sombra raised an eyebrow. "I guess you saw him turn into that thing, hey? One minute he's that skinny guy with the beard, and then he turns into that giant *diablo* monster... right before your eyes..." Crane shook his head, screwing his eyes tight shut and gritting his teeth. A low moan of torment came from between them. El Sombra sighed. "You were already pretty crazy, getting crazier, but now... you're gone, aren't you, amigo? Gone for good."

He lifted his sword, resting the blade in his palm for a moment, considering. Crane only stared, weeping and making his soft, mad noises. El Sombra sighed, shaking his head. "You know, I don't know if I can kill a guy who's already dead. Even if he is one of the bastards."

He lowered his sword, looking around the wrecked laboratory, eyes narrowing. "Hey, you got any glue here?"

LOMAX CHARGED, BARRELLING towards Doc Thunder like a freight train. Doc stood his ground, eyes narrowed. He knew a punch from Lomax's fists could take a normal man's head right off at the neck – what it would do to him, he didn't know, but it wasn't likely to be anything good.

He was used to using his strength, and that wouldn't work here. For one thing, he was too used to holding back, to measuring and rationing his great power for fear of turning every fight into a bloody execution. For another, even if he did manage to overcome his phobia of his own power and attack with all of it, would it actually work? Could he actually put Lomax down for good? Could he even injure him? What if he swung with all his strength and only succeeded in making him angry?

No, strength wasn't going to be the answer on its own. Doc had one advantage as far as he could see. Lomax was so enamoured of his new physical power, that he'd forgotten where he'd got it from. He'd forgotten that the greatest weapon in his arsenal had always been his mind.

It wasn't possible to out-punch him. But it was possible – more possible now than it had ever been before – to out-*think* him.

Doc waited. He waited until the last possible moment, when Lomax was almost on top of him, when he was swinging those bony knuckles back, his teeth already bared in a grin of sheer, animal triumph.

Then he threw himself flat on the floor.

Lomax's feet slammed into Thunder's prone body, sending him flying forward, unable to correct himself. The man-monster slammed hard into the tarmac, his face grinding up big chunks of roadway and gravel, leaving a trench behind him.

Doc rolled to his feet. Hitting Lomax wasn't going to work. He could kick him in the head with enough force to flatten a wrecking ball into a metal pancake, and all it was likely to do was break his foot. He could aim a cobra strike directly to the man's testes hard enough to create an imprint of them in what was left of the concrete and the absolute best it would do would be to make him angry. He was under no illusions about his ability to play Lars Lomax at his own game.

But Lomax was too overconfident in his new body. Just because he was stronger and more resilient, he assumed there was no way for Doc Thunder to defeat him in a fight. Just as in their previous battles, he'd assumed that he would win because he was smarter and had fewer morals. Doc Thunder almost smiled. As always, Lomax's complex, intricate, almost Rube Goldbergian plots fell down because he'd missed something simple. Something as simple as the weak plaster in a Parisian ceiling.

As simple as a wrestling hold.

Doc didn't know that much in the way of judo – an omission he was cursing himself for – but he knew some basics, and had to hope that Lomax, who'd rarely if ever fought hand to hand before now, knew even less. Quickly, he grabbed hold of Lomax's wrists, forcing them up behind his back in a double nelson before he could lock his arms, while at the same time pinning Lomax's legs at the backs of the knees with his own. Lomax struggled, but so long as Doc could keep a tight hold on him, he could keep him in this position for quite some time. The next step would be to put him down for good.

Another policeman would be on the scene soon, carrying a .38, or maybe even a shotgun. At which point, Doc would instruct him to shoot Lomax through the eye at point blank range, maybe more than once. At the very least, that would cause a massive brain hemorrhage. He wasn't happy about the necessity, but he was out of options, and he had a sneaking suspicion that Lomax would heal from even that injury in time.

He had a sneaking suspicion that Lars Lomax would never die. But if he could only hold him a little longer–

– suddenly, Lomax relaxed.

"Oh, why fight it? When you've gotta go, you've gotta go. You win again, Thunder. I'll go quietly to my cell, like a good little felon. I'll rehabilitate. I'll prop up the status quo for you. I'll be a hero too and have a shirt just like yours! Yes sirree, you've shown me the error of my ways!"

He was laughing. Doc frowned, keeping his grip tight. He couldn't let himself be suckered now.

Why was he laughing?

And then the tail wrapped around his throat and squeezed.

"Psyche!" Lomax bellowed, and suddenly Doc realised that this time he was the one who'd forgotten the simple thing. The tail. It wasn't an affectation, it was something Lomax had designed into the serum because he saw exactly this scenario coming. And now he was choking Doc to death with it, and the only way out was –

– let go of one of Lomax's wrists.

Doc tore at the clutching tail with one hand, and that one hand was the undoing of him. Lomax grabbed hold of a fistful of tarmac, tearing it right up from the road and slamming it with all his strength into the side of Doc's head, knocking him sideways. Then Lomax was back up on his feet as though nothing had happened, moving straight into a kick at Thunder's belly that sent him up like a football, followed by a two-handed blow to the rising body that knocked him right back down and made another crater in the ruined road.

It had all happened so fast that Doc Thunder barely even knew where he was. He reached up and touched his mouth, and the finger came away bloody. *Dear God,* thought Doc, *he's actually hurting me. He's strong enough to take me apart with his bare hands.*

I'm going to die.

And in that moment, he was glad that El Sombra had run away.

*　　*　　*

CRANE HAD BEEN no help. All he did was whine and moan and occasionally scratch his face and neck, drawing blood. El Sombra didn't know what the final straw had been, but any sanity he'd once had was long gone now.

Fortunately, El Sombra had found what he was looking for. A tube of fast-acting rubber cement, left by the sink after some long-forgotten bit of mending. Carefully, El Sombra spread the cement over the very tip of the sword, then took the thing he'd been saving in his pocket and attached it, holding it in place for long minutes until he was sure the cement had set.

"Don't let him in here." murmured Crane, his eyes wide.

"Shhhh. I won't let him in," smiled El Sombra in response, trying to be reassuring. "You'll never have to face him again. I promise. It's okay, amigo. It's okay."

It was strange. He knew he should feel hate for Parker Crane, or whatever his real name had once been. It was Djego's job to bear things like pity and doubt, to feel sorrow and shame. That was Djego's role in their team of one. El Sombra was there to take never-ending revenge and to laugh and to never look back. But to know that his murder of Heinrich Donner – his righteous kill – had resulted in so much harm coming to so many... and now to see the leader of Untergang, the man he'd come to New York to kill, just an empty, broken madman, a shell of a person...

El Sombra wondered if he was changing.

Experimentally, he prodded his sword at the steel door, and the thing he'd fixed to the end slid into the steel as if it were made of butter.

Good.

"Don't." whispered Crane, a tear rolling down his cheek. "Don't let him back in."

El Sombra smiled, placing a hand on his shoulder. "It's okay, amigo. I'm going to go and make sure nobody ever needs to see him again. And I couldn't have done it without you." He squeezed lightly. "You didn't mean to, but you did some good. Remember that."

Then, gently, he pushed the tip of the sword through the front of Crane's skull and into his brain.

He was not incapable of pity, he knew. But he was who he was, and he did what he did.

And broken or not, the bastards had to die.

DOC'S HEAD SNAPPED to the left, then to the right as the massive red fists slammed into his jaw. Blood flew from his nose and his split lip. One eye had swollen to the point where he could no longer see out of it.

"You know," Lomax grinned, "I've tried a lot of ways to get rid of you over the years. I've tried bombs, I've tried bullets, I've tried poisons. I've tried to create superhard metals. I've tried to dig up radioactive elements. You know what I've never tried? Beating you to death."

He laced his fingers together and then swung his joined fists up in an arc underneath Thunder's chin, sending him flying back with a crack that sounded like bone breaking.

"It's incredibly satisfying." Lomax laughed, that terrible rockslide laugh. "If only I'd thought of it sooner!"

Doc shook his head as he picked himself up, trying to concentrate, or at least to stay conscious. Lomax's serum was still working. He'd gained at least a foot in height since the start of the battle. Doc doubted he'd be able to pin him again, even if he could somehow circumvent the tail. The best he could do at this point was survive; as long as Lomax was concentrating on him, he wasn't endangering innocent lives. Every moment Doc managed to stay on his feet was a victory.

Of course, Lomax was getting stronger all the time. The fact that he was making Doc bleed now meant that his punches were as strong as exploding shells. How long before they were strong enough to tear his head right off his body? And was Lomax ever going to stop getting stronger, tougher, bigger? Would he eventually become too big and heavy to move, or would he continue his rampage even as he outgrew buildings or even cities?

Lomax smashed another punch past Doc's defences, slamming his jutting bone knuckle into Doc's open eye, and in the white-hot flash of pain, Doc had a nightmare vision of Lomax, the size of

Manhattan itself, using the city as his throne and issuing orders like a dictatorial Gulliver among Lilliputians. The absurdity of the image only made it seem more terrifying.

Another blow snapped Doc's head back, and he found himself sinking to his knees. He needed a few minutes to heal, and it was clear he wasn't going to get them. Blackness crowded his vision, and his heartbeat was a drum pounding constantly in his ears. He waited for the blow that would finish this unequal combat and set the monster Lars Lomax loose on an unsuspecting world.

It never came.

Instead, he heard laughter. Laughter like rocks tumbling down into a quarry. Lomax's laughter.

For a moment, Doc thought the laughter was directed at him. Why not? Hadn't he failed anyone who'd ever counted on him or cared for him? Wasn't he dying because he'd committed one inexcusable act of stupidity after another? Because he hadn't seen what was right under his nose until it was too late?

Then he realised Lomax was laughing at someone else, and a chill shot through him to the pit of his stomach.

El Sombra was about to die, and there was nothing Doc Thunder could do about it.

LARS LOMAX COULDN'T help himself. The laughter just came tumbling out.

El Sombra had run out of the chapbook store and now he was standing there with his puny little sword, pointing it at Lomax as if it would actually do any good at all.

"Really? Seriously? You thought, 'Oh! There's Doc Thunder, the most powerful man on earth, getting his hide handed to him by someone much bigger and stronger than he is! Wow, he needs some help! I know, I'll run forward with my little toothpick and wave it menacingly in the bad guy's face! That'll help!' Oh, you kill me, you really do." Lomax almost bent double, laughter exploding out of him. "I might even have you stuffed."

Then he saw what was cemented to the end of the sword, and the laughter stopped instantly.

"No." He whispered the word, taking a step back, shaking his head. "That – that won't work. My skin's too tough. The cement won't hold."

"Won't it?" El Sombra grinned.

Lomax snarled, moving forward, pulling back an arm ready to smash El Sombra with a single blow, hard enough to pulverise his bones and liquefy his flesh, to turn him into flying specks of red jelly just as if a bomb had hit him at point blank range. And at that moment, El Sombra thrust forward and up.

The augmented tip of the sword slid effortlessly through the crimson skin of Lomax's chest, between his ribs, piercing his heart in one swift motion.

Lomax gasped, blinked, and took a step back. He coughed, once.

"You can't..." Black blood trickled from his mouth. "You can't plan for things like that, can you?"

Then, the look of disbelief froze on his face. He toppled backwards, hitting the tarmac hard enough to fracture it.

The red eyes closed.

Doc blinked, slowly getting to his feet. The blackness was clearing from his vision. He was already starting to heal, but he couldn't quite believe what he was seeing. "How... how did you..."

Wordlessly, El Sombra pulled his sword from the man-monster's body. Glued to the end of his sword with rubber cement, still glistening in that strange, alien way, was a single bullet of inexorium, as sharp and deadly as it had been when it was fired, as indestructible as it had been when the masked man had dug it from one of the marble pillars in Grand Central Station with his sword. He smiled.

"A bullet in the right place can change the world, amigo."

And quite suddenly, Doc Thunder had nothing to say.

EPILOGUE

One Fine Day in New York City

"...AND SO, ONCE again, we can thank Doc Thunder, America's Greatest Hero, for safeguarding our fair city from the machinations of those who would destroy our very way of life."

A cheer went up from the crowd, and Mayor Ambrose adjusted his tie, smiling genially. "Although Doc has asked me to point out that the final blow against the nefarious Lars Lomax, the most dangerous man in the world, was struck by a brave Mexican hero –"

More cheers, a cry of "Viva El Sombra!" from the back of the crowd, then a wave of spontaneous clapping. Ambrose smiled genially, and motioned for silence.

"– a brave Mexican hero who has requested to remain anonymous, lest the worldwide reporting of his deeds interfere with his quest to rid the globe of a certain other enemy of the USSA, who I will likewise refrain from mentioning by name..."

The crowd grumbled.

"...though I understand he only has one ball."

A riotous cheer, a few hats thrown into the air, and another surge of applause, this time lasting for a full minute.

"Naturally, we wish him all the best, and hope his success will lead to Untergang's final exit from the world of terror. I have of course issued a full pardon for any, ah, crimes of violence he may have committed while a guest of our city, and hope that, should he ever complete his task, he finds his home here in Manhattan, where he will always have a place among our heroes."

Another surge of clapping, more "Viva El Sombra!" from the kid at the back.

"Only next time, please, use the flat of the sword."

Polite laughter, some of it uneasy. *Damn it, Darren, the crappy joke goes in the middle, the good joke goes at the end. Jesus. Learn to write a damned speech, why don't you.* Despite his thoughts, the Mayor's smile never faltered. *Okay, time to open it up.*

"'Any questions, ladies and gentlemen of the press? You, sir." Ambrose motioned to a rat-like man in a dirty overcoat.

"Rich Uben, sir, *The Daily Bugle.* What happened to Lomax's body?"

"Well, obviously, since he was stabbed through the heart by Mexico's Greatest Hero –" More cheers and applause. *That's how it's done, Darren.* "– we feel he's no longer a threat to anyone on this side of the grave. However, to make sure, we removed his head from his body by means of controlled explosion. Seventeen controlled explosions, in fact, utilising more than one hundred sticks of dynamite."

The crowd made an appreciative 'ooooh' sound. No doubt most of them were wishing they'd had front row seats.

"The head and the body have been flown separately to Langley, where they are being studied extensively by top men."

Uben narrowed his eyes, looking suspiciously over the top of his glasses. "Uh-huh. And which men might those be, Mister Mayor?"

Ambrose smiled back at him, a trifle frostily. He paused a moment before giving his answer.

"Top. Men."

* * *

IN THE DREAM, Maya was chained to the altar again, and the giant roc was circling overhead, swooping down towards her. This time it had Doc Thunder's face.

"Don't worry," said Doc, as he opened his mouth wide to bite into her naked flesh, "I'm Doc Thunder, America's Greatest Hero, and I never make a mistake."

She tried to scream, but in the dream something had stolen her voice.

At the last second, someone sprang from the rocks, slamming a fist into Thunder's head, knocking the great bird down into the valley below. She couldn't see his face.

"Wake up," said the Stranger.

Maya jerked awake with a start, blinking at the sun streaming in through the window. "Who on earth–" she muttered, shaking the sleep from her eyes.

"Wake up," said Doc, lounging in the doorway. He was holding some sort of bundle in his hands, gently, as if he was afraid he might break it. There was something about him that seemed different, as if a weight had been lifted from his shoulders.

"What do you mean by this intrusion?" she said, frostily, staring ice daggers at him. He only laughed.

"You need to start making a habit of getting up earlier, young lady. You're sleeping half the day away." He laughed again at her look of astonishment. "Come on, get up. You can sleep in when you're back in your kingdom. You are still planning on going back?"

She nodded, slowly, not looking at him. Why on earth did he want to drag this out? "Yes. I'm sorry, Doc... Hugo... whoever you are. But I need to sort a few things out."

He nodded. "Fair enough. Oh, that reminds me, Monk wants to go too."

Maya's eyes widened, and her mouth fell open, and then she laughed despite herself. "Monk's awake?"

"Awake and asking after you. And like I said, he wants to come with you. I figure he might end up being pretty useful if any more viziers or high priests have been plotting. The only trouble is, you might have to wait for him to be ready to travel. And maybe while you're waiting, we could talk a little. Sort a few things out." He grinned, and the thing in his arms moved.

Maya smiled, relaxing on the bed, her green eyes glowing with their familiar warmth. "We'll see. No promises. What on earth is that you're holding?"

Doc smiled. "It's a present for you. Just something to say sorry for... a lot of things, I guess. Keeping secrets. Not being the man you thought I was." He shook his head, then held the bundle out, tugging back the swaddling clothes to reveal the pink face of a baby piglet. "I'm thinking of calling him El Chancho. When he grows up, he can be my new sidekick."

Maya put her hands to her mouth, gasping in delight. "Oh, he's adorable!" She reached to take hold of the little bundle, looking down at the snuffling little snout of the piglet. Then she looked up at Doc Thunder, smirking. Doc raised an eyebrow.

"What's that for?"

"Oh, I was just thinking." Maya smiled wider. "Doc Thunder saves my life from a treacherous high priest armed with a mystic gem and a giant roc. Hugo Donner gives me a pig."

Doc smiled, looking at the floor. "Maybe Hugo Donner wants to make a more realistic impression." He looked up, suddenly serious. "And Hugo Donner wants to come along to Zor-Ek-Narr too."

Maya winced, frowning. "The whole point is–"

"We'll leave Doc Thunder in New York. I promise. It's not like anybody needs him right now anyway. Who's left for him to fight? Besides, I need to get my blood away from all the would-be super-scientists wanting to be the next Lars Lomax. It's either the Forbidden Kingdom or a beach in Malibu and a shave."

Maya's frown lifted. "Hmmm. A holiday at home with Hugo Donner and Monk Olsen, two big, strong and very ordinary men about town." She smiled. "We'll see."

Doc smiled. "No promises."

They looked at each other for a long moment.

"Oh, what the hell." Maya laughed. "Come to bed."

AT THE JAMESON Club, the disappearance of Parker Crane had not gone without comment. Jonah had refrained from participating in the gossip. For one thing, it was not the place of a trusted servant to indulge in idle rumour, or to betray confidences about those he was tasked to serve.

For another, he was getting very worried about the leader.

The Führer had been in touch, through intermediaries. Reports indicated that Untergang had been so weakened by Crane's shenanigans that Hitler was considering pulling all funding and shutting the experiment down for good. He had expected a significant propaganda victory from Operation Blood-Spider, the report said, and instead he had seen Untergang almost bankrupted to feed the whims of a dilettante with an obsession with American masked heroes. As soon as Crane resurfaced, he would have questions to answer in Berlin.

It was Bunny Etheringdon who broke the news.

"Thanks awfully, Jonah," he'd said, accepting his fifth Singapore Sling of the evening. "I say, have you heard the dreadful news about poor Parker?"

Jonah froze. "I'm afraid I haven't, Sir. Nothing serious, I hope?"

"Well, he's dead!" Bunny slurped down a hefty gulp of the Singapore Sling. "They found his body in some ghastly little one-room apartment in the East Village – the bit that was half destroyed in that bizarre business with the monster man. He'd been shot, or stabbed, or some such." He looked left and right, as if checking for spies, and then leaned in with a stage whisper. "There's some talk that he may have been involved with the whole thing. Do you know he was dressed up like that fellow the Blood-Spider? I'm on tenterhooks waiting for the next revelation, I'll tell you."

He leant back, smiling facetiously, as if expecting Jonah to gasp, raise his hands to his cheeks and exclaim "Well! I never!"

Instead, Jonah kept his composure, and only nodded. "If you'll excuse me, Mr. Etheringdon."

Bunny smiled, waving him off. "Oh, of course, Jonah. No rest for the wicked, eh?"

"I have one final task to perform first, Sir." He bowed, walked down the stairs to the Lower Library, let himself in and locked the door behind him.

Then, without any fuss, he placed a loaded pistol in his mouth and pulled the trigger.

The Jameson Club hired a new major domo on the Monday.

"NAME?"

Marlene smiled prettily, looking through the lenses of the glasses she'd bought from the theatrical costumiers. "Mary Watson," she smiled. It was amazing the difference red hair dye and a pair of glasses made. She could have walked right up to anyone from her old life and they wouldn't have recognised her at all.

"Occupation?" She'd gone for a very tight black rubber dress with a rather prominent window onto her chest, a gift from David in days gone by that was paying dividends now. The customs officer couldn't keep his eyes off that cleavage window, which was all for the best as it distracted him from the cheapness of her fake passport.

"Actress." She smiled again, arching her back a little to make sure his eyes remained exactly where they were. She supposed she was being rather dreadful, really, but it wasn't as though she was going to give him her telephone number. Not her real one, at any rate.

"And is the purpose of your visit business, or, ah... pleasure?" The man's moustache twitched as he leered. It reminded Marlene rather of a rat's whiskers. He did have a perfectly gorgeous accent, though, but she supposed they all did here. One of the benefits of her move to London.

"Oh, pleasure, of course," she purred. Best not to let on that it was both. After all, crime was a serious business, but declaring war on it was quite the most perfect pleasure she could imagine.

The customs man laughed, opening up her suitcase and leafing carefully through the perfumed silk negligees and leather corsets she'd carefully packed. Of course, he was far too fixated on those to notice the false bottom of the suitcase, and he certainly wouldn't think to look beneath it to find her twin automatic pistols and the mask Parker had left her. He looked up at her, a twinkle in his eye, his lips parting in a smile that revealed the most unsavoury set of teeth.

"One more thing, Miss Watson – the name and number of your hotel. Just to be on the safe side." He even added a wink.

As Marlene reeled off the name and telephone number of a completely different hotel, and a fictional room number for good measure, she found herself wondering if she would end up seeing the customs officer again after all. He looked like the sort that might solicit a prostitute, or possibly enter an illicit vice den to gamble the night away. There was at least a ten per cent chance, she decided, that he would find himself looking down the barrel of the Blood Widow's automatics.

"See you soon, Miss," he said, grinning and fiddling with his crotch as she wiggled away on her heels towards the taxi rank.

"Oh, I hope so. Perhaps even sooner than you think." Marlene murmured, and smiled.

"I SPOKE TO Hisoka's parents. They said thanks for your help." Inspector West took a long drag on his cigarette, then breathed the smoke out slowly, so it formed a lazy cloud drifting over the railing of the balcony, out towards the city. He watched it for a moment before the wind took it apart. Then he poured another sake.

Okawara's was a tenth-rate sushi joint in the heart of Japantown, a little fish being eaten alive by larger, slicker competitors. But they did a good, cheap, strong sake, and they had a view that those big fancy restaurants would kill for. From here, you could see everything, the whole damned city. You could look down on it with a warm sake in one fist and a Lucky Strike in the other, and pretend for a minute or two that you didn't need to walk those damned streets, to wade through the crap that everybody else has to wade through just to survive.

It must be nice to be able to leap over it, or at least that's what Easton West figured. But maybe that just meant you landed in it harder.

"It wasn't me who... apprehended Hisoka's killer." Doc Thunder danced around the word, but they both knew what he meant. *Murdered.*

"You got him that pardon, right? Get out of jail free?" West tried to keep the bitterness out of his voice. "That masked son of a bitch killed a dozen men, maybe more. We're just supposed to forget about that?"

Doc Thunder shrugged. "He saved my life. He probably saved yours. Probably the President's. The whole USSA, in fact." He looked at Easton, and suddenly he looked tired. "What was I supposed to do? I don't like his methods any more than you do, but there it is. He's the reason the sun came up this morning."

"I don't care if he put the damned sun in the sky to begin with," Inspector West growled. "We're a nation of laws. That's all that keeps us from sliding into Hell." He swallowed another fistful of sake.

Doc paused, looking out at the view. "Crane killed Danny. I'm sure of it."

Easton West nodded. "It was him, all right. But that doesn't change anything." He poured another. "Danny Coltrane was the nearest thing I ever had to a father. I became a cop to get the man who killed him. To *get* him, understand? Get him *right,* by the book. That's how the Ghost would have done it." He downed the shot in one. "Killing Crane like that – that's spitting on Danny's memory. And if I see El Sombra again, he's going down for that. By the book."

Doc nodded. There wasn't much to say. He poured himself a measure of sake he knew he wouldn't feel, then poured one for Easton. He lifted the cup between two outsized fingers, and smiled. "Here's to Danny."

Easton smiled, picking up his cup and draining it. "Yeah. Here's to you, Mister Ghost Boss." He smiled, very slightly, just at the corners of his mouth. "You rest now."

"Sure, I knew the Blood-Spider. Him and me were like *that,* buddy. Like *that.* He knew he could count on Harry Stacey, yes sir. Knew what I'd done *in the line,* keeping the streets safe. Yeah, okay, maybe there were a few minor breaches of the regulations here and there, but opium goes missing from the evidence locker all the time these days – don't know why people pointed at me. Everybody knows your slant is a fiend for the dragon, and we got a lot more chinks on the force than we used to, thanks to that asshole Rickard and all his bullcrap about 'diversity'. I'm just saying, ask them where it went. Christ, 'diversity in policing'... What the hell does 'diversity' even mean, anyway? I'll tell you; anti-white racism, that's what. The most oppressed race in the whole goddamned world is the friggin' white man. Anyway, the Blood-Spider...

"Now listen, you don't want to believe all that crap about Parker Crane being the Blood-Spider. That's just lies. Parker Crane was just one more asshole rich boy, that's all. In fact, I heard he was a fruit. Well, that's *why* he was always seeing those models, they knew he was safe! And let me tell you, the Blood-Spider was no butt-bandit. The guy was all man. Like me. Coupla peas in a pod.

"And don't believe all that crapola about that friggin' wetback saving the day! That's the goddamned liberal media for you. If they're not spending all their time on that son of a bitch Doc Thunder, who is – and this is a *documented friggin' fact* – a friggin' faggot, a liberal *and* a miscegenationist, they're wanting to turn a god-damned illegal into the hero of New York city. You want to know who took that prick Lomax down? The Blood-Spider. Shot him through the heart with a magic bullet, saved all our asses. That's a damn fact.

"And what does he get for it? He gets smeared! Don't believe that bullcrap that he was Crane, or that Crane was a Nazi – that's just the Jew media tryin' to play with your head, friend. Listen, you know you're getting the straight dope from me. I'm a cop. Well, no, I ain't a cop any *more,* now I clean the toilets in this joint, but like I said, that's all because of the damn slants.

"Yeah, like I said, that business with the opium out of the evidence locker. I mean, *someone* signed it out – probably a chink, like I said – and sure, they used my name. And they found the stuff in an apartment that I'd apparently signed a lease for, but look, that apartment belonged to a *hooker,* okay? I'm a happily married man. Well, I was.

"Listen, pal, this too will pass, you know? A real rain's going to wash all the scum off the streets, let me tell ya. A hard rain's gonna fall when the Blood Spider comes back to town. Him and me were like *that*, like I was sayin', and he always looked after his number one guy. That's all I'm saying. He always had a place in his organisation for Harry Stacey.

"The Blood-Spider will rise again, friend. The Blood-Spider will rise again..."

IN THE END, El Sombra was glad to go.

New York had been... fun. He had to admit it. There was magic in this city – a strange energy on every street corner, waiting to be unleashed. The music, the culture, the larger than life personalities... As he stood on the docks, waiting for the boat that would take him to Europe – to the final battle with the creature he'd been born to destroy – he found himself thinking over the little things.

Djego, standing in a coffee house in the East Village, not three blocks from El Sombra's battle with Lars Lomax, reading his old poems and getting a standing ovation, starting to cry as a piece of his heart came back to him.

El Sombra, dancing with the breakers in Times Square, losing himself in the rhythm, free and unrestrained and whole again for a few short minutes.

Djego, in the Metropolitan Museum of Modern Art, looking at Warhol's 'cellphone', a block of black ceramic studded with numbers and a tiny sheet of glass, and for a brief moment being transported to that other world, the world of dreampunk.

El Sombra, squeezing Crane's shoulder, feeling the burning that would forever be in him ease, transforming into sadness for a single moment.

Djego sitting in a futurehead bar, wearing El Sombra's mask around his neck like a bandana, détourning his own personal demons and transforming them into couture, laughing like a boy.

El Sombra, standing on top of the Empire State Building and yelling into the night, scaring the tourists and aggravating the cops and not giving a damn, because whatever the bastards had taken from him, he would always have this one single moment, forever and ever until the day he died fighting.

All of these moments happened, in between and underneath his mission and his adventures and all the craziness and the violence. They all happened, and they were all important, even if they weren't part of that big, complicated story of Doc Thunder and the Blood-Spider and the most dangerous man in the world. Maybe more important because of that.

And maybe that was the lesson of New York City – that all the moments were important, that all the little things mattered. The smallest detail could save the day or destroy the world. It was a good lesson to take into the endgame.

And he had to admit, they'd been very gracious about all the dead bastards.

Still, it was past time to leave. He'd spent too long circling America, while the enemy in Berlin had grown more evil and more dangerous still. Now was the time to end it once and for all. Now was the time to go to the heart of the Ultimate Reich and show them what they'd so thoughtlessly created. What they'd forged in the fires of their damnation.

Now was the hour of final battle.

El Sombra breathed in, focussing on the task ahead.

"Hot dogs! Hot dogs! One dollar five! Wrap a nickel in a bill and eat your fill!"

El Sombra breathed out, laughed his magical laugh, and turned away from the docks and towards the yelling voice in the distance. Well, what choice did he have?

Who could go to their death without a last hot dog?

AND SOMEWHERE IN Langley, Virginia, in the deepest part of a bunker owned and operated by S.T.E.A.M. for the purpose of storing the most dangerous artefacts in the world, there was a large crate and a smaller bottle. Inside the large crate, there was the corpse of something that had once been the son of a mediocre salesman. Something that had grown up to be the most dangerous man in the world, and that had thrown its humanity away to become more dangerous still.

Floating in the bottle, sealed in a solution of formaldehyde, was the creature's head. It floated, eyes closed, the neck ragged and burned from the explosives used to separate it from its body.

It floated that way for a very long time.

And then it opened its eyes.

And if anyone had been there to see the head, they might have been able to read its snarling, sneering lips as they moved behind the thick glass of the jar, showing its fangs. They might have worked out what it was saying, in its dark formaldehyde tomb.

Next time, Thunder.

Next time.

THE END

Al Ewing was born in 1977, three days before Elvis died on the toilet. Indoctrinated into the loathsome practice of comics at an early age by his disreputable brother, the child progressed from his innocent beginnings to the despicable depths of sin represented by the British comic *2000 AD*, long known as a haunt of depravity. He remains ensconced there to this day as a writer of the bizarre and fantastic, when not involved in even more sordid past-times. His previous contributions to the sordid, populist medium of adventure novels include *I, Zombie*, *Death Got No Mercy*, and the first El Sombra novel, *El Sombra*, all published by Abaddon Books.

CHAPTER ONE

The Handover

FOUR HOURS AFTER curfew – in the shadow of the St Paul's Cathedral – an unmarked hansom cab rattled to a halt. The door opened and Dr Victor Gallowglass stepped down onto the street. His heart beat a nervous tattoo against his ribs, although he was concentrating hard so that his nerves and his fear did not show in his face.

A gang of five men, skulking in the shadows, watched him from the other side of the street, their dark clothing making them almost invisible. Except for the debonair gent who stood slightly apart from the others.

"Good evening, Doctor," the man said.

He was immaculately turned out, wearing a fine green frock coat, charcoal grey trousers, spats and a silver-embroidered waistcoat. A gold silk cravat finished off the ensemble, held in place with a ruby-tipped pin. In one hand he swung an ebony cane as if keeping time, like a metronome. His face was as sharp, his brown hair – greying at the temples and slicked back from a pronounced widow's peak – glistened with a copious helping of hair oil.

He looked from the grim face of the doctor to the pall of Smog that hung over the city like a shroud, the glowing yellow streetlamps turning its clammy mantle a sallow tinge. The hazy white disc of the moon struggled through the banks of pollutant cloud that still plagued the city, despite former Prime Minister Valentine's best efforts. Its milky luminescence added an eerie, unsettling quality to the night's illicit proceedings.

"A fine evening, is it not?" the man continued, as if they were all there for no other reason than to pass the time of day.

"Where is she?"

The man raised an eyebrow. "Do not worry, Dr Gallowglass, your daughter is safe."

"I want to see her."

The debonair gent regarded Gallowglass for a moment, an incalculable expression in his eyes.

He turned and nodded to one of the suspicious-looking characters waiting in the darkness behind him.

The darkly dressed ruffian took a step forward. He was of burly build but weighed down by the large sack he was carrying over his shoulder. Carefully, he set the sack down and fumbled with the rope tying it shut. He pulled the sack down around the body of the small girl bound inside.

The girl looked terrified and, on seeing her father, fresh tears began to stream from her eyes, but she said nothing. She couldn't – the gag prevented her from doing so.

"Oh, Miranda, my poor darling," Gallowglass gasped. Tears welled in his eyes too. "It's alright now. It's going to be alright, my darling. This will all be over very soon, I promise." Blinking the tears away he fixed the kidnappers' spokesman with a look of black, unadulterated hatred. "If you have harmed a single hair on her head..." He did not need to say any more.

"I can assure you that she has been as well looked after as Her Majesty might expect to be," the other said, his voice oozing charm and charisma despite the direness of the situation.

Gallowglass reached out his arms to the frightened child but didn't dare take a step towards her.

"I doubt that distinctly," he growled. "Now let her go." His tone was more pleading than he would have liked.

"All in good time, doctor. All in good time." The debonair gentleman slapped the shaft of his cane into his hand. "But before we hand her over to your care you must give us certain assurances."

"What is it you want from me?"

"Your continued, faithful, patriotic service. That is all, Doctor Gallowglass. All that we ask is that you see your vital work through to completion."

Gallowglass's expression didn't change.

"I will continue with my research until my labours bear fruit," Gallowglass conceded.

"And we have your word on that?"

"You have my word."

"Well, we can't ask for more than that, can we? After all, an Englishman's word is his bond, is it not?"

At another nod from their leader, the ruffian freed the girl from her bonds.

An expectant hush hung over the street, the shadowy silhouette of the cathedral on the other side of the barricade a threatening presence nonetheless. It was a silence disturbed only by the Smog-muffled clatter of Overground trains – although there were a lot fewer of them running on the elevated tracks now at this time of night – and the sudden clatter of roof tiles above.

Anxious glances shot to the rooftops of the burnt out buildings on the other side of the wall.

"What was that?" the debonair gent demanded.

"Don't know, boss," one of his unshaven lackeys replied.

The man put a steadying hand to the shoulder of the one still struggling to free the girl and turned cold, black eyes on the equally anxious-looking doctor. "You were told to come alone!"

The debonair dandy took a step back towards the wall, eyes fixed on the rooftops on the other side of the road. His companion took a step back too, pulling the girl after him.

"I did!" Gallowglass screamed.

The unshaven lackey suddenly shot an anxious glance up at the wall behind them. "Here, boss, you don't think it could be –"

"Silence!" the other snapped, never once taking his eyes from the buildings on the other side of the street. "I thought I heard..." The dandy's words trailed off into silence and then: "Look! Up there!"

All eyes followed his trembling finger.

At first Gallowglass could see nothing amongst the shadows shrouding the rooftops, not until one of those shadows detached itself from the darkness and unfurled bat-like wings.

Like some animated gargoyle it leapt from the guttering at the edge of the roof.

Gallowglass gasped and a number of the kidnappers began to whimper. All of them recognising the night stalker for who he was.

The skin of its leathery wings rippling as it dropped from the parapet, the figure swooped towards them.

"Get out of here!" the dandy shouted and took off down the street, keeping close to the wall as he ran. His burly comrade was close on his heels, dragging the terrified girl after him.

As the bat-winged terror came within a few feet of the ground, his legs swung forwards and he planted the soles of two heavy boots squarely in the chest of one of the panicking rogues. The man was hurled onto his back and a solid kick to the head made sure that he stayed there.

Two remained. The crack of gunfire shattered the night.

Gallowglass watched, his jaw slack with shock, as the armoured bat-man bore down on the kidnappers. Their shots must have missed, Gallowglass decided, for the figure did not even break his stride as he closed on them.

But their second volley of shots certainly didn't miss. How could they? The vigilante was right on top of them now. Gallowglass heard the pang of metal on metal and the advancing colossus wavered.

But his hesitation was only momentary. One last bounding stride and he was on top of them. Dully gleaming claws sliced through the night. Blood sprayed black in the darkness.

Another threat neutralized.

The masked vigilante – the one the press had dubbed Spring-Heeled Jack – was the only man who dared stalk the streets of London once the curfew sirens had been sounded. During the hours of darkness he delivered his own brand of justice to those who had taken advantage of the fact that, in the aftermath of the Wormwood Catastrophe, the capital had become a more lawless place than ever. The authorities' resources had been stretched to breaking point and were no longer able to cope with the rise in opportunistic crime and gang-related warfare.

With three down and two to go, the vigilante didn't hesitate for a moment but, leaving the motionless bodies of his victims behind, launched himself after the gang's leader, his burly companion and the still captive child.

The first any of them – doctor, vigilante and kidnapper – knew of the locusts' arrival was the zinging buzz of chitinous wings, as the gigantic insects rose over the west wall and descended on the fleeing felons.

For the first time since taking on the kidnappers, Spring-Heeled Jack faltered, stumbling and losing his balance as he tried to arrest his forward charge. There were two of the things – their bodies as long as a man was tall, their huge wings a blur of movement.

They paused for a moment, hovering several feet above the cobbled street, their mantis-like heads jerking from side to side as they regarded Gallowglass and the vigilante with compound eyes the size of footballs.

As if at some unspoken command, one of the locusts moved towards the vigilante; the second targeted the dumbstruck, paralysed doctor. Regaining his feet, the vigilante put a gauntleted hand to a dispenser on his belt. A second later, he tossed something small and metallic towards the insects. The object hit the road as the giant insects passed overhead.

There was a soft click and then with a great whooshing noise, like air escaping from a punctured dirigible, a thick jet of smoke erupted from the device.

It was as if the locusts had hit a wall. The two insects, buzzing angrily, withdrew, turning away from the expanding gas cloud. Repelled by the smoke bomb they left the vigilante and the doctor, and set off after easier prey.

Even through the smoky haze, Gallowglass saw what followed clearly enough.

"No!" he screamed, his paralysis suddenly gone, his legs carrying him after the insects. But he was too late.

First to be plucked from the ground was the unshaven ruffian, the girl stumbling to her hands and knees as the startled man lost his grip on her. The locust lifted the kidnapper, kicking and screaming, into the air. It took off back over the wall, holding the wailing man fast in its pincer-grip, labouring its way towards the black dome of St Paul's.

Just for a moment Victor Gallowglass thought that perhaps his daughter might escape from her ordeal unscathed. But his moment of desperate hope was short-lived.

The second locust dropped onto her back before he could reach her. With the child clutched in its chitinous embrace, it rose again into the Smoggy air.

Gallowglass was sprinting now, arms outstretched towards his daughter, as if he might somehow still be able to pluck her out of the sky and to safety, but against the airborne assailant, he was utterly helpless.

As the locust rose over the wall after the other, the girl's gag came free and he heard her cry.

"Daddy!"

Hearing her scream his name only made the already desperate situation infinitely worse.

But then his faltering steps found purpose again and, within a few strides, he was at the wall. He had already managed to scramble a good six feet up the barricade when the vigilante grabbed him.

"Stop!" the vigilante's voice boomed from the speaker grille in the front of his goggle-eyed mask.

With one strong tug, Spring-Heeled Jack pulled him off the wall.

"You cannot go in there. The whole area is contaminated!"

With a snarl born of rage and frustration, Gallowglass pulled himself free of Jack's grasp and then, turning, began to pummel the vigilante's bullet-proof breastplate with his fists, until at last, realising that that too was futile, he gave up and fell to his knees. The soul-wrenching sobs came freely now in an outpouring of agonised grief.

"There must be a way!" he wailed through the tears. "And if you can't do it, then we must get help!"

PAX BRITANNIA

Also available

Abaddon
Books

PAX BRITANNIA

UNNATURAL
HISTORY

Jonathan Green

Visit www.abaddonbooks.com for information on our titles,
interviews, news and exclusive content.

ISBN: 978-1-905437-10-8
UK £.6.99   US $7.99

Abaddon
Books

Follow us on twitter: www.twitter.com/abaddonbooks

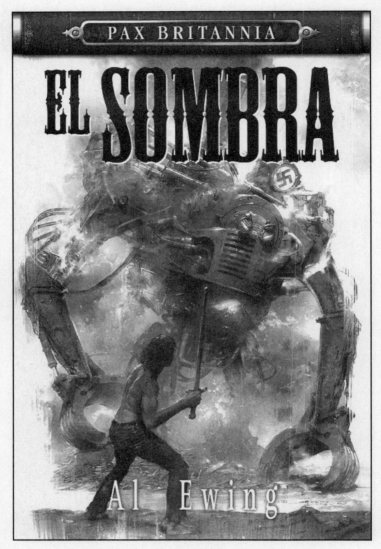

Visit www.abaddonbooks.com for information on our titles,
interviews, news and exclusive content.

ISBN: 978-1-905437-34-4
UK £.6.99   US $7.99

Follow us on twitter: www.twitter.com/abaddonbooks

PAX BRITANNIA

LEVIATHAN RISING

JONATHAN GREEN

Visit www.abaddonbooks.com for information on our titles,
interviews, news and exclusive content.

ISBN: 978-1-905347-60-3
UK £.6.99   US $7.99

Abaddon
Books

Follow us on twitter: www.twitter.com/abaddonbooks

PAX BRITANNIA

HUMAN NATURE

JONATHAN GREEN

Visit www.abaddonbooks.com for information on our titles,
interviews, news and exclusive content.

ISBN: 978-1-905437-86-3
UK £.6.99   US $7.99

Abaddon
Books

Follow us on twitter: www.twitter.com/abaddonbooks

PAX BRITANNIA

"Jonathan Green gets mileage
out of his monsters, with
big action set-pieces that
read like things we'd like
to see in a rip-roaring
summer movie."
– *SFX*

BLOOD
ROYAL

JONATHAN GREEN

Visit www.abaddonbooks.com for information on our titles,
interviews, news and exclusive content.

 UK £.6.99   ISBN: 978-1-906735-30-2
US $7.99   ISBN: 978-1-907519-37-6

The Infernal Game

COLD WARRIORS

REBECCA LEVENE

Visit www.abaddonbooks.com for information on our titles,
interviews, news and exclusive content.

UK £.7.99   ISBN: 978-1-906735-36-4

US $9.99 CAN $12.99   ISBN: 978-1-906735-83-8

Abaddon Books

Follow us on twitter: www.twitter.com/abaddonbooks

'Levene is clearly
a writer operating at
the top of her game.'
THE MAGAZINE

The
Infernal
Game

GHOST DANCE

REBECCA
LEVENE

Visit www.abaddonbooks.com for information on our titles,
interviews, news and exclusive content.

UK £.7.99   ISBN: 978-1-906735-38-8

US $9.99 CAN $12.99   ISBN: 978-1-907519-03-1

Abaddon
Books

Follow us on twitter: www.twitter.com/abaddonbooks

NO MAN'S WORLD

BLACK HAND GANG

PAT KELLEHER

Visit www.abaddonbooks.com for information on our titles,
interviews, news and exclusive content.

UK £.7.99   ISBN: 978-1-906735-35-7

US $9.99 CAN $12.99   ISBN: 978-1-906735-84-5

Abaddon
Books

Follow us on twitter: www.twitter.com/abaddonbooks